Early praise for
Unpretty by Sharon Carter Rogers

"*Unpretty* is the kind of thriller that comes along all too rarely for my tastes: a daring, original plot with rich, fascinatingly odd-ball characters and the sense that even the presumed 'heroes' are only moments away from unraveling completely and spiraling off into the middle distance. Leaves you bound and helpless against the need to turn the page. Great stuff!"

—Gail Simone, DC Comics writer
(*Wonder Woman; Action Comics; Birds of Prey*)

"*Unpretty* is a gripping, fascinating tale fed by a myriad of plot twists that keeps you guessing."

—Nancy Moser, Christy Award–winning author
of *Time Lottery* and *Just Jane*

"In this fast-paced story, Sharon Carter Rogers explores issues of art, beauty, and redemption. She uses historical tidbits to great effect, increasing the tension as a killer's human masterpiece nears completion. *Unpretty* is marked with unforgettable scenes."

—Eric Wilson, critically acclaimed author
of *A Shred of Truth* and *Facing the Giants*

Praise for Sharon Carter Rogers's
debut novel, *Sinner*

"Heart-pounding adventure."

—*CCM* magazine

"A thriller fantastic."

—*Aspiring Retail* magazine

"A gritty mystery that's unpredictable and delightful."

—*InFuze* magazine

"Engaging. Haunting. Innovative. . . . Reminiscent of Dean Koontz on a dark night."

—Alton Gansky, bestselling suspense novelist

"Truly a wonderful story . . . captures the mystery and intrigue of *myth*."

—The Bookshelf Reviews

"A great suspense thriller starring two incredible antagonists."

—Harriet Klausner, Amazon.com's #1 reviewer

"A fantastic job . . . leaves you turning pages faster and faster with each line!"

—1340mag.com

"Rogers deftly weaves an intriguing tapestry, leaving unexplained miracles to enhance the story's sense of wonder. *Sinner* is unique, hopefully the first of many novels."

—*Press & Sun Bulletin*

UNPRETTY

a novel of suspense

UNPRETTY

a novel of suspense

SHARON CARTER ROGERS

HOWARD Fiction
A DIVISION OF SIMON & SCHUSTER

NEW YORK LONDON TORONTO SYDNEY

Our purpose at Howard Books is to:
- *Increase faith* in the hearts of growing Christians
- *Inspire holiness* in the lives of believers
- *Instill hope* in the hearts of struggling people everywhere

Because He's coming again!

HOWARD
BOOKS

Published by Howard Books, a division of Simon & Schuster, Inc.
1230 Avenue of the Americas, New York, NY 10020
www.howardpublishing.com

This book is published in association with the Nappaland Literary Agency, an independent agency dedicated to publishing works that are: Authentic. Relevant. Eternal. Visit us on the Web at www.Nappaland.com

Library of Congress Cataloging-in-Publication Data
Rogers, Sharon Carter.
Unpretty: a novel of suspense / by Sharon Carter Rogers.
p. cm.
Includes bibliographical references and index.
1. Police—Fiction. 2. Kidnapping—Fiction. I. Title.
PS3618.0468U57 2008
813' .6—dc22
2008009119

ISBN-13: 978-1-4165-6649-6
ISBN-10:   1-4165-6649-X

10 9 8 7 6 5 4 3 2 1

Manufactured in the United States

For information regarding special discounts for bulk purchases, please contact Simon & Schuster Special Sales at 1-800-456-6798 or business@simonandschuster.com.

Edited by Liz Duckworth and Lisa Bergren
Cover design by Kirk DouPonce, DogEared Design
Interior design by Jaime Putorti

For Bucky,
a friend to the end

ACKNOWLEDGMENTS

My literary agent, Mike Nappa, keeps telling me that "life is made of stories—and that's the only reason we need to write them down." Well, if that's true, then it's only proper for me to acknowledge some of the characters in my life story that helped bring this book into being.

Thanks to Mike Nappa, of course. You are like a winter soldier to me—always vigilant, always protecting. Always making sure I meet my deadlines (whether I want to or not!).

Grateful appreciation also to Liz Duckworth. Your editorial insights and advice from the earliest stages of this book to the last simply made it a better story.

To the real James Buchanan Barnes (you know who you are!). You stood in the gap when it seemed the rest of my world was falling apart. I wish you success in whatever you do. It's good to have you back in my life again.

Gushing thanks to Gail Simone of DC Comics! I am such a fan. You didn't have to talk to me at all, let alone read my manuscript—but you did. Which, of course, makes you even more of a Wonder Woman to me. Your endorsement of my work is one of the highlights of my life to date. Grateful thanks also to Nancy Moser and Eric Wilson for taking time out of your busy schedules to read, and lend your support for, my book.

Thanks to Todd Michael Green, Chris Well, Kevin Lucia,

Caleb Newell, M. E. McFadden, Deena Peterson, and all my pals at MySpace.com. You guys rock! Your frequent encouragement regarding my first book, *Sinner*, really inspired me to make sure this second novel would live up to your expectations . . . which I hope it does!

To the team at Howard Books/Simon & Schuster: my heartfelt gratitude for bringing me into your family. Thanks especially to Dave Lambert and Lisa Tawn Bergren for all your hard work under increasingly short deadlines!

And to the One, whose first recorded work of art was a garden, my humble thanks. As Jonathan Shelby taught me, You are sometimes silent, but never, ever absent from my unpretty life. Thank you for sharing your stories with me.

P.S. If anybody out there wants to contact me, feel free to send me an e-mail through the MySpace.com social network. My profile page is at: www.MySpace.com/SharonCarterRogers.

"There is a monster at the end of this book.

Oh, I am so scared!

Please do not turn the page. Please, please, please . . ."

—LOVABLE, FURRY OLD GROVER,
THE MONSTER AT THE END OF THIS BOOK, BY JON STONE

Where can I go from Your Spirit? Or where can I flee from Your
   presence?
If I ascend into heaven, You are there;
if I make my bed in hell, behold, You are there.
If I take the wings of the morning, and dwell in the uttermost
   parts of the sea,
even there Your hand shall lead me
and Your right hand shall hold me.

—PSALMS 139:7–10 (NIV)

ONE

A man had three daughters.

The oldest was a treat for the eyes, with long, silky hair, a carefully constructed face, and a workout-toned feminine physique. The middle daughter was the happy rebel, with body piercings here and there, hair that changed color with her moods, and a smile that made her face light up like a sunbeam. The youngest was the plainest—and smartest—of the bunch, with ordinary skin, a studious manner, and a glint of secrets in her eyes.

A man had three daughters.

But only one of them was unpretty.

Do you know which one?

EXCERPT FROM THE MICHELANGELUS RECORDINGS,
TAPE 4,
TRANSCRIBED BY H. J. COLLINS

— — —

THURSDAY, SEPTEMBER 18, EARLY EVENING

Jonathan Shelby heard the concussive crack behind his left knee before he felt the actual blow. Flooding pain made him gasp for breath and briefly wonder if his leg had been broken.

He collapsed onto the gritty pavement of the bookstore alley, the aged slime of a well-used dumpster disgustingly close to his face. A moment later an elbow hammered against the back of his skull and disrupted the functions in the occipital lobe of his brain. Temporary blindness prevented him from seeing the concrete that now rose up to meet him.

Missed that third guy, Jonathan thought. *He must have been standing in the shadows near the entrance to the alley. My mistake.*

Jonathan felt a sticky warmth ooze out of the place where his forehead had scraped along the concrete. He tried to roll over onto his back, tried to blink away the roiling blackness that shadowed his vision, but his captor dug a knee into his back and twisted his arm.

"Check his pockets," a voice said.

Jonathan heard a switchblade flick open, felt it cut the back right pocket of his jeans. Another hand began patting down his jacket and quickly discovered the standard-issue gun strapped next to his ribs.

Not good, he thought. *Not good.*

"How long has he been following us?" A different voice this time.

"Since Sixteenth Street. Maybe longer."

Red and yellow lights began flashing at the edge of Jonathan's vision. He blinked, and darkened shapes appeared again. He had a terrible headache. And it was getting worse by the second.

"Jonathan Shelby," the man holding him read. "Correction. *Detective* Jonathan Shelby."

He couldn't see it, but he heard the soft slap of someone catching the leather wallet that held his badge. Heard someone muttering halfhearted expletives. He blinked again and was relieved when his vision cleared a bit, revealing a dirty streak of oil and sludge inches away from his face on the pavement. He was losing feeling in his arm and fought for breath. He hoped for a split-second opening when the guy on top of him would relax. A quick roll and a kick should be enough to—

"Stand him up."

This voice spoke with authority. Obviously the boss.

Jonathan felt the pressure release on his back. The man, surprisingly strong, gripped the back of his head and dragged him to his feet. He cranked Jonathan's arm harder, behind him. Then, before he could do anything significant, the second guy stepped close and placed a blade under his chin. Jonathan blinked again, letting his eyes adjust to the stark evening gray of the alley.

Okay, he thought. *One guy trying to break my arm and yank the hair out of my head. A second one dangerously close to cutting a second mouth in my neck. Not good at all.*

The boss stepped closer and appraised him. After a moment he reached out and placed a finger under the detective's chin, gently adjusting the position of his profile.

Jonathan started to speak, but the boss frowned and shook his head. Jonathan took the hint.

The boss reached inside his coat and pulled out a cloth—a handkerchief perhaps? Or a bandanna? Jonathan couldn't tell. The throbbing in his leg threatened to make him stumble, but the knife at his throat provided motivation for him to support the bulk of his weight on the right leg. The boss dabbed the cloth at the blood on Jonathan's face, wiping it away from his eyes, brushing it back into his ear and hair.

Jonathan glanced desperately toward the alley entrance and the row of shops across the street. He knew this part of town well. The bookstore. Coffee shop. The sandwich place. A shoe store. The little art gallery on the corner. It was just past quitting time for most folks. Maybe one of those little doors in the back of one of those little shops would open, and a laughing group of employees would discover what was going on in this hidden alleyway. Maybe help would come.

Then again, maybe not.

The boss folded up his cloth now and stuffed it back into a pocket inside his jacket. He spat, carefully avoiding Jonathan's shoes. Finally he spoke.

"He'll do."

Jonathan felt panic finally break to the surface. He screamed for help and shifted hard to his right. The knife nicked the surface of his neck, but he didn't care. He just knew he had to get out of this alley, right now. He could not be taken. Could not.

The third man twisted Jonathan's arm until it loosened in its socket, pushing down until Jonathan's legs gave out, dropping him to his knees. Then the man pressed a meaty forearm against the detective's larynx to silence him.

"Sedate him," said the boss calmly. "And put him in the trunk. We've got some errands to run before going home tonight."

Jonathan felt his tongue go thick when the big man released the pressure on his throat. He tried to take in a fresh gulp of air, ready again to yell for help. Then the sting of a needle in his neck sealed his despair. *But I promised Aurora I'd be home by six,* he thought absurdly.

He fought it for a moment, but too soon his body involuntarily relaxed, and the night came crashing down in pieces. Jonathan blinked again, felt the goon finally let go of his mangled arm, saw the streak of oil and sludge near his face again. He struggled to maintain consciousness, feverishly twitching on the dirty concrete, but he knew it was a losing battle. A soft, electric whine filled his ears, and for some reason, he thought he smelled onions.

"Let's go," a voice echoed hollowly. But Jonathan knew he was already gone.

— — —

At 6:15 P.M., Aurora Shelby was just a little annoyed. True, Jonathan was always late. And true, she'd known this about him when she married him. But still, he *had* promised her—solemnly *vowed* almost—that tonight, for once in his life, he wouldn't be late. Yet here it was 6:15, and once again, her husband was absent from the dinner table.

Aurora let the candles burn and turned the oven down to a setting that would simply keep her chicken cacciatore warm without drying it out. She turned off the stereo midway through the fourth Norah Jones song, took a sip of wine, and sat down to wait a little longer.

At 6:45 P.M., she was downright angry. She called Jonathan's work number, but there was no answer. She tried his cell phone, but all she got was voice mail. She put the wine away and turned off the oven.

At 7:30 P.M., Aurora moved from anger to depression. She picked a bit at her dinner, then wrapped it all in Tupperware and foil and changed her clothes into something more comfortable. She tried to read a magazine.

At 7:45 P.M., she went to the movies. If Jonathan didn't have the decency to call or come home, then she would just go out and have a good time without him. There was a new Kate Hudson movie they both wanted to see, so Aurora opted to view that one, just to spite him.

At 10:30 P.M., Aurora couldn't remember anything about the movie she'd just watched. She entered her apartment and was surprised to see it had apparently remained untouched the whole time she was gone. For the first time that night, a glimmer of worry crept into her conscious mind.

She called Barry, one of Jonathan's coworkers. He told her that Jonathan had left the station around 5:15 P.M., and he hadn't seen him since. Aurora bit her lip then and called her mother-in-law, who immediately freaked out when she heard her son hadn't come home. Jonathan's mother hung up quickly, intent—as usual—on calling hospitals and mortuaries to look for him.

At 11:15 P.M., Aurora finally called 911 to report that her husband was missing.

Of course, by then it was much too late.

— — —

Kinseth Roberts breathed heavily for at least twenty minutes, then finally reached down under the covers to remove their shoes. They'd been in such a rush to get into bed by eleven o'clock—just as they'd promised Elaina they would—that they hadn't had time to change into pajamas, let alone take off their shoes. So when their heart had finally slowed down, when the excitement of barely making curfew had finally worn off, Kinseth had reached down and unlaced their left shoe, then their right one, and flicked them both out onto the floor. They would just have to sleep in the rest of their clothes tonight.

Kinseth also removed the glass eye from their left socket and dropped it into the bowl by the bed. It was too uncomfortable to sleep very long with it in. Out of habit their fingers paused to gently trace the long red scar that dipped below their left eyebrow and stretched out across their cheek. Only when they felt confident that they were ready for sleep did Kinseth allow them finally to reflect on what they'd seen tonight.

Those three men had dragged that other man up to the porch of the house across the cul-de-sac and then waited. Kinseth had moved the telescope out of their closet and back to the window of their second-story bedroom and watched the men through it, wondering if this new man was a guest or a prisoner. Kinseth guessed it was the second, because at one point the new man had appeared to try to jump off the porch, but the others had quickly pulled him back. Then one had stabbed a needle into the prisoner's neck. At least it looked like a needle. Sometimes Kinseth had trouble sorting out details.

The men had waited for several minutes before the door opened and all four slipped quietly inside. That was when Kinseth suddenly realized it was 10:59 P.M. and that they'd promised Elaina they'd be in bed, covers drawn and lights out, by eleven o'clock sharp. Kinseth already had the lights out, so they leaped into bed, clothes and all, and slid under the covers just in time to watch the red numbers on the clock flicker and change.

That was close.

Kinseth let their eyelids close and thought some more about the men at the house across the cul-de-sac.

It sure was interesting to live on this street.

TWO

Dear Ms. Collins, first, let me say that I hope someday soon to be able to comfortably call you by your first name. Perhaps even to get to the point where names are unnecessary between us. But as we are in the introductory stages of our relationship for now, the gentleman in me dictates the formality of my address to you.

EXCERPT FROM THE MICHELANGELUS RECORDINGS,
TAPE 1,
TRANSCRIBED BY H. J. COLLINS

— — —

FRIDAY, SEPTEMBER 19, MID-MORNING.

Hummingbird Collins wouldn't have taken such careful note of a customer—there were twenty or more a day—but he was sweating when he stepped up to the register.

"I'll be with you in just a moment," she said, quickly closing up the large sketchbook she'd spread out on the counter and collecting the colored pencils back into the box to her right.

She tried to sound serene and cheerful, but she was also just a little disappointed, as she'd finally begun to get into that "Hey, the store's empty, might as well draw something" groove that often produced her best artwork. She was also distracted by the fact that she had somehow misplaced a twenty-dollar bill the last

 the lady had bought that book on
Romanian tourist sites.

But that first peek at the man's glistening hairline, moisture
beading on his scalp but not yet dripping down his face, caught
her mercurial attention, and she pushed aside thoughts of her
latest sketch and even the lost cash. It was cold outside today,
unseasonably cold for September. No snow or ice or rain but
cold. Heart attack? The man before her wasn't overweight or out
of breath from any apparent physical exertion.

"Let me get this stuff out of your way." Hummingbird smiled,
setting aside her drawing supplies and sketchbook. The man
nodded calmly and let his eyes wander around the store while he
waited. And continued to sweat inexplicably.

Maybe he's got an electric heater underneath that coat. That
sparked another thought. *Aha! I bet that twenty-dollar bill is underneath the cash tray in the register. I'll have to remember to
check that after I finish with this guy.*

The man carefully brought his hands out of the pockets of his
oversized military jacket and casually let his eyes sweep around
the open aisles of the bookstore's retail space. The sweep took
only a split second, but in that moment Hummingbird found
herself dismissing the sweat factor and becoming increasingly
fascinated by the sculptured face at her counter. He was tall,
taller than Hummingbird even, and at five-foot-eight she was
often considered unusually tall. Still, she found herself looking
up at him; he was maybe six-two or six-three—close in size to
her brother, T.W., though not as beefy. From the neck down he
was simply an ordinary mass of maleness, covered in slightly
rumpled clothes that indicated respectable muscle tone but nothing truly irregular. His face, though, captured the imagination.

The man's skin was not quite porcelain but definitely the
shade of white that comes from European stock mixed with long

days spent indoors. He seemed healthy, though. His hair was thick and cropped short and, in sharp contrast to the pale skin, darker than black widow legs. Oh yes, and moistened with sweat. Still, it was the bone structure that made Hummingbird's eyes linger for a closer look. Cheeks, jaw, and nose were all straight lines and clear angles, hardening the features of the face from behind the skin and making the artist in her involuntarily begin tracing the lines of shadow and light that played across the man's lean expression.

That's the kind of face that would look good on a killer, she thought. *Maybe I've found the model for my Brutus in that Shakespeare playbill I'm supposed to do for the community theater folks.*

"Sir?" Hummingbird asked cheerily, a bit confused at his hesitation. A lifetime of serving customers in her family's little bookstore had refined in her the proper, fake-friendly demeanor of a seasoned sales professional. "Can I help you?"

He smiled, but his soul seemed absent from his gaze. Hummingbird felt the first wave of alarm course through her.

"I'm looking for the Michelangelo exhibit," he said. "I heard it was opening here today." He was studying her now, staring at each part of her face with an intensity that unnerved her.

Hummingbird gave a light chuckle, counterfeit joviality to cover her confusion and fear. "Ah, yes, the Michelangelo exhibit." She walked out from behind the counter and motioned for the man to follow her. "We have some books on Michelangelo, but the exhibit is actually down the block just a bit. We're Collins Galleria of Books. You're looking for Conklin Art Gallery. Just hang a right, and you'll find it."

The man said nothing but returned his hands to the pockets of his pale green coat and followed Hummingbird toward the door. He paused, seeming unwilling to go back out in the cold.

Out of nervous habit, Hummingbird began to fill the empty spaces with conversation.

"We've often wished we didn't have such similar names," she said, "but technically, we were here first. My mom started this store back in the late 1980s, just after Pop died. Back then there weren't all these fancy upscale shops in the North Downtown area. Shoot, back then Lehigh, West Virginia, didn't even have a north downtown. Just downtown with these narrow streets and a few rows of small family businesses selling shoes and jewelry and, well, books!"

Hummingbird smiled and turned back toward the man now framed in her doorway. His expression hardened, and he remained silent, but he seemed to resume his intimate study of her features, as if she were a long-lost classmate or something. Hummingbird unconsciously fidgeted with her long, thick mane of chestnut hair. There was an awkward moment of silence before she finally spoke again.

"Sorry," she said. "My brother always says I rattle on about anything and everything when I really should just answer the simple question." She tilted her head. "Did you need anything else?"

"No, thank you." The man gazed slowly out the door, then let his eyes drift back to Hummingbird. There was another uncomfortable silence, something a veteran salesperson like Hummingbird found nearly unbearable.

"Here," she said at last. "Follow me, and I'll take you right to their front door." She grabbed a heavy sweater off a rack near the door. "Of course, you have to promise to come back after your visit at the Conklin. We've got a great section in the back on Renaissance painters, and I can show you those books about Michelangelo."

A single drop of sweat finally broke free and trickled down

the side of the man's head, just past his right ear. He seemed not to notice but simply let his lips relax into a forced grin as he nodded. "I'd appreciate that," he said quietly. "Thank you."

Hummingbird smiled in return. She called out to a coworker who had taken her place behind the cash register. "Hey, Kacey," she said. "Gonna run down to the Conklin. Be back before you can name all the number one hits on the latest Elvis commemorative CD."

Kacey waved and shouted back, "Let's see, there's 'Love Me Tender,' 'Jailhouse Rock' . . ." Her voice disappeared behind the clanging of the shop's front door.

— — —

James Buchanan Barnes felt as if he were hammering a nail with a doughnut. He looked at the man sitting across his desk and willed himself into mild-mannered mode.

"Do you understand what I've said, Mr. Conklin?"

The man waved a patrician hand dismissively and adjusted his weight in the chair. "Of course I do, Detective Barnes."

"Please, call me Buck."

Mr. Conklin half raised an eyebrow but said nothing.

Buck shrugged. "Lived here my whole life, Mr. Conklin. Almost fifty years now. And people here have called me Buck ever since I can remember. Seemed inappropriate to ask them to call me something else just because I'd finally earned a detective's badge."

Conklin, apparently unmoved by the personal history, simply sighed and glanced at his watch.

"You and your family aren't from around here, are you, Mr. Conklin?"

Conklin frowned. "No, but we've been active in the community ever since we came here three years ago. We've donated to charities, supported book drives at the library, even contributed money to the fraternal order of police."

Buck nodded comfortably. "That's wonderful, sir. Really. But are you sure there's no one who, well, isn't happy with you? Anything controversial unfold over there? Maybe someone disliked one of your recent art shows?"

Conklin shifted his weight again. "Of course not. That's absurd. We have no enemies, Detective, not in this town or any other place. I'm an art dealer, that's all. And because I'm here, with you, I'm missing the grand opening of our latest exhibit— 'The Michelangelo Mirrors' by Siena Beccafumi. Do you know the artist Beccafumi, Detective?"

Buck shook his head.

"Siena Beccafumi is an Italian painter. He was orphaned as a boy and spent time living in the streets of Rome until a priest rescued him, placed him in an orphanage, and discovered an astonishing artistic talent in the boy. He's widely known in European circles."

Buck couldn't miss the patronizing tone behind his words, but he let the art dealer go on. In his experience, people talked more when he stayed quiet.

"Critics are calling him the Picasso of the classics. This exhibit of his surrealist interpretation of Michelangelo's *Last Judgment* is the first to tour in the United States—and it took quite the effort to get it booked at my gallery."

"Sounds impressive," Buck said, barely covering a yawn. "But that still doesn't explain this." He pointed to the newspaper clipping from the *Lehigh Chronicle* on the desk between the two men. It was an advertisement for the first showing of the "Michelangelo Mirrors" exhibit. Someone had apparently cut it out of the paper and written a single word in red across the image: *Unpretty*.

"I told you, Detective," Mr. Conklin said. "This was in an envelope taped to the front door of my home this morning. That's all. I almost threw it away, but it was just unusual enough that my wife thought I should report it to the police."

"You were right to call us, Mr. Conklin."

"But, honestly, it seems to me that this should be your problem now, not mine. I still don't understand why your operator insisted I come down here to talk to you in person. It seems to me you all could have simply sent a cruiser to my house."

"She apparently thought you might be in danger and wanted to get you and your family to safety as quickly as possible," Buck said, waiting for some kind of reaction from the thick-jawed man in front of him. All he saw was impatience in the art dealer's eyes. "When you told her you were on your way to work, she asked you to stop by here because she thought this would be a safe place for you to wait while we checked out your house. However, she expected you and your wife *both* would come by here."

"My wife went to the gallery to begin setup for today's exhibit," he said dismissively. "So you did send a cruiser to our home after all?"

"Yes, Mr. Conklin. Two of our uniformed officers are at your house right now, checking it for signs of forced entry or vandalism or other potentially threatening circumstances."

"Then I am wasting my time here in your office, Detective. You can call me at the gallery if your officers find anything significant."

"Look, Mr. Conklin, this could be nothing—"

"And it likely is nothing, Detective."

"But, as I said before, it carries all the markings of a threat to you, to your family, or to your business. I couldn't live with myself if something happened and I hadn't taken all possible precautions."

"You may consider me warned, Detective. Thank you. May I go now? We're actually expecting a nice turnout for this exhibit, and my wife has need of my assistance."

Buck chewed on the inside of his lip for a moment "Mr. Conklin," he said slowly, "I know it was inconvenient for you to stop. I appreciate that you took the time."

Conklin rose from his seat and pulled on his overcoat.

"But please, I think this could be serious. It is obviously a warning or a protest of some kind. Until we know more about the nature of—"

The ringing telephone interrupted the detective's plea. Conklin nodded toward the phone and simply said, "Thank you, Detective. You'd better get that." Then he turned and walked out the door.

— — —

Hummingbird stood outside the Conklin Art Gallery and briefly considered paying the modest admission fee to go in and view the exhibit. The images on the posters in the front window looked interesting and creative. Then she caught a glimpse of the stranger walking past the window inside the gallery. Something about that man made her uncomfortable; no, it was better to wait and see "The Michelangelo Mirrors" another time.

She checked her watch and smiled. Just enough time to pop in on T.W. across the street. Maybe she could talk him into buying her lunch today. She'd use her cell to call Kacey and make sure she was okay back at the store. Hummingbird turned around and faced the streetlight on the comer, watching for traffic. Her brother's law office was cater-corner from the Conklin. As she was deciding which direction to cross first, she heard the bell ring on the door to the Conklin. She was surprised to see the man she had just escorted into the gallery exit and walk briskly up the street away from her.

She watched him walk away for several steps before it registered that he was no longer wearing that oversized green jacket of his. Like most of the shops on this street, the Conklin kept a coat rack inside the door. *He must have forgotten it in there,* she mused. *Wonder where he's off to in such a hurry.*

Briefly, she considered calling to him, reminding him of his coat, but she'd already gone above and beyond. He'd discover it soon enough, in this cold weather.

She was halfway across Fourth Avenue when she noticed the stranger again. He was now partway down the block, closer to the next intersection than he was to hers. He stood near the edge of the sidewalk, partially obscured by a Chevy Blazer parked on the street.

Was he staring at her?

Hummingbird avoided his gaze and pretended not to notice. *Definitely something odd about that man,* she thought. She stuffed her hands into the pockets of her sweater and kept walking.

— — —

Buck Barnes picked up the telephone on the fifth ring. "Detective Barnes," he stated.

"Buck, it's the captain."

"What can I do for you, Cap'n?"

"When was the last time you saw Detective Shelby?"

Buck thought for a moment, then said, "Yesterday, around lunchtime. Why?"

There was a tense silence on the other end of the phone, and Buck thought he heard the faint sound of fingers drumming on a desk in the background. "We got a call around five P.M. yesterday from someone at the Conklin Art Gallery. Let's see, the caller said his name was . . . yes, Kyle Conklin. Must be the owner's son. Anyway, he reported a few suspicious characters roaming

North Downtown. He said they hadn't done anything criminal, but two of them had been there earlier and seemed to loiter a long time around the gallery. The two left and came back later with a third man. This Kyle Conklin felt uneasy about them. A description on one of the three matched a suspect in a missing persons case that Jonathan was working. He left here last night around five-fifteen to check it out, and no one's seen him since."

Detective Barnes took a deep breath. "Anybody check with his wife?"

"Yep. She's the one who called to report him missing."

"When did she call?"

"Last night, a little before midnight."

"Who's on this, boss?"

"It's still with the uniformed boys. Officer Justins took the statement from Shelby's wife."

"Did Justins start making the rounds in North Downtown? Find out if anyone saw something?"

"Justins got called to a shooting on the west side shortly after he took the call."

Acid rose in Buck's throat. "So this has been sitting on Justins's desk since midnight? And meanwhile who knows what might be going on with Jonathan Shelby?"

"Now you're getting the picture."

Barnes tucked the phone between his chin and shoulder and reached behind his chair to retrieve his coat. "I'm on it."

He reached onto the desk and picked up the newspaper clipping he'd shown to Mr. Conklin moments before. He thought about filing it away in a drawer but decided he didn't want to take time for that, not with Jonathan needing help out there somewhere. He folded the clipping and stuffed it into his back pants pocket.

"If anybody needs me," he said into the phone receiver, "I'll be in North Downtown."

— — —

"T.W., your sister's headed this way."

T. W. Collins reached over and gently tapped the intercom button. "Thanks, Becky. I'll be right out." A moment later he stood in the small reception area of his little one-man law firm, ready to greet Hummingbird's first visit of the day.

"I think it's sweet that you two are so close," Rebecca Proctor said, leaning back in her chair at the reception desk. "And I like that she stops by here once or twice each day. Gives me a nice break when she comes over."

"Baby of the family, you know. We all tend to spoil her." T.W. smiled and looked through the large plate-glass window and watched his sister approach.

"Not in high school you didn't!" Becky said with a laugh. "She used to complain daily about her big brothers and how they messed up her life and all."

"Careful, girl," T.W. teased. "She was your only reference when you applied for this job."

"Hey, you gave me this job because I'm the best—and you know it. Boss? You know that, right?"

T.W. smiled. She was the best and had been like family for almost twenty years. If Humm hadn't lobbied for him to hire her, his mother would have. Briefly, he considered his mother, away on another Rick Steves tour in Europe. With Hummingbird running the store, they could hardly keep her in town anymore.

"Boss?"

T.W. put up his hands in mock surrender. "Hey, I understand. You are definitely the best at what you do. We both know that no one short of Bill Gates could actually pay you what you're *really* worth."

"That's more like it."

A pause. Then T.W. said, "Now, what is it exactly that you do?"

He ducked under the ink pen that came flying his way. Then, by way of appeasement, he said, "Want me to put some hot tea on?"

"Sounds good. But wait until Humm gets here, as she'll probably want to pick out the flavor."

T.W. looked out through the window and saw Hummingbird crossing Hope Street. He walked toward the door, intending to open it for her when she reached it.

But at that moment the massive plate-glass window shattered into pieces.

T.W. felt a wash of warmth spill through the office. He instinctively ducked and wrapped his arms over his head to protect it from shattering glass. He heard Becky's scream mingle with a loud cracking sound and glanced back long enough to see her take cover behind the heavy reception desk. Then he blinked as the world turned in slow motion.

Through the space that used to contain a window, he saw his baby sister wilt like a paper doll, twist and rise in the force of a hot wind, and finally slap silently against the front of a blue car waiting in the street. She seemed to slide like wax paper over the edge of the vehicle and down past the wheel well, until she lay still on the concrete.

T.W. bolted toward his sister. He knew he was shouting her name, but for some reason it seemed as though the sound of his voice had been absorbed by fire.

— — —

Kinseth was eating Frosted Cheerios when Elaina came through the front door holding the morning paper.

"Mornin', little man," she said. Then she corrected herself.

"Of course, you're almost twenty now and not so little anymore, are you?" She leaned over and kissed Kinseth's forehead. "Want the comics?"

Kinseth nodded and pushed aside the cereal box to make room. Elaina unwrapped the *Lehigh Chronicle* and carefully peeled out the section containing the funny pages.

"Thanks," they said through a mouthful of crunching noises.

"How's my baby today?"

Kinseth paused to think. How to answer? Finally they nodded.

Elaina sank into a chair at the table and began to glance at the headlines. "What a night." She sighed. "Some kid got hold of his daddy's pistol and accidentally blew his big toe off. I don't know who was screaming more when they came into the emergency room at the hospital, the mom or the kid." She reached down to loosen the laces on her white, "comfortable" nurse's sneakers and turned a page of the newspaper. " 'Course, I guess I'd be screaming too if one of my kids got hurt like that."

Kinseth looked up from the Garfield comic. "You have kids?"

Elaina snickered ruefully. "No, baby," she said with an absent kindness, as if she'd said this before and expected to have to say it again. "You know that. It's just you and me since the accident, remember?"

"We remember kids."

Elaina sighed. "No, baby. Not anymore." She paused to study the face before her. "You take your medicine this morning, honey?"

Kinseth flushed and set down the spoon.

Elaina frowned a bit. "Look, Kin, I know I'm not Mom, but I am your big sister, and it falls to me to look after you."

Kinseth's chin began to tremble. They looked down at the

table, still chewing cereal, and placed their hands flat on the table.

"It's okay, honey," Elaina said quickly. "It's all right. I will always look after you. You know that. But you have to do your part too, okay?"

Kinseth nodded.

"Promise?"

Kinseth squinted their eyes. This was important, because Kinseth always kept a promise. Always. So what exactly were they promising? To take the medicine? Or to "do their part," which would mean just eating and cleaning and things like that?

Elaina reached across the table and patted a hand. "Finish your breakfast, then go take your medicine."

Kinseth didn't move, and Elaina returned to her newspaper. After a moment she yawned.

"I'm going to take a shower and go to bed," she said. "After I get up we can go grocery shopping. Then I've got another long shift in the ER tonight."

Kinseth nodded.

"You got something to do while I'm out of pocket, honey?"

Kinseth nodded again, carefully picking up their spoon once more.

"Good. Stay close by if you leave the house."

"Greenbelt?" they said, referring to the wide stretch of park-like, undeveloped land that ran behind all the houses on the south end of their cul-de-sac.

"Sure, that's fine, honey. Just don't go farther away than that old church next to the play equipment on the other side of the greenbelt."

Kinseth nodded and started chewing again. That was good. That old church was where they wanted to go today anyway.

--- --- ---

The blaze now burning in the shell of what used to be the Conklin Art Gallery barely registered in T.W.'s vision. All he could see was his baby sister sprawled on the pavement as he made his way to her. The ringing in his ears subsided a bit, and echoes of panic began filling his hearing instead. Several car alarms were sounding along the street. The fire in the Conklin seemed to growl and grumble as it devoured any fuel it could find within the gallery's walls. People were streaming out of the other shops on Fourth Street, shouting to one another, some calling for help.

In front of T.W., a visibly shaken man opened the driver's door of the blue car that had been waiting at the light. "Did you *see* that?" he shouted in T.W.'s direction as he got out of the car.

T.W. ignored the man and knelt beside Hummingbird.

"I mean, what *was* that?" the man continued, oblivious to the fact that a girl was crumpled beside his fender. "Do you think it was a bomb? Or a gas leak?"

T.W. leaned close to his sister and was relieved to see her chest heave with a labored breath. He brushed the hair away from her face and saw her eyelids flutter.

"T.W.?" she mumbled. "What . . . wha . . ." She grimaced, and her hand flew to her temple.

"Shh. It's okay, Humm. I've got you."

T.W. carefully slid his arms underneath his sister, lifting her gently off the ground. Hummingbird rolled herself into his chest, gripping his shirt in her right hand and wrapping her left arm under his elbow and around his back.

"T.W." She gritted her teeth and squeezed her eyes shut tightly. "My head . . ."

Becky held the door open for them. "Is she hurt badly?"

"Not sure," T.W. grunted. "She hit her head fairly hard on the top of that blue car."

"I already called nine-one-one," Becky said. "Had to use my cell phone, 'cause the land lines were apparently knocked out in the blast."

T.W. nodded his thanks and headed toward the long brown leather couch in his back office, intending to place his sister there until the paramedics arrived. But first he stopped and turned to look at the street outside. The fire in the Conklin was now threatening to spread to the building next door. People were wandering in confusion in and around the intersection, with a few brave souls trying to uncap the fire hydrant in hopes of stemming the destruction in the art gallery. Various degrees of first aid were being administered to those who had been too close to the initial blast.

T.W. quickly realized that any rescue workers who showed up here would have their hands full for the foreseeable future. He looked at Becky, who stood mutely by, waiting for some kind of direction from him.

"T.W.," she said after a moment, a scared look beginning to creep into her eyes. "The Conklins had to be inside when . . . when . . ."

T.W. didn't answer. Instead he nodded toward the doorway. "C'mon," he said. "Help me get her to my car. We can get to the hospital long before any firefighters or paramedics can."

Becky nodded and looked relieved to have something to do. She walked quickly to the door and propped it open once more. T.W. followed, carrying Hummingbird in his arms. In the distance sirens finally began to wail.

THREE

James McNeill Whistler once said that an artist is not paid for his labor but for his vision. I believe he was right. It takes great vision to create something beautiful, and I am proud to tell you that my co-laborers and I have dedicated our lives to the pursuit of that artistic vision.

The question that we must ask, though, Ms. Collins, is about the greater benefit of beauty to society at large. Is it better to fill the world with pretty things? Or to erase from it the unpretty elements that so often mar our beautiful vision?

One must strike a balance, I suppose. And that, my dear, is exactly what we are doing.

EXCERPT FROM THE MICHELANGELUS RECORDINGS,
TAPE 2,
TRANSCRIBED BY H. J. COLLINS

— — —

FRIDAY, SEPTEMBER 19, LATE AFTERNOON

Number 26 stood on the wrap-around porch at 1669 Kirby Court and waited. It was a clear, fall day, exactly the kind that 26 liked. The sky was gray, with scattered wisps of cloud cover that stretched like dirty cotton across the heavens. The sun shone but without heat. He'd been smart to layer up before going on his errand this morning, pulling on two T-shirts underneath his plain gray sweatshirt. It had made him a little warm when he was wearing that heavy green jacket over it all, but once he'd gotten rid of that, the sweatshirt and layers were welcome.

He stuffed his hands into his pants pockets and looked up at the little red light hidden above and to the right of the house's front door. If you didn't know the video camera was up there under the porch light, you'd probably never see it. The red light had been added later, for the residents of the house, so they'd know whether or not it was safe to enter.

Number 26 didn't ring the doorbell—he knew it was a fake anyway. And he didn't try to put a key in the lock because there was no lock on the outside. He knew the protocol; in fact, he'd created the protocol. So he simply stood in the cold. And waited.

He closed his eyes and relived the moments of the day so far. She had been attractive, that girl at the bookstore. And helpful. Number 26 smiled in spite of himself and wondered what his father would say if he caught him relishing the memory of the explosion. Dad was . . . 26 paused and instinctively reworded his thoughts. Number 3 was such a "just the facts" personality, which was great when the organization needed a leader but not so endearing when a son wanted a father. No matter. Number 26 had done well today, and he knew it. Dad—Number 3—would be pleased. Ought to be pleased, at least.

Number 26 heard a slight hum and a click. He looked at the tiny light above him and saw it turn to green—the all-clear sign. Seconds later the front door to the house swung open.

"Thank you, 61," he said calmly. He was careful always to appear calm in front of the troops.

"Of course, sir," Number 61 responded with a slight deferential nod. She was about the same age as 26, but she had come to the cause much later than he. Hence the low rank. Still, she was a valuable member of the team, and 26 intended to reward that sooner rather than later.

Number 61 closed the door behind them and waited, gaze slightly lowered to avoid direct eye contact. Number 26 took a moment to appraise his soldier. She was trim, in fighting shape, with the balance of a dancer, always on the balls of her feet as if ready to spring toward, or jump away from, danger. Like all the soldiers, she kept her dark hair trimmed short, though not so much as to lose the femininity of her face. She had her straight hair in a bob that dipped just past her jaw line, and she wore the nurse's apron that suggested she'd been working in one of the basement medical rooms.

"We need more C-4 explosive," 26 said.

"I'll take care of it tonight, sir," the woman responded. "Same amount as usual?"

Number 26 nodded and then glanced around the living room of the house. It had been decorated with normalcy in mind. Gray carpet, a large couch and a loveseat, a big glass coffee table in the center of the room. Art prints hung on the walls—not real art, though. Mundane, mass-produced paintings and framed photographs that one could find in any discount retail store. A coat rack and a bench stood behind the entry, and a narrow wooden table pressed against the back wall. It was routinely cluttered with the most current issues of several popular magazines. Any stranger who was invited into this room for coffee and conversation would never know the house was anything other than a suburban home shared by several hardworking members of the community.

Anyone exiting the living room, however, would have a much different impression of things.

"Where is everyone?" 26 asked casually. His father would be expecting a report soon. He hated making those daily reports to his father, and a little dawdling now could postpone the unpleasantness to come.

"Number 44 is in the barracks, resting, as he'll have night duty." She nodded down the hallway toward a bedroom. "Number 48 is in the studio." She motioned toward the stairs to the basement. "Number 39 is working in the tech room. I think he's following the TV and Internet coverage of the explosion at the art gallery, checking to see if you left any clues behind that might point to us."

"Good."

Number 61 nodded and waited. She was obviously ready to be dismissed, but 26 knew she wouldn't move from that spot until he released her. She was one of the most disciplined of the soldiers and very bright. She'd graduated fifth in her class at medical school, then spent four years as an army medic in Afghanistan before coming back to the family here at 1669 Kirby Court. Number 3 had thought it would be important for her to be a part of the real world before he allowed anyone to recruit her. They had all benefited from his foresight.

"What kind of mood is the old man in today?" 26 said finally.

Number 61 showed her first signs of discomfort, daring a glance up into 26's face before responding. "Number 3 is the same as usual, sir."

Number 26 nodded knowingly. "Chewed you out again, huh?" He gave his soldier a grim smile. "Don't worry about it, 61," he said. "The old man is never satisfied. I don't think he's ever really happy unless he's making one of us miserable."

Number 61 concentrated her gaze on the floor and said nothing.

"I'll go down and talk to him soon," 26 said. "Maybe he'll feel better after he hears about the successes of the day."

"It's almost time for his next dose of medicines," Number 61 said. "Do you want to administer them this time?"

"No," he said comfortably. "You're the real doctor among us. We both know that. And besides," he added, "my interest in medicine is more recreational in nature anyway. But you go ahead and finish your work. I'll be down shortly."

Number 61 nodded, apparently relieved at being released from the conversation. She reached into a pouch in her apron, producing a syringe and a rubber glove, and turned toward the steps to the basement.

"Sixty-one," Number 26 called to her before she exited. "Do you have anything else in that apron?"

"Something for your nerves, sir?"

Number 26 let out a soft sigh. "You, of all of us, know what it's like to spend time with the old man. Just something to take the edge off would be good."

Number 61 dipped a hand back into a pocket and came up with a folded sheet of colorfully decorated blotter paper. "One square or two this time, sir?"

"One."

She tore along perforated edges and handed a square of the paper to her commander. He quickly placed it on his tongue and nodded his dismissal to the doctor.

After she left, he sat on the loveseat and concentrated on the chemicals in the paper as they were absorbed into his mouth. When he'd first started using this drug, he could feel its effects almost immediately. But now he'd built up something of a tolerance, and it often took half an hour or so before he experienced relief. He leaned his head back against the wall, closed his eyes, and began the progressive relaxation, self-hypnosis exercises that helped him direct the effectiveness of the chemicals his body was ingesting. He willed the muscles in his arms to loosen first, then his

chest and torso, then his legs, and finally his head. By the time the
psychotropic had hit his bloodstream, Number 26 was completely
at peace with the world. He opened his eyes and heard the colors
of the room murmuring his name. They were cheering him, he decided. Cheering the success of his mission today. Applauding his
heroism all along the pathway down the stairs and into the private
hospital room where Number 3 awaited.

Number 26 smiled and stood. He was finally ready to meet
with his father.

— — —

Hummingbird Collins lay in the hospital bed trying to make the
room stop spinning. She had already thrown up twice—once in
T.W.'s car—and the waves of dizziness that kept recurring threatened to make her vomit again. She shut her eyes tightly and tried
to breathe normally. A respite from the nausea came soon after.
She kept her eyes shut and tried to relax her head, very aware of
the large and tender bump that now protruded from her skull
above her left temple.

She let her hearing tune into the news broadcast quietly dron-
ing on the TV across the room. They were saying that investiga-
tors suspected a gas leak at the Conklin Art Gallery, though
some—who spoke on condition of anonymity—were suggesting
terrorists had planted a bomb at the gallery. Regardless, eight
people had been inside the gallery when the explosion happened,
and all eight had died—including the gallery's co-owner, Mrs.
Lillian Conklin, and her son, Kyle, who had been working at the
gallery part-time while attending the local university. Mr. Conklin had narrowly escaped death, having just parked when the
bomb went off. A politician had vowed to track down the people
responsible, but so far there didn't seem to be any real clues to
the identities of the bombers and arsonists.

Arsonist. Bomber. The man's sculptured face, his exit from the gallery without his jacket . . . images kept flashing inside Hummingbird's head. *I've got to talk to the police.* But then another wave of nausea hit, and it was all she could do not to throw up on the fancy backless cotton gown the hospital staff had issued her.

She heard a cell phone ringing and heard it silenced before the first ring was over. Then her brother's voice was speaking softly into the receiver.

The voice on the other end was practically shouting and, in a strange confluence of technology and acoustics, sounded louder than her own brother's voice in the hospital room.

"T.W.? Oh, thank God! I was worried sick!"

"It's okay, Peg. I'm fine. Everybody's fine."

"I've been in faculty meetings all day; that idiotic accreditation review is coming up, and the English department head is worried. We didn't get out until a few minutes ago, and then we all saw the news. Thank God you're all right."

"I'm fine, Peggy. I'm fine." Hummingbird could hear the tenderness in her brother's voice. Peggy Harrison had definitely brought out the best in him. He'd been a confirmed bachelor until she came into his life two and a half years ago and settled him down.

"Well, good." Peggy's voice choked, and she gave a nervous laugh. " 'Cause I'm walking down that aisle in seven months—with or without you."

"Hey, I'll be there for our wedding, baby. You can count on it."

"What about Hummingbird? Did the explosion hit her store?"

"No, the blast didn't travel that far down the block. But Humm was outside when it happened, heading over to see me."

"Oh no."

"She got a little scraped up and hit her head really hard. But you know how hardheaded that girl is anyway." Hummingbird tried to swat her brother's arm without opening her eyes, but she missed. He grabbed her hand and gave it a quick squeeze. "She's got a serious concussion," T.W. continued, "but the doctor says that if she takes it easy for a few days, she should be fine. They're going to keep her in the hospital overnight, though. They said I could take her home tomorrow morning."

"Thank God. Are you at the hospital right now? I'll come over."

"Yeah, we're here. But don't come over. This place is kind of a zoo, what with all the people flooding in here after the explosion."

"But T.W.—"

"No, really, hon. You go on home. They're gonna kick me out of here by eight o'clock anyway, so I'll come by and see you then."

"Well, all right. But are you sure you don't want me to come over?"

"I'm sure. I'm just sitting here while Humm pretends to sleep to keep from hurling. Business as usual. I'll see you later tonight."

"Okay. Give Humm a hug for me. Love ya, you big wreck."

"Love you too."

Hummingbird heard her brother's cell phone flip shut, felt him release her hand and rise to lean over her.

"No, please. Don't bother with the hug," Hummingbird said. "My head has almost stopped spinning. Just stay still and keep quiet, would ya?"

Jonathan Shelby couldn't help but admire his wife. For starters, Aurora Shelby was a devastating businesswoman—tenacious, intelligent, and thorough, just how the Cole Corporation liked them. She'd landed in Cole's corporate affairs office barely a week after minting her MBA and now appeared to be on the fast track to success there, even though she was only twenty-six years old.

She was also a stunner, at least in Jonathan's eyes. Long blond hair that hung almost to her waist when she let it down. Thick, natural eyelashes that governed the deep emerald of her eyes. A light pinking in her cheeks that gave the impression of a faint, perpetual blush. Strong cheekbones, a perfect nose. And a figure that was plump in all the right places and toned in the rest. Jonathan loved looking at her.

They'd been married eighteen months now, and Jonathan still didn't tire of watching her mouth crinkle at the edges when she smiled or of seeing her lissome fingers busily at work on some new project. Right now he was enjoying the way she swept across the kitchen and the mixture of perfume and baked goods that filled his nostrils. He watched her from across the kitchen table, seated comfortably in his chair.

"You sure you know what you're doing?" he teased.

She turned away from the stove and put an oven-mitted hand on her hip. "Hey," she said with mock ferocity, "just because I make more money than you doesn't mean I forgot how to cook a casserole for dinner." She flashed him that million-dollar smile and returned to her work.

Jonathan felt an inexplicable sadness envelop him. He wanted to get up and wrap his arms around her, hold her for ages and ages to come. But for some reason his body wouldn't move.

"I love you, Aurora," he whispered.

She straightened up and turned away from the oven, giving him an appraising look.

"I'll always love you," he said softly. "No matter what. I'll always love you. I hope you'll remember that."

The sadness was overwhelming now, stealing his breath, making him weak. He tried to lift his arm, wanted desperately to touch the vision before him. But his arm wouldn't cooperate.

Aurora frowned slightly and bit her lower lip. Then she placed her cooking utensils on the counter and moved toward Jonathan. She knelt beside his chair and tenderly ran her fingers through his hair. His skin felt warm and tingly in the places where her fingers touched his scalp. He felt his face relax and his eyelids flutter.

She was so beautiful.

Her voice touched his ears like a soothing salve. "You're okay, Jonathan," she said comfortingly. "Just relax and enjoy our time together." He nodded and felt the sadness inside him begin to drain away. "Take a deep breath," she continued. "And as you let it out, close your eyes, and feel yourself relaxing."

Jonathan let his breath release in a soft whistle of air, felt his arm and leg muscles twitch.

"That's it," she soothed. "You're doing fine."

Jonathan blinked his eyes open and saw concern in lovely Aurora's face. He tried to slip out of his chair, to embrace her and tell her everything would be all right. But again his body disobeyed. He felt a twinge of heat in his left arm, and when he looked down, he was disturbed to find himself unclothed.

"Aurora," he said shakily, "where are my pants?"

His wife's voice became silk. "It doesn't really matter, does it, Jonathan?" she cooed. "Just relax, and let's enjoy this nice, romantic dinner we're having together. Feel your legs relaxing. Feel the tension releasing from your calves. Let your muscles loosen. Isn't that better, Jonathan, dear?"

Jonathan felt his leg muscles ease, but his forehead crinkled in concentration. He felt the heat in his left arm again and suddenly noticed that his ankles were scraping against something hard. He felt the first effects of a migraine coming on.

His wife now stood up at his side, looking at him carefully, her arms crossed over her chest.

So beautiful . . .

Jonathan felt the sadness returning. A sadness textured by the hopelessness that comes from being totally alone.

"I love you, Aurora," he whispered. "I love you . . ."

Aurora Shelby frowned fully this time, and a clipboard appeared in her hands. Jonathan felt the chair he was in become cold and hard. He looked down and saw a metal contraption bearing his weight. Were those his arms that were fastened with chains to the arms of the chair?

Aurora leaned over and looked deeply into his eyes.

So beautiful . . .

" . . . will feel full and drowsy, as though waking up from a short nap . . ."

Was she saying something?

"Four . . . three . . ." Aurora said.

" . . . two . . ."

Whose voice was that?

" . . . one."

Jonathan's eyes fluttered open, and he gasped at the memories that flooded his brain. A man with a clipboard stood before him, staring deeply into his eyes.

"Welcome back, Detective Shelby," the man said comfortably. "Have a nice trip?"

Jonathan felt the sensations of reality rushing into his pores. His wrists and ankles chafed where the chains had rubbed them raw. His naked torso shivered on the cold metal chair, a chair he now remembered was bolted securely into the cement floor beneath him. His eyes wildly traced the line that formed between the plastic needle in his left arm and the medical IV bag that hung on a stand behind his head.

I am alone in this place, he thought desperately. *I am alone.*

The man stood up and made a note on his clipboard. Then he spoke aloud, as if talking into a microphone hidden somewhere in the darkened room where Jonathan now found himself.

"Subject still shows some resistance to the hypnotic suggestions," the man said. "Increase the potency of the opiate solution and the hallucinogen before the next test."

An overwhelming sense of hopelessness and exhaustion shuddered through Jonathan's frame. The man with the clipboard turned to leave the room, pausing to switch off the lights at the door.

"Get some sleep, Detective," the man said coolly in the darkness. "You're going to need your strength."

— — —

Robby was on the verge of throwing a tantrum. *Why-won't-it-open-why-won't-it-open-why-won't-it-open?* They banged on the weather-beaten oak door of the old Baptist church situated on the edge of the greenbelt.

Because, stupid, we forgot to leave the stick in the door last time we were here.

The church had been abandoned for as long as they could remember. They'd heard it had originally been a little country church built on the outskirts of town a long time ago. Then, as the years went by and the city began to sprawl farther south, newer construction had sprung up around it. The influx of homes in the area swelled the congregation so that ultimately they outgrew this little old building. Elaina said the congregation had moved to a bigger, newer facility ten or fifteen years ago and had been unable to sell this smaller, deteriorating building, so they left it empty.

Eventually the city of Lehigh bought the land next to it and put in a small neighborhood park for families who lived along the greenbelt. Kinseth had been glad about that, because they enjoyed playing on the equipment at the little park. And that was how they'd first begun exploring in this church as well. For a while there had been a tattered sign in the front parking lot announcing that the church was for sale, but that had eventually been taken down as well. Now the building waited and rotted, like a toy a child once played with all the time and then forgot.

Kenny had little patience for Robby's antics and didn't hesitate to make that known. Besides, he didn't really like this old church; it frightened him a little. It creaked when they walked on the wood floors. It smelled funny in there, like oldness and death. And that thing behind the altar gave him nightmares. Secretly he hoped they'd be locked out of the church forever and go back to playing on the swings and slides at the little park like they used to do.

We did put the stick in last time, said Seth. *We remember doing it, and see? There's our stick right there. Somebody knocked it out on purpose. Somebody doesn't want us going into that church anymore.*

Kinseth decided it was time to step in. *All right. Everybody calm down. This has happened before, and we still got in, remember?*

The voices in Kinseth's head grumbled a bit more, but they all knew they wouldn't accomplish much by complaining. They started walking around the church building, looking for windows that were unlocked or cracked open.

We should have taken our medicine, mumbled Kenny. *We always think better when we take the medicine.*

"We go to sleep when we take our medicine," Kinseth whispered. "We can't hear any of us talking when we take our medicine."

Sometimes that's a good thing.

But not all the time.

Most times.

It feels wrong.

Elaina says it's the right thing to do. And Elaina loves us. Elaina saved us after the car wreck. Elaina held our head together with her bare hands until the paramedics came. Elaina says we should take our medicine and just be Kinseth all the time. Like we used to be.

We are Kinseth.

All the time?

All the time. We just can't manage all of Kinseth all the time.

Fragmented personality, we know. We heard the doctors talking too.

Wake up, stupid. Brain damage is what they said. Duh.

That's why we should take our medicine. The doctors think we should take it. Elaina thinks we are taking it.

But we never promised her that we'd take it.

Right, we never promised.

'Cause we always keep our promises. Always.

Kinseth spotted an open window near the rear of the building, back where the church offices had been years before.

What time is it? they wondered suddenly. Kinseth pulled the silver pocket watch out of his jeans and clicked open the cover. They glanced back across the greenbelt toward the cul-de-sac. Elaina would be waking up soon, and she'd said she wanted to go grocery shopping when she did. Would she be mad if Kinseth weren't there when she woke up?

Kinseth scratched their head, brushing away dried grass from behind their ears. "We'll have to come back another time," they said finally. Robby was not happy about that at all. He complained all the way home.

— — —

Number 26 paused at the bottom of the steps to collect his senses. When his father bought this place years ago, it was part of new construction going up all along the block. That meant he was able to persuade the builders to equip it with a few custom modifications that were, as he had said, *better suited* to their family needs.

The first bedroom in the basement needed to be remodeled again only two years ago, after . . . well, after Number 3 had suffered that stroke. It was now a fully functioning private hospital room, complete with heart monitors, breathing machine, oxygen analyzers, a full bathroom, and more. The large cabinet in the corner of the room held more medical supplies—mostly gloves and syringes and IV bags and the like. It was carefully positioned eighteen inches away from the back wall, making a space large enough for a man to squeeze in back there if necessary. When necessary.

Number 3 lived out his days in this hospital room. The stroke had limited his capacity to speak and affected his ability to move the muscles on his right side, so he required twenty-four-hour medical care. That was why Number 61 was such a valuable part of this team. Sure, they all pitched in to help regularly, changing catheter bags, massaging the old man's legs and arms to prevent atrophy, helping to turn and move him to prevent bed sores, occasionally changing IV bags and providing timely injections, all those things. But Number 61 kept him alive and functioning with her careful administration of his prescriptions and physical-therapy needs. Not as if the cantankerous old goat appreciated it. Not once had 26 heard him utter even a word of thanks or appreciation for all this group had done for him. The old man was completely dedicated to the mission, and that was all that mattered to him. When he'd had the stroke, he still refused to relinquish the command of this band of soldiers. So, while Number 26 was the de facto leader in charge, he always reported at least once a day to Number 3. And when his father gave an order, Number 26 was a good soldier and carried it out.

The next room down in the basement was the largest, and they used it as a supply room, where 61 kept her stores of medicines and conducted random experiments and where 39 stockpiled his weapons and technological spare parts. Number 26 only went in there when he was hunting for a certain drug cocktail or when 61 wanted his opinion on some experiment she was running.

The small, office-sized room was where 39 had the computer command center. All of the security alarms and cameras around the house transmitted into here. Also, the row of computers and video-editing equipment lined a wall in this room.

The last room in the basement was 26's favorite, his own private heaven. In there he kept his studio. "Every artist needs a studio," he'd argued to Number 3, "and we are all artists, are we not?" The old man had agreed with him that time, and 26 had taken full advantage of his blessing. It was within the tinted walls of this studio that 26 found his inspiration.

Number 26 felt tremors beginning in his abdomen and recognized the familiar dryness in his mouth. He heard the wind from the air-conditioner vents whispering that he should get today's visit with Daddy over with already. He took an unsteady step toward the door to Number 3's hospital room, then saw 39 step quietly out of the studio.

"Everything all right in there?" 26 asked.

Number 39 nodded and carefully lowered his gaze. "Yes, sir. Almost ready for you, sir. Just need to change the balance of the heroin solution and then run a few more tests."

"Good. Let me know as soon as our model is prepared."

"Will do, sir." Number 39 stood outside the door to the supply room, waiting.

Number 26 stared at him for a moment, knowing there was something he was forgetting. Then he reached inside his pants pocket and pulled out a slip of paper with a name on it. "I left something on the front seat of the car," he said at last. "Make sure it gets delivered. You'll have to look up the address."

"No problem, sir. I can get it ready for delivery right now, if you like."

"You're dismissed then."

After 39 disappeared up the stairs, 26 produced a worn key. When they'd moved the old man into this room, it quickly became apparent he wanted his privacy. So 26 had played the good son. He had his underlings tear out the old door and replace it with a heavy, reinforced metal door and frame. He contemplated putting a deadbolt on the door so it could be locked easily from either the inside or the outside, but in the end he settled for a heavy-duty, dual-keyed door handle, the type found in a mental hospital or a high-security manufacturing company. The knob always required a key to lock or unlock, no matter which side of the door a person was on. Number 26 had made only three keys to the room, one of which he always kept with himself. The second was placed under the old man's pillow. Just in case. The third he had entrusted to 61 so she could perform her scheduled tasks without hindrance. As a matter of procedure, they always kept that door locked, whether inside the room or outside. Number 26's father was almost fanatical about his privacy.

Number 26 fingered the key in his hand for a moment. Then he sucked in a deep breath and stepped into the hospital room, pausing long enough to lock the door behind him as usual.

He was immediately greeted by the frowning face of his father.

— — —

Buck Barnes sat on the curb across from what used to be the Conklin Art Gallery and watched the activity around him. Things were relatively quiet now. All of the paramedics and ambulances were gone, the fire was out, and the police blues had taken over the scene. They'd secured the area, and several officers in plastic gloves were sifting through rubble for evidence. A plainclothes forensics team was there as well, directing the blues as needed, making notes, and running little tests from tools in their briefcases. Most of the witnesses had been questioned and released, and all of the shops along this whole block had been ordered to close for at least the weekend. Some of the merchants complained about lost sales, but most understood the gravity of the situation and cooperated without a fuss.

The detective tugged on the sleeves of his jacket, a nervous habit he acquired not long after he outgrew the coat's midsection a few years before. He'd planned to work methodically down the row of shops, showing Jonathan Shelby's photo and hoping someone had seen him last night. But the explosion that had rocked this little corner put an end to that plan. Most of the people he had talked to were still in shock and unable to remember anything from last night, let alone a single, nondescript man who might or might not have strolled down their sidewalk eighteen to twenty-four hours ago.

Kyle Conklin, the guy who made the call to the station last night, had been the only person to see anything suspicious down here yesterday. And now that poor kid was dead as well, a victim of the blast that took his parents' gallery. Buck felt pressure like a stone wall bearing down on him. Had Jonathan stumbled into the characters Kyle had reported? Were they related to the bombing? And without enough witnesses to interview, where should he go next? He glanced at his watch. Jonathan had been out of communication for more than nineteen hours now.

He rubbed the short brown hair—what was left of it—on top of his head, thinking. Then he reached into his back pocket and pulled out the newspaper clipping—the warning—he'd received from Mr. Conklin that morning. He unfolded it carefully and studied the image it bore. The edges of the clipping were straight and crisp, the sign of a paper cutter, he decided. Someone using scissors wouldn't have been able to cut four such exact lines. He'd had it dusted for prints and found nothing but Conklin's. The advertisement itself was generic, black and white, and about eight inches square. The red ink appeared to have been hand-written on the ad.

Unpretty.

What was that supposed to mean? Was that even a word?

Buck looked more closely at the word, written diagonally with fat strokes across the full ad. "Hmph," he said aloud. "That ink looks kinda funny." He turned the clipping over in hopes of seeing the pen impressions on the back side of the ad, but there was none. "Writer has a light touch," he muttered, flipping the ad back to the front.

Across the street Buck saw a stoop-shouldered man in an overcoat come trudging out from among the wreckage of the Conklin. Mr. Conklin looked like a man whose heart had been crushed within him; he walked around the front of his gallery aimlessly, as if he wanted to leave but didn't have anyplace to call home. He held a charred fragment of a painting in his left hand, but he seemed barely aware that it was there.

Buck pitied the man and felt a twinge of guilt himself. Was there something more he could have done to warn Conklin during their meeting earlier this morning? Should he have insisted on shutting down and evacuating the gallery, despite the obvious protests that would have provoked from Mr. Conklin?

Barnes replayed the meeting in his head and mournfully reached the conclusion that even if he'd acted right away, he wouldn't have had enough time to prevent the disaster. There was no way Buck would have been able to get the place shut down and an inspection team in place before the bomb went off. Besides, he reasoned, he'd had nothing to indicate that an explosion was even planned—no motive, no suspects, no real warning, nothing. All he had was an enigmatic newspaper clipping that Mr. Conklin had found taped to his door that morning. No one could have guessed that it would lead to . . . this.

The detective looked from the charred remains of the gallery back to the clipping. There had to be a clue in there somewhere, a clue he was missing. He studied it for a few more minutes, until the coolness of the curb penetrated the seat of his pants and prompted him finally to stand again. Mr. Conklin was still wearily pacing across the street, still gripping forgetfully that scrap of canvas he'd brought out of the destruction. Buck shook his head. He'd been so preoccupied by the loss of life across the street and by the worry over his missing coworker that he'd completely missed the artistic loss caused by the explosion. "The Michelangelo Mirrors" had effectively been erased from history. He wondered briefly about the monetary value of the work and the many hours that Bertrand artist must have invested in painting his now-obliterated masterpieces.

Barnes paused at that thought, imagining an artist brushing

paint onto a canvas. And suddenly he felt a clue tickling at the edge of his consciousness.

He stared again at the advertisement in his hand, pulling it near his face for a close-up inspection. After a moment he pulled out his cell phone and called an old friend, a professor of art history at the university. She agreed to meet him in half an hour at her office on campus.

Buck closed his cell phone. He would wait for confirmation from the art professor, but he felt reasonably sure he was right anyway. That red handwriting on this clipping wasn't, as he'd assumed, ink from a fat-tipped red marker. It was red paint, expertly applied with a narrow, pen-width paintbrush across the image of the Conklin ad.

— — —

Number 26 met his father's grimace with a tight smile, nodding his respect toward Number 3's rank before sitting down in the chair beside the hospital bed.

The stroke had left Number 3 with diminished speech ability; most of the others could only make out mumbles when the leader spoke. But 26 knew his father's rhythm and intonation, almost knew his thoughts sometimes, it seemed. He alone could interpret the old man's mumblings, though sometimes he wished he couldn't.

The old man grunted. Number 26 automatically interpreted the signals in his head. *Busy day?*

"Successful day," Number 26 said. "You'd be proud."

Number 3 said nothing.

Number 26 gestured toward the muted TV screen on the wall. "Did you see the news?"

Number 3 said nothing.

"The plan worked perfectly. I paid the admission and walked

into the gallery unnoticed. There were already several coats on the coat rack inside the door. Number 39 had packed my jacket with enough C-4 to firebomb the entire inside of that gallery. I took a moment to verify the paintings, and they were ghastly. Absurd distortions of the master's magic. Unpretty. We were right to erase them."

Number 26 paused to assess his father's response so far. For now, at least, the old man was listening. Number 26 half expected to hear a list of flaws in the plan, criticisms of how he'd carried out the plan—their plan. But none came. Not yet at least. He decided to keep going.

"There were other people in the gallery when I tripped the timer and hung my jacket on the coat rack, but that couldn't be helped. Then I went outside and waited. Exactly five minutes later the offensive images disintegrated in a beautiful blast of heat and fire." He waited, but his father still didn't respond. "You'd have been proud, Dad."

Number 3 said nothing, but his frown seemed to relax in severity a bit.

Number 26 felt his face flicker into a happier posture. He'd made the old man proud, he could tell, and that was a rare thing. A thing to be savored.

"More good news," the son said. "We may have found our Minos model yesterday."

The old man grunted. *Another one?*

Number 26 shrugged. "The first one wasn't right after all. We had to wash him out. But this one, well, I have higher hopes for this one. The jaw line is especially good."

Another grunt.

"Well, no, he's not ready yet. But 39 is prepping him for his debut. I hope to be able to begin working with him in the next week or so."

Number 3 breathed a sigh into the oxygen tube, and his eyes became vacant. Number 26 didn't often pity his father, but he did at that moment. The man had been a great artist in his own right before the stroke; he'd taught his son more than all those professors at art schools across the world had taught him, more than all those professors put together. Now he could barely hold a pencil in his deadened hand. Sad.

Number 26 allowed himself to relax into a more personal posture. A leisurely grin spread across his face.

"One more thing, Dad," he said conspiratorially, and felt rewarded by the renewed interest that flickered in his father's eyes. "I met a girl today. She's very pretty. Trim and tall. Long, thick, dark brown hair. Coffee-colored eyes. Smooth skin, tanned. Nice smile. And she's an artist."

Number 3 said nothing, waiting. So 26 continued. "We went for a walk together in North Downtown." He settled back into his chair, warming up to the subject. "I think she likes me."

SATURDAY, SEPTEMBER 20, EARLY MORNING

It was shortly after 3:00 A.M. when the man stood in front of the row of metal mailboxes in the breezeway of the apartment building. The night was silent except for an occasional whistle of cold air that wended its way through wind chimes hung somewhere nearby. The man produced a small flashlight and ran it across the names on each box, finally stopping at the one for Apartment 20.

He walked quietly down the sidewalk to the third entryway, then up the flight of stairs. Apartment 20 was the second door on the left.

From a pocket inside his brown leather jacket, the man produced a roll of packing tape and a small, brown, padded envelope, the kind used to send a CD or DVD through the mail. He hadn't bothered to put a name on the envelope; it was going to be obvious for whom it was intended. With two swift strokes, he tore off medium-length strips of packing tape and quickly affixed the package below the 20 that adorned the door.

Delivery completed, he turned to the stairs and quietly disappeared into the night.

FOUR

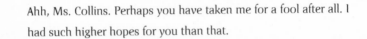

Ahh, Ms. Collins. Perhaps you have taken me for a fool after all. I had such higher hopes for you than that.

EXCERPT FROM THE MICHELANGELUS RECORDINGS,
TAPE 5,
TRANSCRIBED BY H. J. COLLINS

— — —

WEDNESDAY, SEPTEMBER 24, MORNING

T.W. heard the telephone ringing beside his bed and groaned. Not again. Not today. He looked at the brick-red digits that glowed dimly in the clock next to the phone: 5:45 A.M. Right on schedule. He reached out clumsily and pulled the receiver to his ear.

"Hello." He sounded groggy and was happy about that. Maybe she'd finally get the message.

"T.W.? It's Hummingbird."

"Big surprise."

"I couldn't sleep, T.W. I was worried about you. Are you okay? Is everything okay?"

"Humm, sweetie, you've got to stop calling me at awful hours of the morning."

He heard the tremble in his sister's voice and immediately regretted saying that.

"But are you okay, T.W.? Are you okay?"

"Yes, Hummingbird. I'm fine. Sleepy but fine."

"How about Peg? Where is she?"

T.W. sighed. "I assume she's at her apartment. I assume she's still in bed, dreaming sweet things and enjoying the fact that she can sleep."

"But you don't know? When was the last time you talked to her, T.W.?"

"Last night. We had dinner together. We watched a DVD. Then I came home around eleven o'clock." There was silence on the other end of the phone. "Humm," T.W. said, "I'll call her, just to make sure. But not now. It's too early. I'll call her before I go to work, all right?"

"Okay."

"Now go back to sleep, sweetie. I'll come by and check on you during lunch. All right?"

"Okay."

"I'm going to hang up now." He paused. "Humm?"

T.W. waited. He heard Hummingbird's breathing falter, as if she were fighting back tears. He sighed. This had been going on every day since Hummingbird had come home from the hospital. The doctor said it was posttraumatic stress disorder and that they should try to be patient with Hummingbird while she worked through the emotional distress of having survived an explosion where eight other people died.

"T.W., I'm scared." There was a catch in Hummingbird's throat.

"I know, sweetie. I know."

"No, you don't know," she snapped. Then softened. "You don't know."

T.W. rubbed his bleary eyes. "You're right. I don't know. Want me to come over now so you can tell me about it?"

"T.W., I'm scared for you and for Peg."

"You have nothing to be afraid of. Not for us or for yourself."

"That detective came by here again last night."

"I'll call over there again and talk to him. But really, Humm, you should think about answering his questions. He seems like a decent guy, and he's trying to catch those people who blew up the Conklin. He thinks you might be able to help him catch those killers."

"No, T.W., you don't understand. I can't talk to him. I just can't." She was crying now.

"Want me to come over there, sweetie?"

"No."

"You sure? I'm awake now. I can bring you some breakfast or something."

"No." There was a strained silence. "T.W.?"

"Yeah?"

"Will you . . ."

He sighed. "Yeah, Humm. I'll call her right now."

"Thanks, T.W. I love you, you know that, right?"

"Yeah, Humm. I love you too."

"Bye-bye, big bro."

"Get some sleep, little sis."

T.W. hung up the phone and leaned back in bed. Peg wouldn't be happy when he called her this early in the morning. Again. But he hoped she would understand. T.W. reached over to the phone pad and dialed his fiancée's number.

She didn't answer.

WEDNESDAY, SEPTEMBER 24, LATE MORNING

Kinseth Roberts stood on the wraparound porch at 1669 Kirby Court and waited. They knew they weren't supposed to be here, but they had also seen the three meanest men leave the house earlier. That meant the only people left in the house were that lady who never said anything and that other one, the smart man who sometimes came outside to read a book or a stack of papers.

Well, and the man in the hospital bed. But Kinseth weren't supposed to know about him.

And that other man, the prisoner. But Kinseth weren't supposed to know about him either.

Kinseth thought about smiling—so whoever was inside would know they were friendly—but decided against it. Ever since the accident, and the surgeries that had come afterward, Kinseth's smile looked something like a grimace. Oh, Elaina didn't mind. And the folks at the Catholic Center didn't either. They said God liked it when people smiled, and they seemed to enjoy making Kinseth grimace with delight, telling jokes or reading funny stories or showing comic strips they'd cut out of the newspaper. They said Kinseth used to laugh all the time, that the grimacy smile reminded them of happy days and that they should do it more often. Sometimes Kinseth laughed for them even when nothing was funny. It seemed like the nice thing to do.

But other people seemed a little frightened by Kinseth's smile. For them, Kinseth tried to keep a straight face, so it wouldn't make them uncomfortable. That's what they did now, standing on the porch, waiting.

The thing that always made Kinseth curious about this house was the front door. They had learned already that the doorbell was a fake. Pushing that button didn't ring a bell or do anything inside the house. They couldn't simply walk in through the front door either, because there was no doorknob on the outside. There was no lock either. The front of the door was entirely smooth from top to bottom. The only way into this house was to be let in by someone who was already inside.

Kinseth had stood on this porch for an hour yesterday, but nothing had ever happened. Now, today, while Elaina was sleeping, they thought they'd stand here again and see if something might change. They weren't sure why they wanted to stand here, really. But something made them curious yesterday, and even though today they couldn't remember what it was that had made them curious, Kinseth didn't like knowing they'd started something yesterday that was still unfinished today. So they waited.

They had been on the porch for only twenty-five minutes today when the door finally opened. It was the smart man. He was frowning, but it was a tolerant frown, as if he wasn't going to hurt anybody.

"You're not supposed to be here," the man said. "You know that."

Kinseth tried hard not to grimace-smile. But they were feeling very excited about this new conversation.

"You don't want me to tell your sister you've been over here, do you? You know how she feels about that."

Kinseth blinked nervously. They wanted to say something but weren't sure which words to make come out. The man started to close the door.

"How's the patient?" Kinseth asked suddenly. The door stopped moving. "The sick man in the bed. Is he any better?"

The man cocked his head slightly to the side. "Which one are you?"

Kinseth breathed in and made a quick decision. "Robby," they said.

"The kid?"

Kinseth nodded. The smart man seemed to relax a bit.

"There is no patient in here, Robby," the man said. "You must have made him up."

Kinseth nodded and then reached into the pocket of their

jeans and pulled out a small plastic cowboy. "We brought this for the patient," they said. "We thought he might want something to play with."

Inside their head, Kenny was pouting and complaining that the cowboy was his toy and that they shouldn't be giving it away to the strange man in the bed. Outside, Kinseth held out the toy toward the man.

The man's face looked mildly amused, but he shook his head. "Nice of you, kid, but there's no patient in here, so you should keep your little toy and play with it yourself."

Kinseth nodded. Now they remembered why they had come over here yesterday, what it was that had made them curious enough to stand on the front porch of this house.

"How about the prisoner?" Kinseth asked. "Does he want a toy to play with?" It bothered Kinseth that the prisoner might be lonely and that he might not have any friends to play with. Kinseth knew what it was like to be lonely. Maybe they should be friends with the prisoner, and then none of them would feel lonely.

The smart man's face hardened. "Go home, kid."

Kinseth swallowed and held out the cowboy. The man slapped Kinseth's hand and sent the plastic toy flying into the yard.

"Go home, Robby. And stop coming over here. We don't like unpretty things in this house. Unpretty things get hurt here."

The door closed quickly in Kinseth's face. They waited on the porch for forty-five minutes longer, but the door didn't open again. Kinseth wondered what the man had meant when he'd said he didn't like unpretty things. Their hand instinctively touched their face, gently tracing the scar that traveled across it.

Finally they went back into the yard and retrieved the cowboy. They checked the time on the silver pocket watch and figured they still had several more hours before Elaina would wake up.

They took a longing look back toward the front door of the house, then made a decision.

Kinseth followed the path around to the greenbelt behind the cul-de-sac. It seemed like a good time to visit that old church again.

WEDNESDAY, SEPTEMBER 24, EARLY AFTERNOON

Buck Barnes rubbed his bleary eyes and adjusted the recline on his car seat to make more room between him and the steering wheel. Stakeouts, he had to admit, were the most boring part of his job. But they were important. Take this Hummingbird Collins girl, for instance. She had seen the explosion at the Conklin Art Gallery last week, yet she was the only witness who refused to talk to police about what she'd seen. That raised all kinds of red flags for Buck.

He'd called her apartment several times but always got her answering machine. He'd visited her bookstore down the block from the Conklin, but they told her that Ms. Collins was going to be out for a while until she recovered from injuries suffered in the blast. The woman's doctor informed him that she was doing fine physically, but she was now experiencing some emotional distress from having gone through the explosion. Still, she knew something—she had to—and Buck needed to find out what that something was. She was his last hope for finding any information that might lead him to Jonathan Shelby.

He suspected foul play, of course, when it came to Jonathan, but there had been no ransom note from kidnappers, no claim of responsibility, no buzz among his sources on the street, nothing. Shelby's wife was nearly beside herself with worry and grief. Her employer, the Cole Corporation, had even offered a generous reward for information leading to the whereabouts of Detective

Shelby. That led to calls from a few treasure-seeking tipsters, but without exception, every tip proved to be either a wild-goose chase or simply a dead end.

Hummingbird Collins had refused to answer her door—again—when Buck went by last night. But the rolled-up newspaper he'd seen outside her door earlier that day was gone, so he figured she must at least be coming out long enough to pick up her paper. And he figured it was time to find out more about the woman he had under surveillance.

After a few calls to information hounds in his department, he had a nearly complete file on the young woman. He'd set up his stakeout in an unmarked car across the street from her apartment building late last night, making sure he had a clear view of her front door over the balcony at the top of the stairs. Then he bought himself an oversized cup of coffee, read through her file by flashlight, and waited the night away.

Hummingbird Collins, he discovered, was twenty-five years old. Like her older brother, T.W., she'd attended her father's alma mater and become a Mountaineer, graduating from the University of West Virginia with a degree in fine arts a few years ago. She'd been born in Philadelphia, but her family had moved here shortly after her birth.

Her father, Nuncio, had played a little pro football, bouncing around the NFL before finally catching on as a fullback for the Eagles. They called him Nuncio the Night Train, because they said he hit opposing players like a train wreck in cleats. He lasted four years in Philly before a knee injury forced him to retire. Hummingbird had been two years old at the time. Night Train moved his family back to Lehigh then, back to the place where he and his wife had both grown up. Nuncio Collins had died of a heart attack two years later, when Hummingbird was only four years old. Her mother used the life-insurance money to create college funds for the three kids and also to open a "new and used" bookstore downtown. Hummingbird had worked in that store since she was a girl, taking time out to go to college but then returning home—and to the bookstore— after graduation. When her mother retired two years ago, Hummingbird took over the store and had been running it ever since.

Buck had visited the store a few times over the years himself. He remembered the elder Mrs. Collins as a friendly, warm individual. He'd made a note to himself to try to track her down if he still couldn't get to Hummingbird. Maybe she'd be able to help him get some information out of her daughter.

Though it was past midnight, he continued to flip through the pages in his newly created file on Hummingbird Collins and read the rest of the family information. He figured sleep was a luxury he could afford only after Jonathan Shelby had been found.

The young woman had two older brothers. Detective Barnes groaned at the sight of the oldest—the attorney who had called two days ago and threatened harassment charges if Barnes didn't stop bothering Hummingbird. He went by the name of T.W., and Buck enjoyed a wry grin when he saw what the initials actually stood for. Fortunately, this guy, T.W., was primarily just a sports lawyer—meaning he was basically a glorified agent for pro athletes, probably using his father's NFL connections to get clients and spending most of his days schmoozing big egos and reading the fine print in athletic contracts.

The other brother, the middle child, was a freelance photographer here in town. It had seemed to Buck that one of the other guys in the department knew that photographer kid. Maybe worked with him on a case before? He wasn't sure. At any rate, it didn't matter at the moment, because judging from the credit-card bills, the photographer had joined his mother on a tour of Europe, and neither was scheduled to return to the States for several weeks. Detective Barnes closed the folder then and let his bulky form—an imperfect mix of muscle and fat, he conceded—settle into the seat of his car.

Barnes had been dozing in the driver's seat of his sedan when the sound of a car door startled him awake. It was 2:30 in the morning. Trying to slump out of sight, he watched as a large man in a dark leather coat exited a Ford Taurus and walked up the sidewalk toward the building where Hummingbird Collins lived. The detective quickly jotted down the license-plate number of the car, just in case. He watched as the man disappeared inside the entryway, then reappeared at the top of the stairs. The man strode quickly to Hummingbird's front door and appeared to attach something—an envelope?—right under the numbers of her apartment. A moment later he was back but walking away from the Taurus. He quickly disappeared on foot somewhere down the street.

Buck was overcome with curiosity. He pulled up his dashboard computer and tapped in the license-plate number on the Taurus. It belonged to one Hollis Evans, with an address in Shinnstoo, a smaller town situated a little north of Lehigh in upstate West Virginia. That explained why the large man left the car and took off on foot. Obviously, the Taurus had been stolen earlier in the night, used for this errand, and abandoned. Barnes flagged the file so that when it was called in as stolen later in the morning, the operator taking the call would be able to tell Mr. Evans where to find his wayward auto.

Next, the detective exited his car and retraced the footsteps of the mysterious deliveryman. When he stood in front of Apartment 20—Hummingbird Collins's apartment—he found a brown padded envelope taped to the door. The detective was tempted simply to remove the package and examine its contents. That's what they'd do in those TV crime shows that so many people enjoyed. But the honest officer in Barnes won out; he wouldn't break the law by examining Hummingbird's mail without a warrant. He would remember that it had been delivered, and he would make a note to ask about its contents at the earliest opportunity.

Buck had returned to his car then and spent the rest of the night dozing in and out of sleep. A little after 5:00 in the morning the carrier for the *Lehigh Chronicle* woke him up again. Moments later the soft thud of the newspaper hitting the door of Apartment 20 again captivated his curiosity. Barely five minutes later the door to Hummingbird's apartment opened, and the bathrobed woman stepped tentatively out to retrieve the paper. Buck thought about trying to run up the stairs to catch her, but knew he'd be woefully late and would probably just scare the young woman anyway.

Then she'd turned to go back into her apartment, frozen by the sight of the envelope on her door. She looked frantically over the railing and around the steps that led to her apartment but saw nothing. Eyes wide, she stared for a moment at the envelope. At last she seemed to shiver, then reentered her apartment, leaving the envelope where it was.

Ten minutes later the young woman reappeared and, with a shaky hand, retrieved the envelope and carried it inside. Her apartment remained silent the rest of the long, slow morning.

Now it was after lunchtime, and Buck was feeling tired and hungry and desperately in need of a shower. He thought about trying to call Hummingbird Collins one more time but decided against it. Her apartment windows remained darkened all morning, and she hadn't come out again at all, not even to check the legitimate mail that the postal carrier delivered around 11:00.

The good detective had just decided to take a quick lunch break from his surveillance duties when a silver Lexus pulled up and changed his plans.

— — —

Kinseth was glad to see the window at the back of the Baptist church was still open. They had been a little worried that someone had found it and locked it, like the front door. They were bigger now, of course, and sometimes it was hard to fit their new, bigger body through small windows and cracks in walls and things, but Kinseth had had lots of practice at squeezing into and out of tight spaces. This window was creaky and stiff but still opened wide enough to welcome their body into the cool shadows of the church.

They found themselves in an abandoned office, a small, empty room that was probably a pastor's study or something like that. Kinseth couldn't help sneezing when they inhaled their first breath of the musty, dusty air. The sound of that sneeze echoed damply in their ears and caused them to freeze in place, wondering if anyone else was in the church—and if that anyone else might have heard the sneeze of an intruder. But nothing happened after one minute, after two minutes, after four minutes and thirty-one seconds, so Kinseth finally relaxed and stepped out of the empty office and into the hallway.

Seth and Robby wanted to go directly into the auditorium of the church and look at that beautiful scary thing behind the altar. Sometimes it changed, and they were terribly curious to discover if it was different this time. But Kenny argued against it and, in the end, won out.

So Kinseth turned instead toward the rear of the church, following the maze of hallways until they reached the room that had once been the place where a choir must have practiced. They walked carefully over to the back of the room, where a load of old risers had been stacked and left in place. As usual, the risers were exactly eighteen inches away from the wall. They knelt down and pushed, feeling that familiar, gleeful apprehension when the trapdoor swung silently open.

--- --- ---

T.W. parked his Lexus parallel on the street and hurried toward his sister's second-floor apartment. He took the stairs two at a time, then rapped loudly on the front door of her apartment.

"Hummingbird, it's me," he said. "Open the door."

When nothing happened, the lawyer paced in a circle for a moment, then pulled out his cell phone. On the fifth ring the answering machine clicked on. "Hey," Hummingbird's sunny voice said, "why aren't you shopping at the Collins Galleria of Books right now? Well, anyway, leave me a message, and I'll get back to you as soon as possible. Thanks!"

"Hummingbird," T.W. said. "Open the front door. I'm outside waiting in the—"

The door to Apartment 20 opened, and T.W. flipped his cell phone shut.

"Sorry," Hummingbird said. "I was drawing. Didn't hear you knocking."

T.W. looked at his little sister with compassion. She'd showered at least, but her thick brown hair still hung damply, unbrushed, over the shoulders of her bathrobe. She looked tired.

"How's your head?" he asked as he entered the tidy little apartment.

"Fine," she said, closing the door behind him and taking an extra second to secure the deadbolt lock into place. "Hardly any dizzy spells at all now." She seemed to be avoiding his gaze.

"You eat today?" he asked.

She nodded and gestured toward the kitchen. "Macaroni for lunch."

T.W. resisted the urge to pace around his sister's living room. He felt the nagging worry that had been building up inside him all morning, wanted desperately to talk to Hummingbird about it, but at the same time didn't want to make her feel panicked again. He decided to wait.

"What were you drawing?" he said, forcing his tense muscles to relax and sitting down on the couch by the door.

Hummingbird's eyes grew slightly wider, but she covered it quickly. "Nothing, really."

T.W.'s forehead creased. Hummingbird was not the type to hide her artwork. In fact, most times you couldn't keep her from showing you whatever it was she was working on at the moment.

"Show me," T.W. said. "I want to see."

There was hesitation in Hummingbird's face, but it was finally replaced by a look of trust in her eyes. She walked toward her bedroom and returned a moment later with a sketchbook of pencil drawings. She handed it to T.W. without saying anything.

T.W. opened the sketchbook and discovered that it held at least a dozen new pieces, all in pencil, all of the same person. It was a man, in varying poses and seen from varying angles. He appeared to have chiseled cheekbones and a sculpted nose and chin. Dark hair, short and thick. In every drawing, the eyes were the dominant feature, the most detailed and ominous. They seemed slightly narrowed and stared directly at T.W., no matter where he held the page. He flipped the pages and also noticed that the face on them never smiled.

"Who's this guy?"

Hummingbird didn't respond. Instead she sat on the couch next to her brother, leaned her head on his shoulder, and closed her eyes.

T.W. sat in silence with her for a moment, until he felt his sister's breathing even out. Then he reached an arm around her shoulders and lifted her face. She looked at him and, after a second or two, recognized something in his eyes.

"What happened?" she said quickly, stiffening upright on the couch, her eyes searching his face for clues.

"Look, it's probably nothing, Humm . . ."

"Are you okay?" she asked. "Did that detective—"

"No," T.W. said quickly. "No, I'm fine."

"What happened, T.W.? Tell me." She was pleading now.

He sighed. "It's just that, well, I called Peggy this morning like you asked me, but she wasn't at home."

Hummingbird's face creased with concern. "Did you call the police?"

"No, of course not. Not yet. I mean, Peg's a big girl. She's got a life of her own. She might have simply gone into work early today. Or maybe she was sleeping and didn't hear the phone."

"Did you call her at the university?"

T.W. stood. "Yeah, and that's what worries me a little. She hasn't been in her office all morning. No one's seen her. And she's not answering her cell phone either."

Hummingbird stared up at her brother with flashing eyes, as if weighing an important decision.

"Listen, Humm," he said, choosing his words carefully, "I think it's time you tell me what you've been hiding from everybody these last few days. I think it might involve me and Peggy, and if it does, I deserve to know about it."

Hummingbird's face flashed with indecision and then trust. "You're right, T.W.," she said finally. "I should have told you sooner, but I was, well, I was scared. I'm not used to being scared, not of anything."

"I know."

"Come here," she said after a moment. "I want to show you something."

— — —

Jonathan Shelby knew he was dreaming, but he kept his eyes closed and his body still anyway. The swirling darkness of his dream was so much better than the pitch blackness of his reality that he didn't want to do anything to jeopardize the momentary peace.

In the dream he heard himself breathing, a soft, shallow intake and exhale that sounded almost normal. He liked that. It was good to breathe.

He wanted to hear music, but at first there was none. Then he remembered that in a dream you could do anything your mind tells the dream to do. So he ordered the colors to sing. Of course, since black was the only color, it was a mournful song, hushed and full of bass-heavy tones. A funeral song. Jonathan let the music wash over his soul and wondered, briefly, how long he could control this quiet dream before waking himself up with his thoughts.

You know what would be nice. His semiconscious brain floated to the fore. *A visit from an angel.*

He remembered reading about angels in the Bible. Once, when one of Jesus's apostles, Peter, had been imprisoned, an angel had come in the night and led a dramatic rescue. Peter, all the while, thought it was a dream.

If the duct tape had not been pressed so tightly against his mouth, Jonathan would have smiled at that thought. But he knew no angel was coming to rescue him. Not now. Maybe not ever.

Black had stopped singing now, maybe running out of melody. But Jonathan could still hear the shadowy color breathing, matching the pace of his own respiration.

You sing pretty. Even without words.

Jonathan couldn't tell if he had said that to black or if black had said that to him.

Sing more pretty things.

Jonathan heard the low humming of black pick up again. He liked that song. It seemed special. He concentrated on the noise, listened more carefully to the harmony. It sounded like a hymn, like a song he had heard his mother sing when he was scared to go to sleep at night. Almost instinctively he matched the melody with low rumbles in his own throat.

Gradually Jonathan became aware that a new voice had entered the song. It was a plain tone, halting. Barely audible but warm. Sincere. It sang no words either but let its humming speak the lyrics.

For the first time in . . . well, Jonathan didn't know how long, he felt a measure of peace. If only he could sleep forever . . .

Black finally reached out to him. He felt its fingers press lightly into the palm of his right hand. *We thought you might need a friend,* it whispered. And slowly the swirling darkness thickened.

Jonathan Shelby knew he was dreaming. And then, gratefully, his consciousness finally gave way, fully, to black, until once more he was unaware of anything but the rainbow of colors reentering his dreams.

— — —

Hummingbird led T.W. into the bedroom and pointed to the corner where she had set up a large drawing table and lamp, with pencils and inks and even a few tubes of paint. Stacked neatly on the drawing table were five padded envelopes, each one about the size of a CD or DVD.

"The first one came on Saturday," she said evenly. "It was taped to my front door. Mrs. Findley next door took it down when she got her paper that morning and kept it with her until she saw I'd come home from the hospital. We do that kind of thing for each other, 'cause about a year ago there were some kids in the apartment complex who thought it was fun to steal FedEx packages and stuff.

"Anyway, that first envelope contained this." She walked over to the nightstand and retrieved a microcassette recorder. "And this." She reached inside one of the padded envelopes and pulled out a tiny cassette tape. She placed the tape inside the recorder and pressed rewind. "I've been getting a new microcassette taped to my door every morning since."

T.W. nodded grimly. He reached over and took the microcassette player from his sister's hands and pressed the play button.

Dear Ms. Collins, first, let me say that I hope someday soon to be able to comfortably call you by your first name. Perhaps even to get to the point where names are unnecessary between us. But as we are in the introductory stages of our relationship for now, the gentleman in me dictates the formality of my address to you.

I think I might not really have noticed you today, except that I became aware of the fact that you had noticed me. That was a pleasant surprise. I too am an artist, and it is always pleasurable to make the acquaintance of another who dabbles in the craft.

I think you must be wondering by now if I am the person you think I am. Yes, of course, the answer is yes. I am the one who planted the bomb at the Conklin Art Gallery. I suspect you disapprove, but suffice it to say I had my reasons, and my reasons were just.

Now comes the awkward part, Ms. Collins. I would very much like to continue our budding friendship, but I also am aware that you are a witness to something you likely should not have seen. I expect the police will soon be knocking on your door with all kinds of unsavory questions. I seek to protect you, my dear, from any-thing . . . unpretty . . . that you may be tempted to do. So please understand the strength of the warning I am about to give you.

Do not talk to the police. Do not talk to anyone about anything to do with me, with my work, or with the Conklin Art Gallery. I mean this as only a warning, but I must tell you that warnings can quickly turn into actions. Corona Sanchez, Ruth Swanson, Abram Erskine, Jonathan Shelby, and many others can testify to that.

I understand your brother is to be married in the coming months, Ms. Collins. I wish Mr. Collins and Miss Harrison a lifetime of happiness. It would be a shame if something happened to spoil their wedding day.

I look forward to chatting with you again soon.

Stunned, T.W. listened to the microcassette recorder as it moved into the familiar hissing of blank tape. At last he shut off the recorder and looked at his sister. She was trembling.

"Remember Corona Sanchez?" she said softly. "About two and a half years ago? She was that elementary-school teacher who disappeared for three weeks. When they finally found her body in that dumpster, she was naked and had been all shot up with drugs. They said it was the drugs that had killed her."

"It's okay, Hummingbird," T.W. said quietly, but his heart was racing.

"And that detective who keeps harassing me? He says he's looking for someone named Jonathan Shelby. He says he thinks the people who blew up the Conklin might be involved in the kidnapping of this Shelby guy. *Kidnapping,* T.W." She didn't have to say more. T.W. knew she was thinking about Peggy. And he was too.

"It's okay, Hummingbird," T.W. said again. There was determination in his voice. "We're not going to let this psycho killer scare us."

Hummingbird nodded, though she seemed to be fighting back tears. T.W. reached out to hug his sister close. "You're not alone anymore," he said. "We're in this together, and we'll figure out what to do. We always do, right?" She nodded into his shoulder and took in a deep breath.

"You sound like Mom," she said.

T.W. gave a dry chuckle. "Actually, I sound like Dad. But you're too young to remember that."

"I remember little bits of Dad," she said. "I don't want to be afraid anymore, T.W." She took in a deep breath. "I won't be afraid anymore." There was new determination in her voice now.

"It's okay to be afraid, honey," T.W. said comfortingly. "We just can't let being afraid be the thing that stops us from being brave. All right?"

She gave T.W. a quick squeeze, then pulled away from him to wipe away a tear that strayed down her cheek. "All right," she said, forcing a smile. "You're right."

She let her eyes wander around the bedroom. "Now go into

the living room so I can get dressed," she said at last. "I can't hide out here crying anymore." A worried expression flashed across her face. "We need to make sure Peggy's all right."

T.W. felt his jaw tighten. "Right," he said. He reached over and scooped up the pile of padded envelopes off the drawing table. "You get ready. I'm going to listen to these."

FIVE

There are those who have tried to label our organization as a cult. They say that Michelangelo Buonarroti is our prophet, and his paintings our sacred texts. They have even tried to name us with silly designations such as the "Michelangelus Movement" and such.

We, of course, find these accusations to be laughable. True, we have a proper appreciation, and respect, for the Genius of the Renaissance era, but it's absurd to think that we would ascribe a cult-like reverence to Michelangelo and make him our prophet of truth.

A cult, by definition, believes in some sort of God and seeks to worship that deity. We don't believe in God; in fact, we find the idea of him mostly to be an annoyance. Oh, don't get me wrong. We admire God. Well, the image of God, at least. Particularly his ability to create a masterpiece of judgment on the peoples of the earth. But if God ever did exist, he's long since dead by now.

That's why our work is so important. If there is no all-powerful Artist at work in the world, then some of the created beings must fill that function. Without artists like us, who would administer the beauty of justice in the world?

Without us, the unpretty would prosper.

And that, dear Ms. Collins, is something we can't allow to happen.

EXCERPT FROM THE MICHELANGELUS RECORDINGS,
TAPE 2,
TRANSCRIBED BY H. J. COLLINS

— — —

WEDNESDAY, SEPTEMBER 24, EARLY EVENING

Buck Barnes knew he was going to have to give this up before too long. His aging body could only take so much these days, and spending nearly twenty-four hours in an unmarked police car had left his neck, his back, his rear end, and most of the rest of him full of aches and pains. It had been more than four hours since Hummingbird Collins's lawyer brother had showed up. Buck kept thinking he might try to get some information out of the brother when he came out of the apartment, but given the lawyer's last phone call to him, that was an iffy prospect at best. And he couldn't keep sitting here doing nothing while Jonathan Shelby was still missing.

The detective sighed. The longer this woman avoided him, the more certain he was that there was a connection between Hummingbird Collins, the Conklin explosion, and the disappearance of Jonathan Shelby. There were too many coincidences for that not to be true. Shelby disappeared in North Downtown. Hours later the Conklin explosion, and Hummingbird Collins was the only witness unwilling to cooperate with the police investigation. And that Conklin advertisement. The art professor at the university had confirmed Buck's earlier suspicion. It had been red paint—PMS 193, the professor had guessed—that had been used to write *Unpretty* across the ad. And PMS 193 was a color that was well suited for illustrating blood in a painting. There were only a few art-supply stores in town that carried that particular PMS color, so Buck had talked to the managers at all three of those places. And found out that Hummingbird Collins was a regular customer at each and every one.

Detective Barnes had not suspected Hummingbird at first—after all, why would a young woman with all the promise of a great future blow it up in a flash by killing eight people just down the block from her? She had the proximity and access to have planted the bomb. But nothing in her profile indicated an interest in, or proficiency at, explosives. And what was the benefit? What would be the motive? Insurance fraud was out—it was the Conklin that had been torched, not her bookstore. It didn't make sense. But it also didn't make sense that she was so adamantly avoiding him.

Well, he still had options. He'd wait maybe one hour more. Then he'd head back to the station and start the warrant process with Judge Santos. He'd ask for permission to wiretap Hummingbird Collins's phone and also for a search warrant for her apartment and the bookstore. He might also ask for an arrest warrant for the young woman. Even though she wasn't a suspect in the explosion, she still could be categorized as a person of interest. He could hold her in jail for a few days at least, and maybe then he'd get her to talk.

Buck was making a list in his head of the paperwork he'd have to fill out when he got back to the station house and almost didn't notice the large, well-dressed man who crossed the street and stalked directly up to the driver's window of his car.

— — —

Hummingbird peeked out from behind the drapes in her apartment and watched as T.W. strode confidently across the street and walked right up to the driver's side of the tan Malibu. T.W. was an imposing figure when he wanted to be. He had Daddy's size and Mom's savvy about interpersonal relations. It felt good to have him on her side, but she still worried that maybe both of them were in over their heads.

And she was worried about Peg.

T.W. had called the university again but got only voice mail. He had called her three closest friends, who hadn't heard from her. Then had he called her mother. It was her mother who had called the police to report her daughter missing—only to find out she had to be missing for twenty-four hours in order for a report to be filed.

"We have to tell them, Humm," T.W. had said, sitting down across from her. "They're more likely to share our alarm over Peggy if they hear this maniac on tape. He talks about us."

"And he talks about me," she had said miserably. "If they have her, and we report the tapes, it will only be worse for her. And if they don't have her, then they might come after me."

T.W. had rubbed his temples in frustration and listened to the rest of the tapes. Then he had handed Hummingbird a small yellow pad and made her listen to them again.

"Write down anything that might give us a clue to who this guy really is or where he is or what it is he really wants from you," he had said. And then T.W. had done the same.

When they had finished, it seemed to Hummingbird that their lists were woefully short. But it was a start. And then it was time to formulate a strategy.

"The first thing we have to do," she had said, feeling her confidence grow immeasurably with the simple knowledge that she finally had someone with whom to talk about this situation, "is figure out a way to get Detective Barnes to stop nosing around me. He doesn't realize how much danger he is putting us in simply by trying to contact me. Maybe if he understood, he'd back off a little. At least not be so obvious."

"What do you mean?" T.W. had said.

In answer she'd pointed toward the window.

"Tan Chevy Malibu," she'd said tiredly. "He's been there since last night. Don't know how he's gone to the bathroom— guess they teach you how to hold it in detective school."

T.W. had snorted at that. But he had seemed relieved that

Hummingbird was regaining her sense of humor and, for once, declined to comment on her inability to make a "real joke." After he had checked the window, T.W. had come back and sat down on the couch, fingers tapping impatiently on the coffee table in front of him.

"Still," he had said, "this Detective Barnes is the one guy who might really be able to help us. If he doesn't get us killed first."

Then Hummingbird had had an idea. "Think Detective Barnes is a fan of football history?" she had asked.

A moment later, T.W. had smiled and made a call on his cell phone.

"Tomorrow morning," he had said when he hung up, writing down a time on a sheet from the yellow pad and tearing it off in his hand. Then he had glanced toward the window and said, "Well, I guess now's as good a time as any."

Now Hummingbird's brother was standing in the street, about to confront the good Detective Barnes and tell him—politely, she hoped—exactly where to go.

— — —

Ready hung up the receiver and hit a button to scramble the phone number again. You could never be too careful. And with the wall full of technology he'd amassed, he could easily track the old number and switch it over to the new one if the situation warranted. But it rarely warranted. One-use phone numbers were the best way to go, he'd decided years ago. Besides, he'd given T.W. a new number to use if necessary. He liked to keep in touch with Night Train's son. The kid had been a decent football player during his days at the University of West Virginia. Not the best, mind you, but certainly good enough to get picked up as a free agent somewhere in the NFL. Ready had always admired that T.W. had opted to pursue a career in law instead.

Ready chuckled to himself. T.W.—and many like him—often joked about the way Ready was so obsessive about his privacy. They lumped him into the "cadre of conspiracy theorists" who lived in the cracks of this town. Well, he didn't consider himself a conspiracy theorist. But he wasn't above using the network those guys had set up for his own benefit from time to time. Or for the benefit of his best friend's children. Which was why, even though they made jokes about him, they always came to him when a situation got dangerous. When you can't trust anybody, you always end up trusting the guy who never trusted anybody to begin with, right?

Ready logged onto an e-mail account and sent off a quick note to an address that immediately came back as undeliverable. He nodded. That meant Galway was watching. Now he hoped the old man would respond in time.

━ ━ ━

T.W. tried to act confident, but inside his stomach buzzed like a beehive on a hot summer day. Still, he didn't hesitate. He kept both his fists clenched and a frown on his face as he approached the tan Chevy Malibu that held a disheveled and tired-looking Detective Barnes. T.W. had a fleeting thought that the police department ought to be able to afford a nicer style of sedan for its officers to drive, but then he decided he paid too much in taxes already and wondered why the force didn't drive "preowned" Ford Escorts or something cheap like that. He had to stop himself from smiling at the thought of a high-speed police chase conducted with Escorts.

He was halfway across the street when Detective Barnes sat up in his seat and caught T.W.'s eye. The lawyer motioned for the detective to roll down his window, and Barnes complied. A quick read of the detective's eyes showed curiosity and an utter absence of fear.

"Detective Barnes," T.W. said. He hoped the policeman noticed that he was speaking more loudly than necessary in this situation. "I think it's time we talked face to face."

"My thoughts exactly, Mr. Collins," the detective said calmly.
He started to exit his car, but just as the door unlatched, T.W.
slammed it shut from the outside. Detective Barnes raised his
eyebrows. Still curious. Still no fear.

T.W. rested both hands, in fists, in the open window of the car
door. He held his head back away from the car, however, and
continued speaking in a louder-than-necessary voice.

"First," he said, "you will stop harassing my sister, or I will
have a half-dozen lawsuits on you before you can think to
breathe again. Lawsuits against you personally, against your department, against the city and anybody else I can think of.

"Second, you will break off surveillance of my sister, effective
immediately, and won't return to her home or her place of business unless invited.

"Third, you will leave now. Right now." T.W. finally leaned in
close and lowered his voice to a normal level. His eye flicked to
the right, behind the detective's car.

Detective Barnes appeared to allow himself a small smile.
"Now wait just a minute, Counselor," he started, but T.W. cut
him off.

"Leave now, Detective," he whispered. "Please." He opened
the palm of his right hand slightly, releasing a crumpled piece of
paper—he hoped surreptitiously—and dropped it into the detective's lap.

Barnes's gray eyes betrayed nothing, and at first T.W. was
afraid the detective hadn't noticed the covert drop. But then the
man's right hand swept over and covered the paper in his lap.
There was a moment of silence between the two men, then a curt
nod.

"As you wish, Counselor," Detective Barnes said. He started the engine, gave a short salute, and drove away.

T.W. stood for a moment in the middle of the street, feeling both relief and excitement. He glanced around the neighborhood, wondering from where—or even if—the right people had been observing that little exchange.

He took a deep breath and turned back toward Hummingbird's second-floor apartment.

He had just sent away the only man who might be able to offer some sort of protection for his sister, for his fiancée, and even for T.W. himself. He shook his head. He hoped that wouldn't prove to be as big a mistake as it seemed.

— — —

Hummingbird stood by the window and was startled when the telephone began to ring. She felt torn. Should she keep watching T.W. as he confronted the detective or answer the phone? She saw her brother stand up and take a step back into the street, heard the engine of the Malibu fire up. She decided to ignore the telephone. It stopped sounding after the fourth ring anyway, one before the answering machine would have answered.

The Malibu drove slowly away, and Hummingbird didn't know whether she felt relief or apprehension at the sight. T.W. stood in the middle of the street for a moment longer, probably collecting his thoughts. Then he turned and started back toward Hummingbird's apartment. As he reached the curb, he stopped and dipped a hand into his coat's inside pocket, pulling out a cell phone and flipping it open to answer. He spoke for a moment, then practically collapsed on the curb.

Hummingbird let out a soft cry and raced to the door. She grabbed her housecoat on the way out but didn't give herself time to find her shoes. Her bare feet slapped on the cold concrete of the stairs as she ran down to meet T.W. He was waiting for her at the bottom of the stairs, smiling.

"It's okay," he said, the relief evident in his voice. "She's okay."

"Peggy?" Hummingbird felt her spirits lift immeasurably.

"Yes, Peggy," he said. Then he grabbed his sister in a big bear hug and spun her around. "She spent the entire day at a conference center in Weston. They're working on some accreditation review at the university, and the department head thought all the tenured professors should go off-site for a meeting today to hammer out the details of their presentation to the review committee next week."

"So they just canceled all English classes and took off for the day?"

"Yep. Seems kind of counterproductive, if you ask me. But Peg says it actually turned out to be a good thing and that they're all feeling much better about the accreditation meetings next week."

Hummingbird sighed. "I have to admit, *I'm* feeling much better knowing Peggy is safe."

"Me too. And by the way, she's headed over here right now. Says she tried to call you, but there was no answer. She wants to take us both out to dinner but said that I should bring my credit card to pay for it. But hey, why quibble over details, right?"

Hummingbird smiled. "Just let me get my shoes."

WEDNESDAY, SEPTEMBER 24, LATE NIGHT

Jonathan Shelby was still in utter darkness, but he could feel his eyes open and shut. His whole body was sore from having been manacled to this torturous chair for . . . well, Jonathan didn't know for how long. His brain floated and fluttered, confusing him as it tried to make sense—again—of the environment around him.

By sensation alone he knew the hospital IV was still attached to his arm. His arms and legs were still locked securely to the chair. He was still unclothed. But the catheter they'd attached previously had now been removed. He wondered absently if that was a good sign or a bad one. A fresh strip of duct tape covered his mouth; the old one had been a bit more loose. He felt like sobbing again but knew that no more tears would come.

Jonathan couldn't tell how long he'd been staring into the darkness before he became aware of another presence. It was the breathing that tipped him off, a light, comfortable inhale and exhale that seemed to come from somewhere in front of where he was sitting.

He tried to make his eyes focus in the darkness and felt a re-newed pang from the headache that lately seemed to be his con-stant companion. After a moment he thought he distinguished movement directly ahead of him. He leaned forward, peering into the black, frustrated that he couldn't see clearly, that his brain seemed sluggish and waterlogged. He didn't know whether to be glad or frightened by the fact that he wasn't alone.

"So you're awake then," a voice said calmly. "I thought you might have been, but I wanted to make sure before I said any-thing. After all, you need your rest."

Jonathan remained silent.

The shadowy figure unfolded itself from the wall and casually walked toward the imprisoned detective. It was a man, medium build, medium height. But Jonathan could make out little else about him in the darkness.

The man tugged at a corner of the duct tape on Jonathan's mouth. "You know," he said serenely, "if you'd take your medicine instead of spitting it out every time, there'd be no need for this little inconvenience."

Jonathan couldn't remember what the man was talking about. But it filled him with anger anyway. The man gave a quick pull and ripped off the duct tape, like a person pulling a Band-Aid off sensitive skin. Jonathan grunted at the stinging that followed. The man moved to a desk lamp and turned on a dim bulb.

"How long have I been here?" Jonathan finally whispered.

The man simply smiled and turned away.

"I have a family," Jonathan said hoarsely. "A wife."

"Not anymore, Detective."

Jonathan stopped to let this news muddle through his syrupy thoughts. Had they hurt Aurora? Or worse—

"Tell me, Detective Shelby, do you believe in God?"

"Wh-what? Yes."

He was surprised at his lack of hesitation in responding to this question. Yes, he decided, he did believe in God. Still. In spite of all that was happening to him. That thought seemed to calm him a bit, to help clarify his thinking ever so slightly. *Aurora.*

"That's good to hear, Detective," the man said. "Because I am now your God."

Jonathan snorted. "You're just a bizarre freak."

The man said nothing but turned around to face his prey.

"And a pervert," Jonathan continued. "Where are my clothes?"

The man laughed lightly. "Obviously my interest in you is not sexual, Detective," he said. "Surely you remember that much."

"Then where are my pants?"

The man walked back to the wall, leaned against it, and slid to the floor until he was merely a shadow in the darkness again.

"What spirit is so empty and blind," he said from the dim-ness, "that it cannot recognize the fact that the foot is more noble than the shoe and skin more beautiful than the garment with which it is clothed?"

"What?"

"Michelangelo Buonarroti said that, Detective. Perhaps you've heard of Michelangelo?"

"Of course. But—"

"Have you also heard of Biagio da Cesena?" the man continued. "No? Because, Detective Shelby, you bear a striking resemblance to him. Oh, not the hair, of course. But the chin, the nose, the eyes. Striking."

Jonathan said nothing. This conversation was causing the pounding in his head to increase. He struggled to maintain a grip on reality. What was that in his hand?

"Biagio da Cesena was the master of ceremonies for the Vatican in 1541, at the time when Michelangelo painted his *Last Judgment* masterpiece on the altar wall of the Sistine Chapel."

This was beginning to sound familiar to Jonathan, though he couldn't tell why. He had never been interested in art, really. And he didn't even know that Michelangelo had painted anything on the walls of the Sistine Chapel. Hadn't he just done the ceiling? Jonathan began to sweat, and a slight tremor ran through his legs.

"When Michelangelo first showed the *Last Judgment* to the venerable Biagio," the man continued, "the Vatican's master of ceremonies was displeased, to say the least."

The man stood again and walked toward Jonathan. This time, however, he busied himself checking the line on the IV drip attached to the detective's arm. He produced a syringe and fitted the needle into a preset spot in the tubing that flowed from the IV bag and into Jonathan's veins.

"What's that you're giving me?" Jonathan asked tensely.

"Oh, nothing unusual," the man said evenly. "I think we've finally got the opiate solution at its optimal distillation for your body chemistry."

Jonathan felt a burning in his arm as the man injected the drug into the IV, a burning that he realized was familiar. How long had he been here? How long had they been drugging him? He was going to end up a junkie if he didn't get out of here . . .

"We'll let that settle in a bit," the man said after giving the injection. "And then, Detective Shelby, you'll be glad to know that I'll be removing this medical setup completely." The man leaned in close and unexpectedly produced a small flashlight that he shined directly into Jonathan's left eye. Jonathan cringed and squeezed his eyes shut, feeling completely blinded by the tiny light.

"You must relax," the man's voice soothed. "You are feeling calm and at peace."

Jonathan felt the muscles in his face reflexively loosen at the sound of the man's voice, felt the man's thumb prying open his left eye, then his right. The rest of his body, however, remained rigid.

"You see," the man's voice continued in that soft, comforting tone, "Biagio da Cesena objected to the nudity present in Michelangelo's masterpiece, and he made his objections known, in no uncertain terms, directly to the artist."

Jonathan's mind felt as if it was filled with a thick cloud of mist. He struggled to concentrate on his captor's words.

"Michelangelo responded by immortalizing Biagio. By painting his face on the figure of Minos—you might know him as a Satan figure from Greek mythology. He painted Biagio as Minos in hell."

The man squeezed open Jonathan's jaws and quickly placed one, then two squares of paper on his prisoner's tongue. Jona-

than tried to spit the papers out, but the man was too fast, forcing his lips together and covering them with a fresh strip of duct
tape.

"Of course, the good Biagio objected to this kind of depic-
tion, appealing to the pope himself and demanding that Michelangelo change the image. The pope, however, refused him,
pointing out that a pope's authority was in heaven, and since
poor Biagio was consigned to hell in the painting, there was
nothing the pope could do."

A recurring vision of snakes flitted through Jonathan's mind.
He vaguely felt the IV being removed from his arm and pressure
applied.

"In the hell that Michelangelo envisioned for Biagio da
Cesena, a serpent coils itself around the devil's naked frame."

In his mind, the bevy of snakes hissed and twisted, like strands
of a rope being woven together, until they became a monstrously
large serpent edging around the outskirts of the room.

"And that serpent is forever striking," the man continued in
that soothing, singsong voice. "Forever loosing its venomous
poison directly on poor Biagio da Cesena."

Jonathan felt a sudden heat fill the room. He heard snakes
hissing outside his head, in the walls, on the floors. He heard his
captor, unscrewing the dim lightbulb from the lamp.

"You look so very much like him," the man murmured in his
ear. "The spitting image of Biagio da Cesena. Of Minos. Of
Satan himself."

Jonathan jerked toward the voice. He heard the sound of
manacles falling off his left hand, then his right. He felt an icy
coldness slither around his left ankle.

"Biagio da Cesena was an unpretty man," the voice breathed.
"A devil, according to Michelangelo." A pause. Then a whisper.
"You are an unpretty man. A devil." The man was backing away

now, almost to the darkened doorway of the room. "Be careful, Biagio," he said in a hushed tone. "I understand snakes like unpretty things."

The shadowed man disappeared through an opening in the darkness.

Behind the duct tape, Jonathan Shelby screamed.

— — —

Number 39 sat in his technology room and watched the progress of 26 with infrared-aided cameras. He felt certain the subject was ready—he had done the tests on the opiate and hallucinogen dosages himself. But he was not the hypnosis expert that 26 was, and it never ceased to amaze him how quickly and effectively his boss could implant a hypnotic suggestion in a subject.

Of course, his boss certainly had help. The first thing they did with each subject was to administer the heroin solution repeatedly, fine-tuning it each time, to make the subject drowsy and accommodating. The opiate solution conditioned the subject to relax, making him or her more susceptible to the hypnotic suggestions. This was important, because an agitated, mentally active subject was nearly impossible to hypnotize. But a relaxed, drowsy subject was much more malleable and open to the power of suggestion. The repeated heroin and morphine doses also played with the subject's memory, blanking out some of the more invasive medical procedures that were necessary when keeping a person bound to a chair for days on end. Fortunately Detective Shelby had required only an enema procedure and a catheter. After that, nutrients in the IV drip kept his body working and hydrated with diminished need for typical bodily functions.

Next they experimented with the LSD dosages. Number 61 had suggested administering this drug through the IV, as with the heroin solution. But the boss seemed to enjoy using the squares of blotter paper himself and preferred that method for his models as well. A few days of LSD, and the subject was often hallucinating on his or her own, even without the prompt of a new dose of the drug.

When the subject had been conditioned, Number 39 began his experiments, testing dosage combinations and using his own hypnotic suggestions to see what the effect would be. Once or twice he had lost a subject before 26 could use the person as a model. The boss's retribution had been swift and severe each time. Number 39 had quickly learned that it was much better to administer tests to subjects in the chair than to be a subject in the chair himself, so now he kept his mistakes to a minimum. Or to himself, as circumstances dictated.

Number 39 stood quickly to attention when the boss entered the room.

"At ease," 26 said comfortably. He leaned over and peered into one of the monitors.

"Ease up the red lights slowly," 26 said.

Number 39 obeyed, putting them on the timer that made their increase seem almost imperceptible to the subject.

"Add the orange lights in the mix too," 26 said.

Number 39 obeyed.

"Are all four cameras operative?" 26 asked.

In response, 39 switched the monitor views, going first to the video camera on the south wall, then the east wall, then the north, then the west.

Number 26 nodded his approval. "Set the cameras on a thirty-second rotation."

Number 39 complied. Then both men sat back to watch the progress.

"This is a good model," 26 said after a few minutes. "Number 3 will be proud."

"How long shall I leave the duct tape on the subject?"

"Give it a little longer. I uncuffed his hands. I don't think it will be long before he figures out that he can take the tape off all by himself."

Number 39 nodded.

"But if it's still on when he's in the full delirium, you'll need to go in there and get it off. Otherwise I can't get the complete facial expression."

"Yes, sir."

The two men watched the model for a moment, but 26 was apparently feeling conversational. "Number 3 didn't approve of using live models at first, you know."

"Yes, sir."

"But then I showed him the difference. The intangible emotions, the hints of eternity in the facial expressions. The purity of fear and rage captured in a living, human moment. You can't get that unless you use a live model."

"Yes, sir."

"It has to be this way. I told him that. To do anything less than that would be . . . unpretty."

"Yes, sir."

"He finally agreed. He is an artist too, after all. He could see the difference with his own eyes." A contented sigh. "Yes, it has to be this way."

Number 39 didn't respond, as it seemed the boss was now talking to himself instead of his companion.

"Bring up the volume on the fire now," 26 commanded. He sounded calm, confident, like a news producer calling for camera angles and effects on a live broadcast.

Number 39 set the timer on the audio tracks, slowly increasing the volume of the fire sound effect similar to the way the red and orange lights were gradually increasing.

"Ahh, there it goes," 26 said, noting that Jonathan Shelby had finally torn off the duct tape that covered his mouth. The subject stood and tried to run, but his feet were still firmly chained to the base of the chair. He writhed a bit on the floor, clawing at the manacles around his feet before crawling painfully back into the chair that was his prison.

"Now the heat," said 26. The boss was obviously captivated by the spectacle unfolding before him. "Turn up the heaters in relation to the increase of the audio on the fire." The assistant obeyed without comment.

"Good work, 39," the boss said after a few moments of staring into the monitors. "You had this model well prepared for his studio time."

"Thank you, sir."

"Oh, and before I forget," 26 said, never taking his eyes off the screen before him. "This needs to be delivered by tomorrow morning." He reached into a pocket and pulled out a newspaper clipping with red writing across the front. Then he put his hand into a second pocket and retrieved a microcassette tape. "And this," he said, "as usual."

"I'll take care of it during one of our breaks tonight, sir."

Number 26 nodded his approval. Then they both settled in to watch Jonathan Shelby. If past experience were any indicator, it would be a long night for them all.

— — —

Kinseth sat by the window watching the night go by. It was almost midnight, but Elaina had forgotten to make them promise to be in bed by a certain time, and since they weren't tired, they had decided to sit by the window for a while.

The house at 1669 was entirely dark tonight, something that rarely happened. Kinseth knew they were all there, and when they were all at home there was always a light on somewhere in the house. But not tonight. Kinseth thought maybe something special happened when all the lights were out in the house across the cul-de-sac. It made them nearly crazy with curiosity not knowing what it was that damped the lights over there, but there was really nothing they could do to find out what was going on tonight.

Of course, Elaina hadn't said they couldn't leave the house. All she'd said was "Good night" and "Sleep tight." Nothing about staying inside all night.

Kinseth felt the familiar temptation beckon him. Elaina still didn't know they often snuck out at night. At least they didn't think she knew.

A car drove slowly into the cul-de-sac, headlights off, engine idling softly.

Kinseth sat up in their chair and turned their telescope toward the car. Maybe this would be interesting enough to keep them indoors tonight.

The front door of the house at 1669 opened, and the woman came out. Kinseth wondered if she ever smiled. She might be pretty if she smiled, they thought. The woman ignored the driver and went directly to the trunk of the car instead. The trunk popped open when she got close to it, and she immediately started pulling boxes out of it. When she had placed four square boxes on the curb next to her, she reached inside her coat pocket and pulled out what appeared to be a wad of money. She dropped it into the trunk and then slammed the cover. The driver immediately pulled slowly away, still keeping the headlights dark until the car was out of the cul-de-sac and onto the connecting street.

The woman picked up two boxes and walked them inside the front door of the house. Kinseth wished now that they'd gone outside earlier so they could run over and inspect the remaining two boxes while the woman was gone. But she returned so quickly that Kinseth knew they would have been caught—and possibly punished—before they would have had a chance to get a good look at them. A moment later, the house was sealed up again.

And still completely unlit within.

Kinseth hated mysteries like this, so they decided to think of something else. They pushed aside the telescope and opted finally to go to bed. Elaina had promised them a trip to North Downtown tomorrow, so it was probably a good idea to sleep anyway.

When they lay in bed, Kinseth thought about their adventures earlier in the day. They thought they might have made a new friend today. And that thought made Kinseth smile while they drifted off to sleep.

— — —

Jonathan Shelby heard someone gasping for air, sucking in oxygen as though it were a river pouring down his throat. His fists clenched almost uncontrollably, causing a prickling pain in the palm of his right hand.

I am an unpretty man.

He heard—no, felt—somebody's heart racing, like a rabbit running through a den of wolves. Or snakes.

The serpent was here, unseen but present nonetheless. Jonathan could sense the beast, feel it sneering through fanged jaws and forked tongue.

I am a devil. Destined for hell.

He longed for a drop of cool water, for something to relieve the overwhelming dryness in his mouth.

I am Biagio da Cesena. I am an unpretty man.

He smelled the stench of urine, vaguely aware that it was his

own, that it was mixing with the sweat that now slicked his
naked skin.

Snakes like unpretty things.

Jonathan felt something sinister licking his ankle. He screamed
and kicked, but the metal restraints held his feet in place.

The serpent seemed to enjoy his frightened state. It hissed delight as it curled around Jonathan's chair. Jonathan heard that
sound of gasping again, felt the heart racing, smelled the putrid
mixture of perspiration and urine, tasted the fear that permeated
his own breath.

The cold of the serpent's skin on his calf contrasted with the
fiery heat that filled the air around him. It did not squeeze—not
yet—but simply twisted up Jonathan's leg until it had undulated
its muscular thickness around his torso, under his arms, and
around his chest. Jonathan tried to shove a fist down inside the
fattened coil, tried to push it off, to scratch it away from his skin,
away from the cracking pain that grew within his rib cage, clawing at the smooth roundness that threatened to steal the air from
his lungs. But the harder he fought, the tighter the serpent
clutched, and soon Jonathan's body was frozen in the grip of the
serpent's mighty coils.

I am Biagio da Cesena . . .

He heard the hungry hissing as the serpent's head hovered
close, so close.

I am an unpretty man . . .

He screamed as the snake struck at last.

And I am in hell.

SIX

When the great Michelangelo Buonarroti unveiled his painting of the *Last Judgment* on the altar wall of the Sistine Chapel in 1541, it was by far the largest single painting of its time. It covered more than one hundred and sixty square feet of wall space. Prior to that point, paintings that required that much space to be filled—such as the ceiling of the Sistine Chapel—had been broken into distinct subdivisions that spread out across the overall space. This approach, of course, created something more like a mural of smaller paintings which then connected ultimately to make up the whole.

Not so with the *Last Judgment*. Michelangelo painted this image as all one piece. In it he depicted the triumphant return of the Christ, the God-Man rescuing his elect and bringing them to heaven while also condemning the lost to their eternity in hell. This painting contains more than four hundred active figures within it—angels, demons, humans. And nearly all of those figures were painted without clothing—after all, what use are the latest fashions at the end of the world?

It is said that when Pope Paul III first saw the *Last Judgment*, he fell to his knees in awe, praying that he might be spared the inferno pictured on his chapel wall.

More than a decade later, a new church leader, Pope Paul IV, looked at the same painting and took offense at the nudity it displayed. He insisted that Michelangelo "tidy up" the images on the wall of his church by adding draperies to cover the exposed geni-

tals of the figures in the *Last Judgment*. The artist famously refused, telling the new pontiff that he would tidy up the painting
only after the pope had succeeded in tidying up the world.

Interesting, isn't it?

One pope looked at the *Last Judgment* and saw the awesome
truth of God displayed as a work of art.

Another looked at the same image and saw only pornography.

Who do you think was right?

EXCERPT FROM THE MICHELANGELUS RECORDINGS,
TAPE 6,
TRANSCRIBED BY H. J. COLLINS

--- ---

THURSDAY, SEPTEMBER 25, MORNING

Buck Barnes hurried into the police station with too much on his
mind. He had watched the news this morning, like everyone else,
he assumed, and had seen the report on the murder of Dr. Jonas
Mecklinburg the night before. Dr. Mecklinburg had run the Institute of Cosmetic Surgery for the last four years, specializing in
face work and liposuction procedures. He was well regarded in
the community, and his doctors often donated their services to
victims of accidents and fires. Apparently there were enough rich
women with a beauty fixation to fund the good doctor's clinic
and his charity work as well. And apparently someone out there
didn't like the doctor's work. He had been found around 5:30
this morning, unclothed, strangled to death, and tied to the front
door of his clinic.

The murder of Dr. Mecklinburg was disturbing enough, but
as Barnes watched the news cameras survey the activity at the
crime scene, another image had caught his eye. Fortunately
the news cameras didn't know exactly what they were filming

at first, and their reporters failed to comment, except in passing, on the newspaper clipping that joined the cluttered flyers and posters outside the clinic's front door. But Detective Barnes saw it.

Taped to the window of the clinic was a half-page newspaper advertisement extolling the virtues of plastic surgery at the Institute of Cosmetic Surgery. And written carefully in red across the advertisement was one word: *Unpretty.*

Buck Barnes had immediately called the precinct. He was patched through to the officer in charge of the crime scene, but before the officer could get to it, one of the smarter reporters also spotted the crimson-stroked ad. Suddenly it seemed all cameras were aimed at the specimen, and then everyone's suspicions were raised when the detective on scene quickly walked over and removed the advertisement while the cameras were rolling.

"Too late," Detective Barnes had muttered to himself. "Now we'll have nothing but questions about that advertisement and what it means." He shook his head. "Oh well, maybe the press coverage will give us the lead we need in this case—and in the Conklin case."

Then he'd remembered to check his watch and realized he was dangerously close to missing an important appointment. The crumpled yellow paper that T. W. Collins had given him last night said simply, "8 A.M., your office." Detective Barnes had decided to give the sports attorney the benefit of the doubt on this one. The man obviously thought someone other than the police was watching his sister. So Barnes had planned to get to work early today, wait for the meeting, and go from there.

When he walked into the precinct building at 7:55 in the morning, he was lost in thought about the events of recent days, knowing they all connected somehow but frustrated that he hadn't yet found the connecting point.

"Good morning, Detective." Sunny Yan smiled at him from the reception desk.

"Morning." Barnes nodded a greeting toward the young woman, pausing long enough to decide he didn't want coffee this morning. That was enough of an opportunity for Sunny.

"Hey, Buck," she said warmly, "you're kind of a football nut, right?"

He shrugged. "I guess so."

"How about football trivia? You any good at that?"

Detective Barnes grinned. "Secret's out, huh?" he said. "Yeah, I've been known to win a game or two of *Sports Illustrated* trivia."

"Okay." Sunny grinned back. "Here's a stumper for you. Who ran back the longest interception—without scoring a touchdown—in NFL history?"

"That one's easy," Buck said. "Champ Bailey, Denver Broncos, 2005 season. In the playoffs against the New England Patriots."

"Good!" Sunny said. "And how about the second-longest interception return without a touchdown?"

Buck thought for a moment, and then it came to him. "Also easy," he said. "The answer is Charles 'Ready' Robinson, Philadelphia Eagles, 1985 season. Against the St. Louis Cardinals. And," he added with a flourish, "Ready was a hometown boy, one of our own. Went to college at the local university here in town before jumping to the pros after his junior year. But of course that was way before your time, youngster."

Sunny dimpled. "Glad you know that, Buck," she said, " 'cause Ready Robinson has been sitting in your office waiting for you for the last half-hour."

– – –

Hummingbird Collins waited for the answering machine to pick up the phone, screening her calls, just to make sure.

"Hey, sis," said a warm voice, "pick up the phone."

"Hey, bro." She smiled into the receiver.

"You ready for the day?"

That was the code phrase she and T.W. had worked out last night. Since they couldn't be sure if someone was listening in on the telephone line, they figured this would be the safest tactic. If she said she was running a little behind, it meant something was wrong, and he should call the police immediately. If she said she hadn't slept well, it meant nothing was obviously wrong, but she felt scared. If she said anything else, then everything was going as planned.

"I think so," she said with confidence. "I'm actually looking forward to going back to work today. Seems like forever since I was in my own little store, selling my own little books, with my own little Kacey teaching me something unexpected and new about the life and times of Elvis Presley."

"Glad to hear it, Humm." T.W.'s voice seemed noticeably less strained. "Come by and see me after you have a chance to get settled in at the bookstore. They put in the new plate glass on my office front, and it looks all sparkly and clear, almost like nothing's there."

"I will, T.W." She felt her spirits lifting at the prospects of the day. Then she turned and saw the new padded envelope that had been taped to her door that morning.

"One more thing, Humm," T.W. said. "Any, um, deliveries today?"

She sighed. "One. As expected."

"Well, you know what to do with it," T.W. said.

"Right." She brightened a bit at the reminder of their plan. "I'll take care of it right now, then I'll head out to work so I can get the bookstore opened by ten o'clock."

"See you soon then."

"Thanks for calling, T.W."

She hung up the phone and stared at the padded envelope. Then she powered up her laptop and set to work. She'd already stayed up late to transcribe the other tapes. Transcribing this new one shouldn't take her more than half an hour or so. She and T.W. had decided that it would be important to have transcripts of every word on every tape. There was no telling when those transcripts might be needed as evidence.

- - -

Number 26 was exhausted—and happy. It had been a long, difficult night but also one that had rewarded him with, he hoped, exactly what he was looking for.

The model had passed in and out of consciousness during the early part of their session before finally passing out for good at around 4:30 A.M. Number 26 wasn't sure at first if the model was still alive, but that had been a secondary concern anyway. Number 61 checked in on the model at around 6:00 A.M. and found him to be alive but in a drug-induced coma. She expected him to regain consciousness sometime during the day and asked if 26 had finished with him yet.

Number 26 told her to go make coffee, a deliberate insult to her, but he needed to put her in her place. Couldn't she see that he was working? And wasn't it obvious that he wasn't through with the model until he said he was through? She had taken the rebuke without a word and fifteen minutes later returned with a steaming cup of coffee, black. Number 26 left her standing at the door waiting for the next two hours, forcing her to do nothing while he and 39 sifted through the night's video images, often going frame by frame.

At around 8:00 A.M. he'd paused to check their progress so far and discovered that they'd identified at least a half-dozen frames that would be usable. A half-dozen! That was a treasure trove of material, as sometimes in the past he'd had to make do with only two or three clear images.

Number 26 felt positively giddy, and when he was in this kind of mood, he was also forgiving. He looked at 61. She stared impassively at his chest, careful to avoid direct eye contact. Somehow she understood the purpose of his gaze, and after a moment she produced a colorful sheet of paper from a pocket.

"I think one square should be plenty, 61," he said. She nodded and tore off one square of the drug-soaked paper, which he quickly placed on his tongue.

"It's been a good night's work," he said to 61 and 39. "Time in the studio is always taxing on everybody. Why don't you two go get some sleep?"

Number 61 and Number 39 each gave a slight head bob to signal gratefulness. Number 61 walked quickly out, but 39 hesitated.

"And you, sir?"

Number 26 waved him on. "I'm going to enlarge and print out these six frames so I can show them to Number 3. Then I may get right to work on them. Minos has been waiting quite some time for his face."

"And the subject?"

"Tell 44 and 48 he's their responsibility now. If he lives."

Number 39 nodded and exited the technology room.

Number 26 looked at the video monitors and saw the model, now spent and collapsed in the studio. This had been a good one.

He spent a few moments enlarging and printing out the six facial close-ups they'd captured during the night and was thrilled when he also heard the colors begin to sing his praises once again. He wondered, as the room swam in a beautiful dance, if Daddy could also hear the colors sing. Then he decided that even if he could hear them, Daddy wouldn't admit it, since they were singing about the son.

Still, when Number 3 saw the images he'd just printed out, the old man would be proud, whether he said so or not. Number 26 was sure of it.

— — —

Detective Barnes felt a little like a nervous football fan when Ready Robinson stood to shake his hand.

"Sorry I'm late, Mr. Robinson," he said.

"No need to apologize, Detective," Ready said. "You're not late. I was just early. I find that it's sometimes helpful to check out a situation before committing to it."

Ready Robinson still looked to be in good shape, and it annoyed Buck just enough to make him feel uncomfortable. After all, they had to be about the same age, and it had been a few *decades* since the man had last played ball. But there he was, dressed like a sportscaster, still lean and muscular, with the only real sign of age a slight graying at the temples of his tight, curly black hair.

Buck involuntarily sucked in his gut. "Well, I appreciate you sticking around long enough to chat with me, Mr. Robinson."

The former footballer smiled graciously. "Please, call me Ready. Everybody else does."

"And you feel free to call me Buck. As you say, everybody else does."

Formalities out of the way, Detective Barnes took his seat

behind the desk while Ready Robinson took the chair on the other side.

"Can I assume that Hummingbird Collins sent you?" Buck asked.

Ready reached into his coat pocket and produced a manila envelope folded in half. "She sent this for you."

Detective Barnes opened the envelope and found a micro-cassette tape as well as what appeared to be a transcript of some sort and a pencil sketch of a white male with short dark hair.

"This tape—and the others that Hummingbird has received—are the reason she can't talk to you. Well, the reason she can't speak directly to you."

Detective Barnes spread the three items on his desk.

"Hummingbird has transcribed the contents of this first tape and sent you a copy of the transcription because she wasn't sure you would have a microcassette player handy. Plus, we thought it would be wise to dust them for prints."

Detective Barnes nodded and began scanning the pages of printed text. His face flushed a bit when he came to Jonathan Shelby's name, especially since it was mentioned in the same context as Corona Sanchez. He had worked peripherally on the Sanchez case, and they had never been able to solve that one. It now languished in the cold-case files of the department. He didn't recognize the other two names.

"Detective Barnes—Buck—Hummingbird Collins and anyone she is associated with are now targets in the sights of this psychopathic murderer. And every time you pressure her for more information you draw the circle around her a little tighter."

Buck nodded. "I understand your concern, her concern," he said. "But I can't simply let this killer off the hook." He stood up and paced behind his desk. "You see, Ready, this guy has one of our own. A personal friend of mine and a detective on our police force."

"Jonathan Shelby."

"Yes. And I owe it to Jonathan and to his wife, Aurora, to pursue every lead, to dig up every clue, to do whatever it takes to bring that man home."

Ready gave a nod. "Then we are on the same page, Buck. We just see different ways of getting to our desired destination."

"Go on."

"Hummingbird has shown good faith by sending me to you and by sharing evidence with you. This tape and the transcript. She has even gone a step further by giving you this." He pointed to the sketch on the desk.

"She saw him? She saw the bomber?"

"Yes. Not only saw him but studied his face. She thought she might use elements of his features for a poster she was commissioned to draw."

"I heard she was something of an artist."

"She's quite good, Buck. And she's spent nearly a week refining this drawing so you would have a face to look for."

Detective Barnes studied the drawing. The man wasn't familiar to him, but he would scan the drawing into the department's database and run a face-recognition program on it. When they cross-referenced it against the national database, chances were good it might yield a name to go with the face.

"She is good," Barnes said after a moment. "We should be using her as a police sketch artist for wanted posters."

"Now, Buck, I think you owe us something."

Detective Barnes frowned, lowered the sketch onto the desk, and leaned back in his chair. "I'm not going to negotiate with you, Ready," he said with narrowed eyes. "Not with you or T. W. Collins or Hummingbird Collins or anyone else. Save the negotiations for your sports contracts. My obligation is first to Jonathan Shelby and to catch this psychopathic killer. Not to do favors for spoiled kids with a connection to a sports celebrity."

Ready's lips grew tight, and Detective Barnes could see him making assessments in his mind. Then he dipped his head slightly in deference and gestured, palms up and out, toward the detective.

"Fine, Detective Barnes," he said coolly. "No negotiations. But perhaps you would allow Hummingbird to make a request or two?"

"I'm listening."

"First, she would ask you to break off surveillance of her."

Barnes said nothing.

"Second, she would ask that you call her home and leave a message on her answering machine indicating that she is no longer being pursued for questioning. She believes her phone is bugged and wants her stalker to hear that you've given up pursuing her."

"What does she expect me to say is the reason we no longer wish to question her?"

Ready shrugged. "You're a college graduate. Figure something out. Third," Ready continued, "she would like you to work on identifying the man in her sketch—without making that sketch public."

"Ridiculous. If we put this out to the press, chances are good we'll get someone to call in who has seen this guy and knows where he is."

"Actually, Detective, if you publicize that drawing, you not only make it clear to the killer that Hummingbird has betrayed him, you also make him disappear—likely with the body of your Jonathan Shelby in tow."

Buck started to say something in anger, then decided to stay silent instead.

"Fourth," Ready said, "Hummingbird would like to ask that you contact the press with some misinformation about this case. Perhaps suggest that you got an anonymous tip that the bomber has left the state or that the bomber is a woman or something like that. We feel confident that this killer is monitoring not only Hummingbird Collins but also your efforts in pursuing this case. If we can make him feel as if you are way off his trail, he may relax and make a mistake that we can use."

Buck took in a deep breath. "You use the word *we* quite liberally."

Ready stood up and, unexpectedly, swept the contents of the envelope into his coat pocket again. "Detective Barnes," he said evenly, "the entire Collins family means something important to me. I owe their father quite a bit. And I owe T.W. something as well. I certainly don't intend to sit idly by while you blunder about like a bull in a china shop."

"I'd like those materials, please. The sketch, the tape, all of it. The other tapes you mentioned. And anything else Hummingbird Collins might be holding back."

"At present those items are all the private property of Hummingbird Collins. You'll need a warrant to get them, unless she was to offer them to you of her own free will."

"I can have a warrant in my hands in twenty minutes," Buck growled.

"Which, interestingly enough, would likely be nineteen minutes after these materials might have disappeared forever."

Ready opened his suitcoat. Even though Buck had seen him put the bulky materials directly into the inside pocket, there was obviously nothing in there now.

What is this guy, an amateur magician too? he thought. Aloud he said, "I can charge you with withholding evidence, obstructing a police investigation, criminal tampering, and several other crimes that will keep you in jail and out of my hair for many years to come."

"You can *try,*" Ready said with a ferocious grin.

Something in the man's voice and manner made Detective Barnes hesitate. Ready Robinson was known for two things. One was his stellar play as a defensive back for the Philadelphia Eagles. The other was his uncanny ability to avoid the spotlight, regardless of which paparazzo or reporter or whoever was trying to track him down.

"I can arrest you right here, right now, Mr. Robinson," Barnes said quietly.

Ready simply grinned. "As I said, *Detective* Barnes, you can *try.*"

There was a moment of tension. Buck, deciding, relaxed a bit and said with mild cordiality, "Please, Ready, have a seat. Can I get you coffee or something?"

"Why, thank you, Buck," Ready said with formal amiability as he slipped comfortably back into the chair. "But I'm not thirsty at present."

Buck hesitated a second longer, then picked up the receiver on his phone and made a call. After a moment Ready nodded his approval, and suddenly the evidence from Hummingbird Collins magically reappeared on Barnes's desk.

When he hung up the phone, Ready was already standing to leave. "How will I contact you?" the detective asked.

"You won't," Ready said. "But we'll keep in touch. I promise." He held out his hand as a peace offering. Detective Barnes shook it and then watched the visitor leave.

A moment later Buck slapped his desk and uttered a quick

curse. "Forgot to get his autograph," he muttered to no one in particular. "I must be getting old."

Buck listened to the phone ring five times before the machine picked up. Was she screening her calls, letting this call be heard by interlopers as planned? Or had she actually left her apartment at last?

"Ms. Collins," he said on the tape, "this is Detective Buck Barnes. I wanted to call and let you know that we have turned our investigation into the Conklin gallery bombing in a different, and we hope more productive, direction. So we no longer need your testimony regarding that incident. Now, please tell your brother to call off his lawsuits against our department so we can all move forward. I wish you the best, Ms. Collins. Goodbye."

Ready Robinson walked away from the police building with a good feeling. He didn't necessarily like Buck Barnes, but he did admire that the detective wasn't intimidated by anyone or anything. This detective could be trusted to do what was needed in order to end the threat the bomber and stalker posed.

Of course, Buck wouldn't be working alone. The list in Ready's back pocket—the one Galway had given him and which Ready had conveniently forgotten to show the detective—was already providing valuable insight into the mind of the murderer.

Good old Galway, Ready thought. *Guy's marginally insane but a reliable friend if ever you need one.*

It had taken Galway only four hours to come up with a list of missing-persons cases across the state that fit the modus operandi of the Sanchez, Erskine, and Swanson kidnappings. There were forty-five cases in all, going back at least a dozen years. If Jonathan Shelby was dead, he would make forty-six. Of those cases, only twenty-one had been solved. Eleven of those convictions were based on confessions taken under questionable circumstances, and six resulted from charges tacked onto criminals with long histories and imminent convictions for other crimes. The other four convicted criminals had gone to prison loudly protesting their innocence and demanding DNA testing to clear their names.

Ready had studied the cases during the night. All had involved an abrupt kidnapping. None of the kidnappers had communicated with the families of the victims. No ransom notes, no demands, nothing. None of the kidnappings had lasted longer than six weeks. More than half of the victims were dead when they'd finally been found at locations across the state; the others were often as good as dead. All showed signs of severe drug abuse and possible torture. Some had suffered irreparable brain damage. Those who didn't have brain damage still had difficulty remembering anything about their ordeals except for recurring nightmares about God's ultimate judgment.

And some of them, at least a dozen, mentioned one unique word: *Unpretty.*

That word intrigued Ready Robinson. He would have to do some homework on it when he was safely ensconced in his private little monastery at home again. His computers were networked in so many ways to so many unsuspecting sources that he was certain he could dig up something sooner or later. Sooner, he hoped.

The old football player laughed to himself. Most people thought he was simply a guy who got tired of fame and used the fortunes he'd earned in the NFL to live the sequestered life of a recluse. *No one knows the real truth, except maybe Galway. And my seminary professors.* After all, most people were not aware that there even was such a thing as the Order of the Urban Monk. Which was, of course, exactly the way Ready and the others in his loose-knit little group liked it.

Still, when Night Train's son called for help, Ready didn't hesitate to fulfill his vow to the father and to the Father.

The former football player felt the sun warming the skin on his face and paused long enough to thank God for the day. Then he got down to business with the Creator.

"Okay," he prayed, "it's time for you to intervene on behalf of Hummingbird Collins and her family. And I am happy to help out in any way you see fit."

Ready stopped praying then and took an involuntary survey of the sidewalk and streets around him. He had just had a unique premonition that Christ would indeed use him in this situation.

And that it was going to hurt.

— — —

"The queen returns!"

Hummingbird couldn't help the warm feelings that flooded her soul when she heard Kacey welcome her back into the Collins Galleria of Books.

"Thanks, Kace," she said. "It's good to be back."

"You know, this reminds me of the time when Priscilla Presley—"

"Oh yes," Hummingbird said quickly. "I remember that too. Wow, what a time that was, huh?"

Kacey gave her a hug. "You've been convalescing. I'll give you a break from Elvis trivia."

"Thank you."

"But after lunchtime you're fair game again!"

Hummingbird shook her head and smiled.

"Got a new load of used books from the Harkinson auction

out in New Hampshire last week," Kacey continued happily. "Probably have to donate half of them to charity, but there are some good graphic novels in the collection and at least three collectible books from the British Romantic period, so that was an unexpected treat."

"Great. How long before we're able to integrate them into the inventory?" She kept moving toward her office in the back room.

"I should be able to get them done by early next week."

"You're the best, Kacey."

"I know, but keep telling me anyway. You know how I love to hear it. And it's been lonely around here!"

"What are these?" Hummingbird shouted from the back room.

"What?" Kacey was now busying herself getting the register ready for the day's business.

"There's a stack of little pink papers thumbtacked to the wall in my office."

"Oh, those. Mostly phone messages or notes from people who called in to see you or to send their wishes for your speedy recovery."

"Ahh. Nice."

"Oh, and one is from some local mystery author who wants us to host a signing for her new book. I told her you'd call her back if you wanted to do it, but otherwise she shouldn't hold her breath."

Hummingbird appeared at the doorway to the back room and gazed comfortably around the bookstore's main floor. She took in the rows of books, the tables and comfortable chairs carefully spaced out around the shop, and the brightly colored children's section at the back, near where she now stood.

"It's good to be home," she said softly.

"It's good to have you back," Kacey said. "Now brace your-self! It's ten o'clock, and I'm opening the doors!"

A few customers were already waiting outside the door when Kacey opened it. Hummingbird peeked around Kacey and saw two people come in: a sensible woman in her thirties and a young man with a horribly scarred face.

SEVEN

I was eight years old when my father first took me to the Sistine Chapel. The other tourists spent most of the time staring at the ceiling, at the images of creation and past history that Michelangelo frescoed above. But my father and I spent the entire day staring at the wall behind the altar, at the future history painted there.

I can't say I believe entirely in the *Last Judgment*. After all, the venerable Michelangelo felt it necessary to mix mythical figures from ancient Greece into the images of his masterpiece of the Christ's second coming.

But even as an eight-year-old I was awed by the thundering beauty of judgment upon a sinful world. Beauty is the purgation of superfluities, Michelangelo said, and he depicted it forever in the violence and redemption of the *Last Judgment*. And that is what we of the so-called Michelangelus Movement (though we are not a cult, as I mentioned before) have dedicated our lives to. Enacting the violent beauty of judgment upon our world.

My father was one of the original three who first vowed to pursue this noble goal. I was the twenty-sixth to take the oath and have spent my life from age eight to today as a disciple of the great Renaissance artist, studying the truth, defining the art of life, and purging unpretty superfluities wherever they may be found.

It is, I must say, a glorious existence.

EXCERPT FROM THE MICHELANGELUS RECORDINGS,
TAPE 3,
TRANSCRIBED BY H. J. COLLINS

THURSDAY, SEPTEMBER 25, MID-MORNING

Hummingbird Collins tried very hard not to let her expression register the shock that her mind was feeling. She had seen these two before—they came in once or twice a year, it seemed. But the damage to the left side of the young man's face was always startling. She felt both sympathetic and repulsed every time she saw him. Regardless, she put on her best smile, strode out from the back room, and said, "Good morning!"

The woman smiled her acknowledgment but seemed too preoccupied with helping her companion remove his jacket and hang it on the coat rack to respond otherwise. Hummingbird took the cue, stepping away from the pair and heading toward the counter instead.

"If you need anything," she called over her shoulder, "don't hesitate to let me know."

Hummingbird couldn't help listening in as the woman spoke to the young man. "I have to go two stores over to pick up those work shoes I ordered. I'll be back in about fifteen minutes."

"Okay," the young man said.

"You look at the cartoon books in the back. You remember where they are?"

"Uh-huh."

"When I get back, you can pick one out, and we'll buy it, just like I promised. Got it, Kinseth?"

"Got it."

The young man stared placidly at the woman. She looked toward Hummingbird, as if asking permission to leave him in the store for a few minutes.

Again Hummingbird took the cue. "Here," she said brightly,

"let me show you where the cartoon books are." She came out from behind the counter and walked toward the young man, intending to take his arm and lead him down the rows to the appropriate section near the back of the store.

The woman smiled at the obvious invitation but said, "Oh, it's okay. Kinseth has been here enough times that he knows where the cartoon books are." Then she turned back to the young man. "Go ahead and start browsing, baby. I'll be back shortly."

She nodded toward Hummingbird and turned to leave while the young man began a casual march toward the humor shelves. Hummingbird smiled and retreated to the counter, where Kacey was now trying to load a CD into the store's sound system.

"Look what I got yesterday," Kacey said happily. It was a CD with Bugs Bunny dressed as Elvis Presley on the cover. "*Bugs and Friends Sing Elvis!*" she said. "Talk about a match made in heaven. Life is good sometimes, huh?"

Hummingbird shook her head. However, a few minutes later she had to admit that it was kind of fun to hear Marvin the Martian singing "All Shook Up" with cartoon abandon. She'd started to rearrange the front-window display of new and used bestsellers when she realized that she'd lost track of her one and only customer. She did a quick scan of the store but didn't see the young man in the humor section where she expected him to be. She decided that maybe he needed help finding the cartoon books after all, so she headed toward the back to offer assistance.

Partway there, she spotted Kinseth kneeling in front of a lower shelf in the art and art history section. He seemed transfixed by a book on the shelf but unwilling or unable to pick it up and look at it. Hummingbird was unsure whether to interrupt him, but customer service instincts overruled her doubts. She walked slowly toward her customer.

"See something you like?" she said comfortably, but the young man didn't respond.

As she moved closer, she saw that he was looking at a large, full-color coffee-table book. Though it was displayed in the face-out position, someone apparently had looked at it and then returned it to the shelf backward, leaving the front cover hidden and the back cover on display. Hummingbird tilted her head to sneak a peek at the spine of the book and saw *Michelangelo, The Last Judgment: A Glorious Restoration*. The back cover of the book had no words and was filled from top to bottom and side to side with only one image: Michelangelo's famous *Last Judgment* from the altar wall of the Sistine Chapel.

She knelt down beside the young man and took the book off the shelf, offering it to him to hold. He took the book wordlessly but immediately pulled it closer to his face, peering intently at it and gently brushing his fingers across the image.

"Do you like art?" Hummingbird asked.

The young man shrugged.

"This is a famous painting by a great artist who lived a long time ago. The artist was named Michelangelo. Do you like Michelangelo?"

Again just a shrug.

Hummingbird had almost decided to give up and leave the young man alone, but something in the way he studied the back cover of the book intrigued her. "Do you like that painting?" she asked.

The young man nodded. "It scares us," he said. "But it is still beautiful."

"I can see what you mean," she said thoughtfully. *Why does he refer to himself as 'us'? Maybe he has some brain damage.* "Have you seen it before?"

He nodded.

"At school or in an art museum or something?"

He shook his head.

"Where did you see it?"

The young man suddenly looked at her, searching her eyes. He clutched the book to his chest and stood up. Hummingbird stood also, a bit unnerved by the way his good eye plumbed the depths of her own eyes while his other eye—a glass one apparently—stayed limp and lifeless in its socket. He seemed to make a decision and, without a word, walked past her and toward a table and chair nearby. He laid the book down and began carefully turning its pages, looking at the various insets and details of the *Last Judgment* pictured within.

"Okay," Hummingbird said at last, trying to make her voice sound breezy and unconcerned in spite of the snub. "Well, let me know if you need anything."

THURSDAY, SEPTEMBER 25, EARLY AFTERNOON

Jonathan Shelby was afraid to open his eyes, afraid that if he did, the sunshine he felt on his bare skin would somehow disappear into darkness again. He curled into a ball, chilled by the cold air and the dry grass, but even fall's frigid breeze couldn't stop him from reveling in the open warmth that seemed to surround his frame. He shivered and wondered if he were still dreaming and, if so, how long it would be before he woke up. He jabbed his fists under his armpits and took in a deep breath, coughing when little bits of dry grass flickered into his nostrils and down the back of his throat.

He felt a pain digging into his right palm and realized that he'd felt that same pain recently, during . . . He instinctively shifted his train of thought. Still, his fingers were cramping around something in his hand. He pulled his right fist out and put it near his face.

Slowly, and with arthritic convulsion, he opened the frozen fist. And slowly, wincing at the effort, he opened his eyes just enough to take in a pinch of the dazzling light. After several moments the light and colors finally melded to form a coherent whole. He stared into his palm, his mind registering mild surprise.

There, bent and bloodied by scrapes and freshly formed cuts in his palm, was a small plastic toy. A cowboy?

Jonathan closed his palm painfully over the toy and shoved his fists under his arms once again. He seemed to remember something about a cowboy. And an angel. But he couldn't quite figure out what it was. And until he could, he was going to hold on to that cowboy, no matter what.

He shivered again. Somewhere, vaguely, a thought urged him to get inside, to get to a warmer place. He needed the sun, he decided. He would stay where he was.

His teeth chattered and his eyes fluttered when a cloud passed overhead, but still he didn't move. Then he had another thought.

I am . . . unpretty.

Jonathan Shelby roiled in the dry grass and listened to someone screaming.

THURSDAY, SEPTEMBER 25, LATE AFTERNOON

T. W. Collins looked up at the clock and suddenly realized it was already 4:15 in the afternoon, and Hummingbird still hadn't come by to see him. He had been so busy trying to catch up on the work he'd missed over the past few days that he'd burned up most of the day. He was just reaching for the telephone to call Hummingbird at the bookstore when the intercom sounded.

"Hey, T.W.," Rebecca Proctor's voice cooed over the speaker. "Your better half is on line one."

"Thanks, Becky," T.W. replied. "I'll pick it up in here." He punched the flashing button on his telephone. "Hey, Peg," he said warmly. "How's my favorite fiancée?"

"Good, honey," she said, "but turn on the TV."

"What?"

"Don't you have a TV there in your office? You know, that nice plasma screen that ought to be in my apartment but that you insist on keeping at work so you can show highlight reels of your clients, even though all you really do is watch ESPN?"

"Right, sure," he said, reaching for a remote control in his desk. "What channel?"

"Any of the major networks. Doesn't matter which one, because all the local stations are carrying it. There's a press conference going on about the Conklin explosion. After what you and Hummingbird told me last night, I thought you'd want to catch this."

"Okay, thanks, hon," he said as he flipped the channels.

"I gotta go," she said. "See you at dinner tonight?"

"Wouldn't miss it."

"Loveya."

"Loveyarightback."

He hung up the phone and increased the volume on the TV. Detective Barnes and a few other men were holding a press conference.

" . . . have determined it was the result of a bomb planted inside the premises," Barnes was saying. "Our forensics experts suspect C-4 was the explosive used and that it was somehow sewn into the lining of a cloth or a coat or something like that."

"Detective, do you think it was foreign terrorists?"

"Although we can't rule out anything at this point, none of the evidence so far points to any known terrorist organization."

"Do you have any suspects?"

The detective hesitated, glancing back at a colleague standing nearby. Then he looked directly into the camera. "No. At present we have no credible leads, and we invite the community to call us with any tips they might have regarding the person or persons responsible for the bombing." He turned back to his colleague. "Captain Philips?"

The captain stepped forward. "Right, and that's why we called this press conference today. We want to let everyone know there is now a twenty-five-thousand-dollar reward for information leading to the arrest and conviction of the people responsible for this horrible bombing."

"Captain Philips," a reporter shouted. "What do you have to say to the taxpayers out there who expect their police force to do more than simply offer a reward for others to do the job you all are actually paid to do?"

The captain's jaw line grew visibly tighter. "Only that we are doing everything we can with the resources we have. Thank you. No further questions, please."

"Captain Philips! Detective Barnes!" another reporter shouted. "Is there a connection between the bombing of the Conklin Art Gallery last week and the murder of Dr. Jonas Mecklinburg this morning?"

But the two lawmen ignored the clamoring reporters, backed away from the microphones, and walked stonily out of the room.

T.W. muted the volume when the manicured newscaster in the studio filled the screen. *That must not have been easy, especially since it reflected negatively on the police department,* he thought. *But that detective has bought us all some valuable time.* He made a mental note to thank Ready Robinson for his persuasive efforts with Detective Barnes.

He was just reaching for the telephone again when the intercom buzzed once more. "Hey, T.W.," Becky said, "your sister's headed this way."

T.W. reached over and gently tapped the intercom button. "Thanks, Becky. I'll be right out."

— — —

Number 61 stood at attention when she saw 39 come ambling out of the barracks room and into the kitchen. He took a quick look at the coffee and toast on the table and the open newspaper beside them and nodded for her to be at ease. When she hesitated, he said, "It's okay, 61. The boss isn't here. He's off working on his project. My guess is he'll sleep over there and keep working well into tomorrow. He was really excited about that last model, you know."

Number 61 glanced toward the hallway to the barracks.

"Number 44 and 48 are disposing of the last subject. They won't be back for another hour at least."

Number 61 nodded and sat back down in her chair. "Right, 39," she said finally. "Just don't want to take any unnecessary chances. Especially not if those two goons of his are nearby."

Number 39 reached for a section of the paper, then caught 61 looking at him thoughtfully. "Something on your mind?" he asked.

She hesitated, then decided to speak. "He's crazy. You know that, right?"

"He's also a genius."

She acknowledged that fact with a nod. "Yes," she said, "Johann Smidt is an artistic genius. But he's also growing progressively insane and becoming more erratic with each new subject."

A look of frustration flashed over 39's face. "So what are you saying? That we should dump our research and start over?"

"No. Of course not."

"Then what? We've got twelve years invested in this guy and at least ten more to go before we can have a truly workable prototype to mass-produce."

Now it was 61 who felt the frustration. She had trusted 39 for many years, and she disliked arguing with him. But she also had a brain of her own, and she knew she was right about their fearless leader.

"He's addicted," she said at last. "I tried cutting the potency, but then he ingested a higher quantity of the drug-soaked paper squares."

Number 39 nodded thoughtfully. "Well, that explains a few things."

"He shows signs of impaired memory functions. He has decreased appetite and trouble with sleep, mood swings, flashbacks. And have you seen him with the old man?"

"Of course. But that's harmless."

"*Might* be harmless."

"Look. This is not a problem. Not yet."

"How can you be so sure?"

"Did you see the boss with that model yesterday?"

She nodded. "And I heard the model. All. Night. Long."

He gave a hungry smile. "The boss is a master of mind manipulation. An artist in more ways than one. And we made him that way."

"We also have driven him insane."

"Which is why we need to continue our research. We said we were in this for the long haul, remember? He's off track, yes, but we're still furthering our goals for the Movement."

She sighed. "We might not even finish this research in our lifetimes."

"But we might. We'll never know if we quit."

"You're right. I know you're right. We've been in this too long, broken too many laws to quit now."

Number 39 patted his partner's shoulder reassuringly and grinned. "Let's hope there is no afterlife, right?"

She said nothing. But the thoughts that swirled in her head were not nice ones. Finally she said, "Regardless of the long-term goals, we still need a plan for the short term. Number 26 is deteriorating, and we can't sit by and do nothing forever. He already has trouble distinguishing fantasy from reality even when he's not taking the drugs."

"How much longer do you think he has?"

She shrugged. "Could be a year. Could be a month. Could be tomorrow. No way to tell for sure."

"All right then. We wait him out. Give him what he wants. And when the time comes that he is no longer an asset to our research, then we do to him what we did to his father."

She nodded. That, of course, was the logical thing to do. She felt better just hearing 39 say it out loud. "Okay then," she said. "We have a plan." She stood. "Guess I'd better get more blotter paper."

— — —

Buck Barnes slammed the door to his office and kicked a chair before sitting down. "'Taxpayers out there who expect their police force to do more,'" he mimicked scornfully. "If the taxpayers out there only knew all we do for them, day in and day out, they'd . . . well, they wouldn't let joker reporters ask moronic questions at press conferences."

He slid open a desk drawer and pulled out his file on the Unpretty investigation. He stared at the pencil drawing of the bombing suspect and wondered for the hundredth time if they'd done the right thing by not publicizing that sketch. But he had talked it over with Captain Philips, and the captain had agreed with Ready Robinson's assessment. To catch this guy, they'd have to mislead him into thinking he was safe. They'd have to work the quiet contacts, stay out of plain sight until they had the suspect in the crosshairs. Then they'd go in guns blazing, so to speak.

He logged on to his computer and checked the data reports from the face-recognition requests he'd set in motion. So far the face in the sketch had been entered into the statewide database. A sheriff's department down in the southeast corner of the state had a police sketch that identified a John Doe suspect with similar facial features around the eyes and cheekbones, but the nose and lips were different, so nothing was conclusive. The fact that the police sketch was of an anonymous figure also made it a dead-end lead. But Buck promised to keep the sheriff in the loop if they did indeed find out the identity of their mystery bomber.

The next step was to go into the national databases with the illustration Hummingbird had provided. That would take some time, but it might yield at least a name to go along with the face, even if it was only an alias. If there were any kind of name attached to the bomber, their chances of catching him would increase immeasurably. Names, even fake names, left trails, and a trail could be followed to the real name that the fake name was concealing.

Meanwhile Buck stared hard at the sketch before him. *I will memorize this face,* he thought stubbornly. *So that if I see it anywhere—out getting coffee, buying gasoline, even delivering letters from the mailroom—I will recognize it. And when I recognize him, I will capture him.*

The graphite-shaded eyes of Hummingbird Collins's sketch seemed to mock him.

"I'll find you, you sick devil," Buck said aloud. "And you won't like it when I do."

The telephone on his desk rang just as Captain Philips burst into his office unannounced.

"Yes?" Buck acknowledged both the telephone and his boss.

"Detective Barnes?" a voice said on the other end of the phone line. "This is Marty Haas over at the Haas Art and Craft Supply store."

"Detective," Captain Philips said. "Hang up the phone. This is important."

Buck raised a finger toward the captain and said, "Mr. Haas, listen, right now is an inconvenient time—"

"Hang up the phone, Buck. That's an order."

"Right, Detective. I wanted to let you know that someone came into my store about ten minutes ago and bought a tube of PMS 193."

Detective Barnes stood up and covered the mouthpiece on the phone. "What is it, Cap?" Then, uncovering the mouthpiece, he spoke into the phone. "Do you know who it was?"

"No, Detective. The man paid cash for the purchase. But he looked kind of tired, like he'd been up all night or slept in his clothes or something. He bought several colors of paint, but I noticed that one of them was that red color you'd asked about before, so I thought I should call."

Captain Philips was starting to look very impatient, and when he was impatient, he was unpleasant.

"You did the right thing, Mr. Haas. Thank you. Now, I really need to put you on hold—"

"That's all right, Detective," Haas said. "You can call me back when you get a chance. But I did want to tell you that this guy was in a happy mood. Downright chatty. So I pretended that I needed to get his zip code to enter it into the register before I could ring up his purchase. And, well, he gave it to me. I thought that might be helpful for your investigation or something."

"Buck. Hang. Up. The. Phone. Now. Or. You're. Fired."

Buck flushed and spoke fast. "Excellent. Thank you, Mr. Haas. Look, I'll come by your store within the next twenty minutes, and we'll talk more then. Goodbye." He hung up the receiver without waiting for a response and turned in exasperation to his boss.

"Okay, Captain," he said. "What is so important?"

"Buck," he said. "We've found Jonathan Shelby."

THURSDAY, SEPTEMBER 25, NIGHTTIME

Kinseth Roberts sat on the floor of their bedroom and rocked back and forth, occasionally tapping the back of their head on the wall next to the window. On their bed lay *Michelangelo, The Last Judgment: A Glorious Restoration*. When Elaina had returned from buying shoes, she'd been surprised to find them looking at this art book instead of reading Garfield or Foxtrot comics. She'd been even more surprised when Kinseth insisted on buying this book instead of another cartoon treasury to add to their collection. She'd tried to talk Kinseth out of it—after all, the big hardcover coffee-table book cost three times what a flimsy paperback of Peanuts would cost—but they'd been undeterred. In the end she'd given the book to the nice lady at the bookstore, written a check, and then allowed Kinseth to walk out of the store with the art book tucked protectively under an arm.

Kinseth hadn't bothered reading the text in the book, but they had looked carefully at each picture on each page. They'd started at the beginning, looked at each page all the way to the end, then started at the end and worked their way, page by page, back to the beginning again. Now the book lay open to page 114, where a goat-eared man grimaced while a snake wrapped itself around his naked torso.

Kinseth had seen that man—except for the ears—first chained to a chair in 1669 Kirby Court.

And then on the wall behind the altar at the Baptist church across the greenbelt.

— — —

Buck Barnes sat in the hospital lobby, leaned his head back against the wall, and let his eyes close.

After hearing that Jonathan Shelby had been found, he'd sped over to the Haas Art and Craft Supply store and spent ten minutes getting every tidbit of information he could out of the helpful Marty Haas. The store owner had seemed terribly excited to think he was helping the investigation, almost as if he were an extra in a detective movie. Barnes was content to fuel that excitement as long as it delivered leads in this case. Haas had described a customer who seemed to fit the appearance of Hummingbird Collins's sketch, but when Barnes had showed him the drawing, he seemed less sure.

"Yes, I think that could be him," Haas had said after a moment. "But, you know, he was wearing a cap, so I don't know if that's the right hair color."

"How about the face, Mr. Haas? Does that look familiar?"

"Yes. I mean, I think so. Well, now it's all getting jumbled in my head. It's so exciting, though, isn't it? A mass murderer may have actually come into *my* store. I can't wait to tell my friends at the next Lehigh Business Buddies meeting."

"Tell me about the zip code," Barnes had said with a sigh.

Haas had explained again how he had "tricked that criminal" into thinking he needed to enter a zip code in the register in order to conduct the cash transaction. The suspect had supplied the zip code immediately, apparently without thinking twice about it, maybe unwittingly giving the store clerk his real zip code.

The detective had jotted down the five-digit number, then thanked the art-supply dealer and hurried out the door to rush over to the hospital.

Despite Haas's vacillation and fan-boy enthusiasm, Buck was certain that Haas had seen the suspect. That meant two things. First, the killer was still in the city—*my city,* Buck growled to himself—and second, he was likely hiding somewhere within the limits of a zip code covering the southeast section of Lehigh.

The hospital staff still had not let him see Jonathan Shelby, but just knowing he was here and that he was alive was enough to keep Buck at the medical center. He had thought about going home and coming back in the morning, but in the end he decided that if Jonathan did reach a moment of coherence during the night, Buck wanted to be there. A man in his condition might have only intermittent lucidity, and when it came, the detective wanted to make the most of it. After all, Jonathan Shelby was not only a friend, he was also the man with perhaps the best knowledge of the inner workings of the mad bomber they were now tracking down.

Aurora Shelby had gotten there long before. They let her see Jonathan only briefly, thinking it might spark something in the patient, but it had been traumatic for everyone involved. In the end they sent Aurora out to wait in the lobby, allowing her to re-enter the patient's room only when he was subdued or sleeping. She was with him now, a nurse had told him in passing, sleeping in the chair beside her husband.

Captain Philips had assigned two uniformed officers to stand guard in the hallway outside Jonathan's room and had tried to talk to Jonathan personally, until the doctor threw a fit and demanded privacy for the patient and for his staff. Chester Philips accommodated the doctor on the condition that he would provide updates to the police guard every four hours, sooner if there were significant changes in the patient's status. The doctor had kept his word, and every four hours one of the uniformed blues came out and relayed the doctor's assessment to the captain in the waiting room.

Buck opened his eyes just long enough to read the display on the wall clock across the waiting room. It was now after midnight. At times like these Buck Barnes was glad he'd not given in to the temptation to settle down, get married, and start a family. Oh sure, someday he hoped to find true love and all that. But right now his mistress was his work, and being single meant more time for that. And it meant he could, on a moment's notice, spend a cheerless night in an uncomfortable hospital chair without having to get permission from a wife or any other family member.

He let his head relax and tried to doze off. He was just feeling as if he might actually fall asleep when he heard a voice, closer than it should have been to his ear, say quietly, "Don't you need a permit to sleep in a public place?"

Detective Barnes's eyes flew open. He rolled his head to the left and saw the grinning face of Ready Robinson close enough to kiss. He sighed and sat up in his chair, rubbing the sleep out of his eyes with weary fingers.

"Mr. Robinson," he said. "Always a pleasure."

"Please, Buck. Call me Ready."

"Of course."

Ready leaned back in his chair, elbows up on the armrest.

"What brings you to the hospital tonight, Ready?"

"Jonathan Shelby."

Now Buck was wide awake. "How did you know Jonathan

Shelby was here?" he asked. "We deliberately asked the hospital staff not to make that information known to the public."

Ready didn't answer but instead asked a question of his own. "Where was he when they found him?"

Buck was silent.

"I understand," Ready continued easily, "that he's suffering from a drug overdose. That your doctors have found significant amounts of heroin, LSD, and morphine in his bloodstream."

The silence that followed communicated that Ready Robinson knew more than he was saying and that he was saying just enough to see if Buck would trade some information.

"They found him about fifteen miles outside Lehigh," Buck said. "He was lying naked in the grass near an exit off the freeway. A motorist thought he was a homeless person, thought he was dead, and called the highway patrol. They brought him back here."

"Hypothermia?"

"Yeah. Could have died if he'd stayed out there overnight," Buck said softly. "And judging from the amount of drugs in his system, he *should* have died before he ever got out there."

"How's he doing now?"

"In and out of consciousness but never really lucid. Appears to be having flashbacks to a bad experience while on the hallucinogen."

Ready nodded thoughtfully.

"So," Detective Barnes said, "how did you know Jonathan Shelby was here?"

Ready nodded in the direction of the hallway. "She told me."

Detective Barnes looked up and saw Aurora Shelby coming through the doorway to the waiting room. The woman smiled with relief when she saw Ready Robinson stand up to greet her. She gave him a warm hug and said, "Father Robinson, I'm so glad you could come." Buck raised his eyebrows at her odd address of Ready, but the former football star ignored the look. "I wasn't sure you'd get my message," she said softly. Then a tremble. "It doesn't look good, Ready. It doesn't look good at all."

Ready put an arm around her shoulder and led her to a chair. Ready sat on one side of her, and Buck sat on the other. "You know Detective Barnes, I assume?" Ready said by way of introduction.

Aurora nodded. "Buck is a friend of Jonathan's." She favored the detective with a short smile. "A friend of our family's, I mean. He's been searching for Jonathan ever since he disappeared."

"Aurora, I mean no disrespect," Ready said next, "but I have to ask you a question."

"Go ahead, Father," she said. "I can take anything at this point."

"Has your husband ever experimented with drugs in the past? Any kind of drug?"

Aurora shook her head emphatically. "No. Never. He'll have a drink with dinner every once in awhile, but that's it." She smiled ruefully. "He's always been more likely to bust a drug user than to join him."

Ready nodded. "How's he doing right now?"

Aurora's eyes started to mist up, but her voice remained calm and controlled. "It's just terrible, Ready. He's awake now. He goes in and out of consciousness. Sometimes when he wakes up he simply stares into space, seeing things that aren't there. Then all of a sudden he starts screaming and flails around like he's fighting some terrible beast. The doctors finally had to strap his arms and legs down because he kept tearing the IV out of his arm."

Ready stared hard into Aurora's face. After a moment, he held out his hand.

"What are you doing?" Buck asked. Was he asking this grieving woman for money or something?

"What did he give you?" Ready said.

Aurora flushed a little. "He said it was from an angel. He said he wanted me to have it. That it was special."

Buck had new respect for Ready Robinson. How had he known about this?

She reached into her pocket and pulled out a bent and stained small plastic cowboy, a child's toy. Ready examined it closely and passed it to the detective. Barnes also looked at it, wondering what it might reveal. When he was finished, he passed it back to Aurora. She fiddled with it absently while she talked.

"He keeps saying a word—'unpretty.' I don't know what it means, but whatever it is, it makes him so agitated and frightened I don't know what to do."

Both Buck and Ready Robinson came to attention when Aurora mentioned the word.

"Who would do this?" Aurora continued, directing her question to both Buck and Ready. "And why would God allow somebody to hurt my husband like this?"

Buck felt uncomfortable with the silence that followed her questions. "I don't know, Aurora," he said quietly. "I've never been much of a religious man. I don't think I know enough about God to trust him—or ask questions of him."

A faint grin passed quickly over Ready's face. He glanced at Detective Barnes and then looked back at Aurora. "I think the real question is, can you trust God even if he never tells you why this happened?"

Aurora's face mirrored the faint grin that had been Ready's. "Seems like I've heard that from you before, Father," she said. "I don't know the answer to either of our questions. So for now, I'll let them worry about answering themselves." She stood. "Meanwhile, I'm going to go see if Jonathan has calmed down yet."

Ready stood and gave her a quick hug. "We'll find some answers sooner or later, Aurora," he said. "Whether we like 'em or not."

"Thanks, Father," she said. She turned and headed back toward the doors that led to her husband's room. Partway there, she stopped, returned to Ready Robinson, and placed the plastic cowboy in his palm. Then she left the lobby to rejoin her husband.

Buck and Robinson sat in silence for a while in the waiting room. Buck leaned his head back against the wall and closed his eyes again, hoping for a quick snooze before morning came, but his mind was filled with questions. How did Ready know Aurora and Jonathan? Why hadn't Jonathan ever mentioned knowing the famous defensive back? And why did Aurora call him Father, as if he were a priest or something? All of his questions made Buck feel defensive, but something about Ready Robinson made the detective feel it was important to work with the man rather than against him. He turned his train of thought from the puzzles surrounding Ready to the bigger issues at hand.

"We might have a lead," he said suddenly. He heard no response from Ready. "A zip code." He recited the number from memory. There was still no response from Ready.

Barnes opened his eyes and checked the clock. It was almost 1:00 A.M. And Ready Robinson was nowhere to be found.

— — —

Hummingbird Collins lay awake in her bed and worried. It was easy to worry in the nighttime, when the natural silence made every little bump and creak seem like a shout of danger.

She felt good about the day, though. She and T.W. had opted for a "return to normalcy" approach, and it had yielded positive results for her, at least emotionally. Going back to work at the bookstore felt like a homecoming, and it hadn't been long before she became immersed in the daily routines she found so comforting at Collins Galleria of Books. Several times during the day she'd even forgotten that a strangely evil man had killed eight people only half a block away from her, that this same killer apparently had begun stalking her and leaving her daily recordings of absurd philosophical meanderings that were tinged with threats of violence if she turned them over to the police.

But now, at night, alone in her bed, those thoughts returned.

"We can't live in fear," T.W. had told her yesterday and again this afternoon when she'd finally broken away from her work to visit the comfortable confines of his office. "We won't live in ignorance," he added. "But we won't live in fear either. If we die, we die. We are the Collins family, and a Collins never runs away from anyone or anything."

Hummingbird knew T.W. was right. Mom always said he was just like their father—strong, principled, loyal, and fearless. And Hummingbird figured if that's what her daddy was like, and that's what her brother was like, then that's what she would be like as well. So she took precautions—locking the deadbolt on the door, reinforcing the window locks before she went to bed, making check-in calls to T.W. and Peggy to let them know when she'd arrived home and just before she had gone to bed. And for all his tough words, it was T.W. who sent an alarm specialist over to arm her windows and doors and handed her his old baseball bat to tuck under her bed. "If anyone dares to break past the alarm go for a home run," he had said, looking down at her. She had protested, but the bat and the alarms made sense. They were Collinses. But they weren't stupid in their courage. She'd live her life normally, come what may, and trust that God wouldn't allow more than she could bear. For one day at least, she'd been successful.

She felt an inexplicable comfort knowing Ready Robinson was involved too. Ready was rarely seen but was always present in her family's life. Mom said they were closer than brothers when Daddy was alive. In fact, when Hummingbird was a little girl, she'd taken to calling him Uncle Ready, until Mom finally made her stop. He had disappeared sometime during that period in her life, but Mom said he was never far away. And when T.W. had missed out on that college athletics scholarship he'd been counting on, it was a check from Ready Robinson that paid his way to school until he could prove himself as a walk-on for the Mountaineers football team.

Still, Ready Robinson was also a mystery. He rarely spoke of himself or what he did since retiring from football. But Hummingbird had decided he was a comfortable mystery, someone who had proven more than once that he could be trusted.

Hummingbird rolled over and looked at the clock beside her bed: 11:55 P.M. In the silence of the night, she could hear her heart beating in her ears. In spite of everything, she still felt apprehensive about the morning, because in the morning there would likely be another one of those cursed padded envelopes, containing another one of those microcassettes from the madman who stalked her. She wished there were some way she could send him a message, some way she could tell him simply to go away, that she wouldn't be bullied and didn't want to be bothered by his rantings any longer.

She glanced toward the shadowed table across the room, to the place where she knew a stack of microcassette tapes—minus the one she'd sent with Ready—lay in the darkness. T.W. had brought over new blanks and another recorder so she could copy the tapes. A line from Psalm 121 flashed unbidden through her mind: *He who watches over you will not slumber.* She felt the familiar comfort that came from Scripture and then the clarity of mind that often accompanied her Bible reading.

An idea came.

A message, she thought. *A way to communicate to this madman exactly what I think of him.* She smiled. She knew it was a risk—who knew how he might react?—but it was also better than worrying passively in bed every night and doing nothing.

She got up and went to her drawing table and collected some of the new microcassettes, carefully setting the originals aside with a handkerchief—T.W. had said they might want to fingerprint them or use them as evidence at some point. Her copies were already in a neat stack.

Then she went into the kitchen and pulled out a freezer bag and her meat-tenderizing hammer. She dumped several new cassette tapes—noting with satisfaction that they were the same brand as the originals—inside the freezer bag and zipped shut its seal. She started hammering. While her neighbors probably didn't appreciate things going bump in the night in Hummingbird's kitchen, she felt an intense satisfaction as the plastic cassettes cracked and broke and crumbled under the repeated pounding of her hammer.

When the contents of her freezer bag were appropriately destroyed, Hummingbird found a roll of packing tape and went to her front door. A moment later she closed the door, locked it, deadbolted it, and went back to bed. She was asleep in minutes.

— — —

At 3:15 A.M. a man in a dark leather coat crossed the street outside Hummingbird's apartment building and quietly ascended the stairs to her front door. When he came to Apartment 20 he stopped and stared. He had planned to deliver yet another padded envelope to this door, but tonight he found something waiting for him instead. A plastic freezer bag filled with what looked like the tattered remains of several microcassette tapes was attached to the door.

There was a moment of indecision, then a nod acknowledging that a message had been sent and received.

The padded envelope in his interior coat pocket was forgotten. Instead he removed the bag of crushed microcassette tapes from the door, stuffed them into an outer pocket, and with soft footfalls that belied his size, quietly descended the steps, crossed the street, and disappeared between two buildings on the other side.

He never even noticed the other man dressed in gray sweats, a dark knit cap, and a charcoal wool jacket, who silently shadowed him.

— — —

When Hummingbird Collins came out at 6:40 A.M., she found—for the first time in a week—a front door empty of anything except the numbers that were assigned to her apartment. She picked up the newspaper at her feet, looked at the empty space on her door, and tried to decide whether she should be happy or simply afraid.

EIGHT

What is beauty, Ms. Collins? I cannot tell you definitively. I doubt anyone could. But I can tell you that it captivates the soul.

Michelangelo once said that beauty was a flame that had been ignited in his heart, one that tortured him without end through the days of his life.

I think that sounds about right.

Beauty is a torturous thing, is it not? Sometimes torture is required to further the cause of beauty. Sometimes it is beauty itself.

I can also tell you what is not beautiful, Ms. Collins. Anything that masks true beauty. Anything that hinders the beautiful from its necessary expression. These are the unpretty things.

Let me clarify, however. The unpretty need not be ugly. In fact, the unpretty can often seem a beautiful thing to the untrained eye. A fashion model, for instance, with a finely shaped face, a feminine figure, a flattering set of clothes, may appear to be beautiful. But she is often only a forgery of cosmetic surgery, abusive diets, and heavily tailored clothes that accent her strengths and hide her weaknesses. To the novice she is proclaimed beautiful. But you and I know better, don't we?

A surgically altered beauty is no beauty at all. It is, like so many other things, unpretty. And unpretty things must be eliminated so that the truly beautiful may thrive.

Which brings us back to you. Do not think the contacts between you and that detective from the police force have gone unnoticed. Ahh, Ms. Collins. Perhaps you have taken me for a fool after all. I had such higher hopes for you than that. After all, I would hate to see you do something that would be considered, well . . .

Unpretty.

EXCERPT FROM THE MICHELANGELUS RECORDINGS,
TAPE 5,
TRANSCRIBED BY H. J. COLLINS

— — —

FRIDAY, OCTOBER 3, EARLY MORNING

The life of an Urban Monk was more flexible than that of a Benedictine monk but no less disciplined. Ready Robinson reveled in the discipline and in the freedom it gave. When he'd retired from football, he knew that something inside him wanted more than life as just another "former football player who now runs a car dealership/restaurant/life insurance agency" or whatever else his former teammates were doing now. After years of dealing with the pressure of fame and celebrity, he was ready to hide away from the world as well. The life of a Benedictine monk was terribly appealing for Ready; it fit with who he was and what was most important in his life. But after attending seminary he felt God leading him in a different direction.

Ready had been successful in the NFL and even more successful in the way he invested the money he made during his playing days. So he had returned to Lehigh and waited for God to make a move. After a few months of waiting he discovered, through an old professor at seminary, the loose Order of Urban Monks that dotted the nation. The connection was almost instant, and Ready had been dedicated to the lifestyle ever since.

The Urban Monks he knew were few and far between. Some

were Catholic. Some were not. Some were priests. Some were pastors, elders, or simply teachers. All were dedicated and, regardless of their background, generally unseen. They were a free bunch, largely autonomous but committed to a similar set of vows. Recently he and Jonathan and Aurora had been talking about the Shelbys joining the Order, serving in their unique capacities while on the job. Was there any correlation between their talks and the Order's long hunt for the Michelangelus Movement? Had Jonathan been singled out because of it?

At 4:30 in the morning Ready gave up on sleep and, as was his custom, rose from the bed and kneeled beside it to recite his daily vows.

Today, he prayed, *I will serve Jesus Christ with all my heart, soul, and mind, to the honor of God the Father, by the grace of God the Son, through the power of God's own Holy Spirit.*

Today I will pursue a life of obscurity, hiding myself behind the veil of anonymity whenever and wherever possible, to the honor of God the Father, by the grace of God the Son, through the power of God's own Holy Spirit.

Today, within the limitations of my obscurity, I will incarnate my life in the life of my chosen city, understanding interacting, and influencing it as God gives me opportunity, to the honor of God the Father, by the grace of God the Son, through the power of God's own Holy Spirit.

Today I will offer myself as a loyal and living sacrifice to my Lord, to my friends, and to my community, to the honor of God the Father, by the grace of God the Son, through the power of God's own Holy Spirit.

May the Lord Jesus Christ bless and enable me to keep these, my vows, today and every day. Amen.

Ready paused to breathe after reciting his vows. This was his favorite time of the day; the ritual both calmed and energized him. It was a rare morning when peace did not accompany the vow of the Urban Monk. After this morning prayer Ready simply waited, keeping his mind in an attitude of prayer and listening. Sometimes he felt no different after waiting. Other times he felt a special burden to pray for a friend or a city leader or another person with whom he had contact in the community. Sometimes he felt distinct impressions of God guiding him toward a certain course of action for the day or away from a previously planned task. Regardless of what was to come, he always waited—for however long was necessary—until he felt comfortable with God's presence and strength for the day.

Sometimes he waited only a few minutes. Other times an hour or more. And on rare occasions he spent nearly the entire day kneeling beside his bed, breaking away only for the normal functions of the human body and returning again to wait.

Today he was prepared to wait for some time. It had been more than a week since he'd followed that nighttime visitor to Hummingbird's apartment. He'd followed the man when he left, watching from a distance as the man crossed streets and parking lots for about two and a half miles before getting into a dark-colored sedan and driving away. Ready had kicked himself for not following in a car himself, but by the time the stranger had reached his car, Ready remembered that his own car was still parked two miles behind them both. He had pulled out his cell phone, activated its camera, and snapped a quick photo of the car as it drove away. Only later had he noticed the car didn't have license plates attached to it. He had figured they'd been removed for this little nighttime errand and that they'd be replaced as soon as the driver got to a place he considered safe. Ready had been disappointed, but at least he had a photo image of the car itself—an Oldsmobile Alero sedan. The photo was dark, but the

paint appeared to be either blue or dark green, enough information to start searching.

It had been more than a week, and Ready had hit a dead end
in his search for the car and the man who drove it. Detective
Barnes had given him a zip code, and Ready had pulled up a map
of that area from the Internet, studying it for clues to where the
unknown stalker might be hiding, but so far his vectoring algo-
rithm had come up inconclusive, which was not surprising as it
lacked several important variables.

He'd used a contact (and a significant chunk of cash) to gain
access to the motor vehicle records but had been unable to match
conclusively the car in his picture with an address in the zip code
the detective had provided. He'd also tried to use his conspiracy
network to pull in some kind of lead, or at least an idea of where
to start, but again that had not resulted in any real, actionable
information.

So now he waited, praying. He was determined to wait until
God responded. He would wait all day if necessary, and if there
was still no response, he would do the same thing again tomorrow. And the next day. Besides, he actually liked the peace and
stillness that came with waiting. He loved the solitude. He smiled
at the thought. *Guess I'm not an Urban Monk for nothing,* he
thought.

He'd been on his knees in the waiting posture for nearly forty-
five minutes when he heard an instant message request ding into
his computer screen. There were only two people Ready could
think of who knew how to track down his computer address and
successfully override his message-blocking software, and he was
one of them. He got up to check the message and saw a Web address he didn't recognize.

Thank you, Lord, for Galway, Ready prayed. Then he
tapped in the address on his browser, and his eyes lit up with

renewed enthusiasm. This might be exactly the lead he was looking for.

— — —

Number 26 sat in his father's hospital room, deafened by the roar of noises. Dad was not happy today, and he'd let 26 know all about it from the moment he'd stepped into the room. When 3 was in one of those moods, the only thing 26 could do was sit there and take it. There was simply no arguing with the old man. There never was.

Oh, he'd been pleased with the assassination of that plastic surgeon and even happier that the police still had no real leads on the Conklin bombing. But he was furious that 26 had let his last calling card be filmed by the local news stations. And 26 had to admit the old man was right He shouldn't have left it open and taped to the window where everyone could see the red letters that spelled *Unpretty* across the clinic's advertisement. He should have obscured it in an envelope, left it where others would find it first and where it may or may not have ever come to the attention of the TV reporters. But it was too late for that now.

"It was a temporary lapse of judgment," he said aloud. Then he sat back in his chair, closed his mouth, and endured the lecture that followed that admission.

Fortunately he'd been extremely careful with the other details. It was highly unlikely that anyone would connect the Mecklinburg murder to the house at 1669 Kirby Court. And even Dad finally had to admit that.

When the dressing down was finished, there was a time of silence between father and son. Then the obvious question arose.

Number 26 acknowledged the freezer bag with a look of disgust. There was no use trying to hide the obvious. The old man wasn't stupid. Number 26 shook his head ruefully. "Remember that girl I told you about? The one who went for a walk with me? She sent these to me." He grimaced. "We had just a little lover's tiff, really." He shrugged. "You know how women can be."

Number 3 didn't say anything, and 26 slowly realized that his father was actually interested in this.

"I think she was a little jealous of how much time I spent on the last project," he said. "She probably wants to see me again, not just hear from me on the tapes. When we bring her here, when she knows the power of what we do, she'll understand. Our work is turning out beautifully. This last model was superb, although I had to repaint the figure several times before I was satisfied with it. Still, Minos now sits prepared to lord it over hell itself. It gives me chills just to think about it."

He stopped short of inviting his father to come view the work of art. After all, that wasn't terribly practical anymore.

"Of course, the girl and I will kiss and make up soon enough," he said. "She can't stay mad at me forever, right?" He closed his eyes and listened to the humming of the colors in the walls. Were they singing a love song? "Anyway, I'm thinking of paying her a visit sometime soon." He winked toward the old man. "Maybe I'll bring her back to meet you this time. That would be nice, wouldn't it? She'll either be a new addition to our ranks or serve as a model. She is beautiful, so . . . human. If she doesn't fall into line, she could serve as our final sacrifice when we rededicate the church upon completion of our project." He leaned closer to his father, whispering now. "But I do so hope she will fall into line."

— — —

Jonathan Shelby opened his eyes and recognized nothing at first. Then comprehension slowly began to fill his senses. The beeping sound of a heart monitor chirped nearby. A gentle whirring of machinery, the hushed breath of heating vents. He felt an itch and reached for it, only to discover that his arms were strapped to a bed. That led him to conclude that he too was in a bed, in a white, sterile room. A hospital room?

"Where am I?" he asked, except his vocal cords didn't respond the way he'd expected them to, so the words came out more like a slow gurgle of water than a sentence that meant something.

His muscles seemed to ache from too much effort, and he felt weak, terribly weak. His head felt like a hundred-pound watermelon. Immovable.

He blinked.

A vision filled his eyes. Thick blond hair was twisted and pulled back from her face with large plastic hairclips. Wide eyelashes flickered over emerald orbs. A light pinking in the cheeks . . .

"Aurora?" He cursed the gurgling sound.

"Jonathan?"

The voice. He remembered that musical voice. But he could not trust his senses. He felt a warning within him, as though he had been hurt by this mirage before. He closed his eyes and waited for darkness.

"Jonathan," the voice was urgent. "Don't leave me again, Jonathan."

He felt a tingling on his face. It was a good feeling.

He opened his eyes again, and she was still there. There were dark circles under her eyes, a weariness within. How many tears had she cried? Still, a hopeful smile tugged at the edges of her lips. She leaned in close and pressed those lips against his forehead. The tingling spread to his whole body now.

"Are you back with us, Jonathan?" she asked quietly. "Honey, it's me. It's Aurora."

He said nothing but dared to allow himself the freedom to drink in the beauty before him. He studied her, memorizing again her lips, her nose, her eyes, her face.

"Aurora?" It sounded almost like a word this time. "Is it really you?"

"Yes, Jonathan. Yes." A single tear escaped her eye.

"Thank God," he whispered. "Where am I? Where are we? What's going on?"

"What do you remember?"

He tried to shake his melon-heavy head. His brain felt blank, like a chalkboard that had been erased and cleaned with soap. And a part of him wanted it that way, though he couldn't explain why.

"I remember that I love you," he finally gurgled softly. "No matter what happens, I'll always love you, Aurora."

FRIDAY, OCTOBER 3, MID-MORNING

Buck Barnes hung up the phone and breathed a sigh of relief. "We're still not out of the woods yet," Aurora Shelby had said. "But the fact that he is conscious and communicating coherently again is a positive thing. The doctors are very optimistic."

Buck was glad to have even a glimmer of good news. It had been two full weeks since the Conklin bombing, and up until now Barnes had had little reason to be grateful. He opened a file folder—a worn file folder now—and stared again into the face of Hummingbird Collins's sketch. The suspect drawing had been through all of the national databases now, as well as state and local ones, and there still were no conclusive matches. It was almost as if the bomber had erased his face from the public. Or as if he had never existed in the first place.

They had definitively tied the Mecklinburg murder to the

Conklin bombing, however. Whoever this guy was, Detective Barnes was certain he was behind both crimes—and likely several more with similar circumstances across the state over the past dozen years.

This nutcase is a serial killer, Buck said to himself for the hundredth time, *and I've got to find him. And stop him from hurting innocent people ever again.*

His thoughts wandered back to Jonathan Shelby. Aurora had said he was drifting in and out of sleep, and he was generally peaceful and coherent. Apparently he remembered only snatches of his experience over the past few weeks—probably a good thing considering his condition when they first found him. The doctors had said the memory gaps could have been either a result of the heroin found running through his system or the mind guarding itself against psychological trauma, or both.

Buck shuddered when he remembered how near his friend actually had come to death. The people who held Jonathan had shot him up with heroin, morphine, and LSD. Too much of any one of those drugs could kill you. Why give him a cocktail of all three? Even though Buck didn't consider himself a religious man, he had to admit that it was a miracle that Jonathan had not died. Even in the hospital he had come close, suffering a mild heart attack and then lapsing into a coma triggered by the overdose of LSD. The doctors had worried about possible lung failure as well, but the danger of that had passed.

Buck could only imagine the hell his friend had gone through before they found him. He had looked up a little of the history behind LSD and included photocopies of a few important details in his file on the Conklin bombing. He had been surprised to discover that it was a relatively recent drug. Swiss chemist Albert Hoffmann had first synthesized it during World War II. As a test he administered to himself what appeared to be a small, relatively harmless dose of the synthesized chemical. The results were horrifying. For the next fourteen hours the scientist was in hell.

"Everything in my field of vision wavered and was distorted as if seen in a curved mirror. Pieces of furniture assumed grotesque, threatening forms," Hoffmann wrote later. "Even worse than the demonic transformations of the outer world were the alterations that I perceived in myself, in my inner being. Every exertion of my will, every attempt to put an end to the disintegration of the outer world and the dissolution of my ego, seemed to be wasted effort. A demon had invaded me, had taken possession of my body, mind, and soul. I jumped up and screamed, trying to free myself from him, but then sank down again and lay helpless on the sofa. . . . I was seized by the dreadful fear of going insane. I was taken to another world, another place, another time. My body seemed to be without sensation, lifeless, and strange. [I] perceived clearly, as an outside observer, the complete tragedy of my situation."

Detective Barnes skimmed Hoffmann's notes again and decided that whatever Jonathan Shelby had gone through, he hoped the poor man would never have to remember it.

Buck glanced at his watch. It was almost 10:00.

Though he still didn't trust Ready Robinson, he had to respect him. The man—priest?—had promised to keep in touch and had been true to his word. He called in every morning at ten to give the detective updates on the Collinses, and he sometimes threw in other leads as well. He even called in when nothing had changed, just to say that nothing had changed. Barnes appreciated the man's thoroughness.

According to Ready, their little misinformation at the press conference, frustrating as that had been, had worked. The Hummingbird girl hadn't received any more of the threatening microcassettes since. Ready had shadowed her to and from work as

well and reported that, except for the two men Barnes had assigned to keep an eye on her from a distance, she didn't seem to
be under surveillance by any other suspicious characters. He was
certain her telephone was still tapped, though, and had advised
Hummingbird to act accordingly when talking on the phone.
Buck's own men confirmed Ready's assessment.

In return for that information, Buck had told Ready that his
men also had been shadowing T. W. Collins and his fiancée,
Peggy Harrison, and neither of them appeared to be in any
danger. In fact, he was discontinuing the surveillance on T.W.
and Peggy, effective this morning. They would still watch Hummingbird from a distance, however, as she was the only person
who could visually identify the bomber in a police lineup. Ready
had responded to that show of goodwill by dropping off copies
of the transcripts of the remaining microcassettes. They were
currently being analyzed by a psychological profiling expert upstate, but of course, Buck also had kept copies of all of the transcripts for himself. Given how sterile the first cassette had been,
he suspected all remaining cassettes would also have been han-
dled with rubber gloves, giving them no lead on the perpetrators.
Still, Ready assured Buck that the cassettes and recorder were
being treated as evidence and were safe in Hummingbird's apartment.

Barnes spread the contents of his investigation folder on top
of his desk, staring at them while he waited for Ready Robinson
to call. His eyes flicked from Hummingbird's sketch of the suspect, to the two newspaper clippings that had "Unpretty"
painted in thin lines on them, to the police photo of the blown-
out front doors of the Conklin Art Gallery.

He felt certain he was missing something.

He thumbed through the pages of transcripts again, noting
the things that kept popping up in his mind.

For starters, that whole reference to a cult of the Michelange-lus Movement. If there were such a cult, somebody somewhere had to have written something about it. But try as he might, De-tective Barnes couldn't find any trace of it, not on the Internet, not in libraries, not in records of cult-watch organizations, noth-ing. Of course, if you were running a supersecret cult, you might hide your group within a front organization that wouldn't arouse immediate suspicion, like some Islamic terrorist cells hid them-selves within a religious school or mosque. Or you might do your best to disassociate yourself completely from that name. Or you might simply give yourself no name and proceed that way. Hadn't the suspect said something about names being unneces-sary in that first tape? That could be relevant; at this point, how-ever, Buck just couldn't be sure.

He rearranged the pieces of information on his desk. He looked at the advertisement for the "Michelangelo Mirrors" ex-hibit at the Conklin, then at the words painted over the ad. Next he stared at the sketch of his suspect. A few pieces began falling into place within his head. In the background somewhere a phone began to ring, but Buck ignored it. He was busy at the moment.

— — —

It had taken a good portion of his morning, but Ready Robinson finally felt optimistic. He'd tried making his morning call to Buck Barnes, but the detective had been unavailable. No worries, though. He would connect with Barnes later, and by then he could have something more tangible to talk about.

Meanwhile he clicked the mouse on his computer and decided to review one last time the streaming video on the Web site Galway had sent him. He had not been able to copy the video—some kind of encrypting protection on the other end prevented that—and if he knew Galway, the Web site itself was time-encrypted, meaning it would take itself offline after a certain number of hours. So Ready did his best to memorize the important elements of the video, jotting notes on a yellow legal pad nearby.

The video had been dated September 26, and a running clock in the bottom right-hand corner showed the time progressing from 3:38 A.M. and following. Ready adjusted his mental perspective to that of the camera angle, from atop the traffic light. As expected, the streets were nearly deserted at that hour of the morning. Then, after a moment or two, the traffic camera registered a dark-colored sedan driving through the intersection. It took Ready only a second to recognize the car as an Oldsmobile Alero. When he saw that it had no license plates, Ready knew it was the car he was looking for. The Alero stayed only a few seconds in the range of the traffic camera, then the camera angle switched, and Ready could see it moving away from the intersection and down the street toward the next stop light.

Ready had drawn a little map of the car's progress from intersection to intersection, tracking each time it turned or went straight until at last it had turned into a residential area on the southeast side of town. At that point the video screen had split into four quadrants, with each showing itself as a traffic camera posted at one of the four main entrances and exits into this residential neighborhood. The cameras continued their surveillance for thirty more minutes of film, but the car never reappeared, and finally the video blanked out.

It was not exact, but at least Galway's pirating of the traffic cameras had narrowed down the search.

Ready minimized the Web page that held the video and pulled up a street map of Lehigh, carefully zooming in on the area of the city in which the car had last been seen. After positioning and cropping the map, he printed out a copy. Then, though he felt sure it would be the case, he checked his map against a map of postal zip codes and confirmed that the neighborhood into which the Alero had disappeared was indeed zoned under the zip code he'd received from Detective Barnes at the hospital.

Ready marked out the edges of his new map, highlighting streets within that area and estimating how many houses they contained. In the end he figured four square miles of area was out of sight of the traffic cameras, and several hundred houses, duplexes, and condominiums inhabited those four miles. It was still like searching for a needle in a haystack, but at least now Ready knew where to find the haystack.

He maximized the Web site window, intent on reviewing the traffic videos one more time, but when he did, he got an error screen in his Web browser. He tried retyping the original address, but again it yielded only an error screen. Ready was disappointed to lose the video so soon, but he understood. In the world of conspiracies no one could be trusted for very long.

— — —

Hummingbird Collins walked out the front door of the law offices of T. W. Collins with two hot cups of cocoa and a warm feeling in her heart. It had been more than a week since she'd had any contact from the madman who bombed the Conklin, and she and T.W. both were beginning to sense that this was a good sign.

"Look," T.W. had just said this morning, "the guy has to know that the police and good citizens of our fair city are looking in every nook and cranny to find him. Now that he feels you are no longer a threat, he's probably long gone. My guess is he's at some safe house in New York or Canada or Mexico or somewhere."

Hummingbird didn't want to throw all caution to the wind, but she was at least beginning to think T.W. was right. Ready had said he'd not seen anyone unusual following her, and T.W. said the police also had been shadowing her and had not seen anyone either.

She crossed Hope Street, then Fourth, and walked down to the bookstore entrance. "Hey, Kacey," she hollered when she came in, "Becky sent you a cup of hot chocolate."

There was no answer, but a woman who was browsing in the art and art history section glanced up toward Hummingbird. The woman had carefully trimmed dark hair pulled back into a short ponytail and a trim physique that reminded Hummingbird of a dancer. There was a moment of silence between them. Then the woman shrugged and said, "I think the other lady went into the back, to the bathroom or something."

Hummingbird smiled her thanks and said, "Anything I can help you find?"

The woman allowed herself an appraising look and then shook her head. "No thanks," she said, "unless you can tell me where I can get one of those steaming cups of hot chocolate? It smells so good."

Hummingbird gave a light laugh. "Sorry," she said. "My brother's secretary gave them to me."

"Oh well," the woman said without mirth. "Can't have everything in this life, can we?"

Hummingbird set the hot chocolate on the counter and meandered back toward the only customer in her store. "Well," she said, "if you need anything bookwise, don't hesitate to let me know."

The woman nodded and returned to her browsing.

Hummingbird stuck her head into the back room and hollered, "Kacey? You back here?"

The door to the bathroom opened slightly. "In here, Humm," a beleaguered voice called back. "Be out in a minute."

"You okay, honey?"

"Just feeling a little sick to my stomach this morning. Not sure why. I felt fine when I started that cinnamon roll on the counter. Then I went to wait on a customer, and soon after that, well, just felt like I needed to come back here, if you know what I mean."

Hummingbird's face creased in maternal concern. "Anything I can do for you, Kace?"

"No, not really. Except I think there's a lady still out there on the bookstore floor. You mind waiting on her for me?"

"I'm on it, girlfriend."

She turned and stepped back onto the bookstore's main floor and was surprised to find the woman standing only a few feet away from her.

"Is that other girl okay?" the woman said. "She seemed as if she wasn't feeling well before you came in."

Hummingbird put on her best fake smile. "Oh, she'll be fine. Some bad pastry, I think." She noticed that the woman had a book in her hands. "Looking for a good novel?"

The woman cocked her head and said, "I like historicals. Especially those set during the Renaissance. You are a pretty young woman," the customer said strangely, "but I don't see your resemblance to our painting at all."

Hummingbird wasn't sure what to make of that off-the-wall comment, so she simply gave her fake smile again and said, "Would you like me to take that to the front counter for you?"

"No, thank you," the woman said, handing the book carefully to Hummingbird. "I think I'll be going now."

"Well, thanks for stopping by," Hummingbird said in her officially friendly salesperson-type voice. "Come back and see us sometime."

The woman stopped partway down the aisle, long enough to turn around and look Hummingbird in the eyes.

"Oh, I will, Ms. Collins," she said comfortably. Then she continued out the front door and was gone.

Hummingbird stood thoughtfully, tapping a finger on the name badge that hung around her neck and wondering at the strange way of that woman. She seemed nice enough, but some of her comments didn't really make much sense. Hummingbird walked up to the counter and took a big gulp of hot chocolate—though by now it was only lukewarm chocolate.

"No wonder it's not hot anymore," she said to herself. "I should have left the lid on the cup to keep the warmth in longer." She took in another mouthful of her lukewarm drink and grimaced at the bitter aftertaste.

"It smelled better than it tastes," she muttered. "But at least it was free."

She tried one more sip of the bitter fluid and then decided simply to give up on it. She picked up the cup to pour it down the sink in the back, then realized she couldn't find the lid to the cup. She checked the floor behind the counter but didn't see it there either. In fact, she couldn't find a lid for either of the cups of hot cocoa that she'd brought back from T.W.'s office.

"Funny," she muttered. "I don't even remember taking the lids off."

She was so preoccupied with the whereabouts of the lids that she didn't notice the small square of paper that dropped into the sink when she poured the contents of her cup down the drain.

NINE

Do you believe in heaven, Ms. Collins? I can't say that I believe in the traditional view of heaven, but I have seen something of heaven here on earth from time to time. And sometimes it is a bit frightening.

Still, as the great Buonarroti once said, "My soul can find no staircase to heaven unless it be through earth's loveliness."

You are lovely, Ms. Collins. I thought so when I first noticed you. What I haven't decided yet is whether you are pretty.

EXCERPT FROM THE MICHELANGELUS RECORDINGS,
TAPE 2,
TRANSCRIBED BY H. J. COLLINS

- - -

FRIDAY, OCTOBER 3, LATE MORNING

Buck Barnes clicked on one of the early results of his Google search: Buonarroti Accademia of Fine Art, Roma, Italia.

He surfed through the links of the school's Web site and discovered exactly what he wanted to find. There, hidden away in the hills of Rome, was a small college dedicated to the study of classical art, with an emphasis on works and techniques of Michelangelo Buonarroti. Among its programs the school even offered a degree in art called a Michelangelus Certification, apparently bestowed on those who finished a four-year intensive program that culminated in a detailed replication of some great work by Michelangelo himself. The school indicated that most of its graduates went on to be professional artists active in the art community or teachers of art and art history at some of the finest universities around the world.

He looked again at the materials spread on his desk. His mad bomber was obviously an artist. Based on his repeated references to Michelangelo in the tapes and the fact that he bombed a surrealist interpretation of Michelangelo's art, the bomber had a fixation on the great Renaissance artist. If that were true, then he probably knew of the Buonarroti Accademia of Fine Art. And if that were true, it was just possible that the Accademia also knew of him.

Detective Barnes quickly jotted down a number from the "Contact Us" page of the school site. Then he picked up his phone and dialed his receptionist. "What time is it in Rome?" he asked hurriedly when Sunny Yan picked up the line.

"Hey, Buck," she said warmly. "Is this another trivia quiz thing?"

Detective Barnes tamped down his impatience. "No, Sunny. I really need to know. Can you find out for me?"

"Sure, hang on." She put him on hold.

Buck thought about hanging up and simply walking out front to talk to Sunny face to face but decided that would be rude, so he waited, fingers drumming on the partially cracked keys of the number pad on his computer keyboard. Fortunately Sunny was fast at gathering information. After only a minute she was back on line. "It's just after five P.M. in Rome right now. Can I ask why you want to know?"

"I need to send a fax to Italy," he said, "and I'm hoping someone will still be there to receive it."

Hummingbird Collins did not feel well.

She had already sent Kacey home sick—the poor girl had thrown up so much she could barely stand up, let alone wait on customers or unpack books for the bookshelves. Now Hummingbird herself was feeling a little, well, *unreal*.

Fortunately it had been a slow morning at the bookstore. In fact, no one had even come in after that strange woman. About half an hour after she had left Hummingbird felt dizzy, then heard a buzzing in her ears. She had pulled up a stool and sat down behind the counter, closing her eyes to help settle the flashing and curling that seemed to be messing with her vision.

At one point she'd considered closing the store completely for the day and just going straight to a doctor to find out what was happening to her, but when she tried to stand up the entire floor and ceiling seemed to switch places, causing her to lurch back onto her stool and hold on for dear life.

"What is wrong with me?" she whispered now, as a creeping fear washed over her consciousness.

She felt her stool begin to wobble, then take flight over the stacks of books in the bookstore. She was too frightened to scream and could only tighten her knuckles around the edges of her flimsy little chair. She still couldn't open her eyes, afraid of the dizzying blur that would accompany sight. After what was either a minute or a month, she felt her stool tumble over onto the floor, dumping her with it. She lay on the ground, eyes tightly shut, for another month, or another minute—she wasn't sure—until the world seemed finally to settle into stasis.

She opened her eyes and saw a woman—the woman who had been in the store earlier—and two large men looking down at her.

"Help me," she said. "I'm not well."

They didn't seem to hear her. One of the large men leaned in close to her face, inspecting. Then he turned to the woman. "She doesn't look like anyone in the painting," he said matter-of-factly.

The woman nodded, then shrugged. "I guess the boss has a personal, rather than professional, interest in this one."

The other two men also shrugged.

"Flip the closed sign on the front door."

Hummingbird watched the sound of the woman's voice erupt from her mouth into bright, wild colors that swirled overhead and then through her own body. She saw the noise of the big man as he grunted and lifted her to her feet.

"She's going to scream sooner or later." The words formed blocks of ice that crushed themselves on her head and around her shoulders and finally chilled at her feet.

"Fine." More words of ice, this time from the woman. "Sedate her then. And get her into the car. As the poet says, we've got miles to go before we sleep."

Hummingbird felt the small prick and subsequent burn of a needle in her hip. She had a hard time caring, however, since she was already frozen and shivering from the ice words that covered her with shards of winter.

She wanted to call for T.W., for Ready, for anybody to come and save her, but her lips were frozen shut as well. So she spoke words in her soul instead. *Help me, Jesus,* she said wordlessly. *HelpmeJesus, helpmeJesus, helpme . . .*

— — —

Kinseth Roberts stood in the paling light and stared at the scary beautiful thing on the wall behind the altar. They knew it wasn't finished. They could tell because there were blank spaces that appeared to have been deliberately left that way, as if they were to be filled in later when the artist was ready.

They held the book under their arm, gripped it tightly as if it were their only protection against the frights that leaped off the wall and almost into reality. When they had first seen this huge painting on the wall of the abandoned Baptist church, they hadn't known what to make of it. It was both frightening and fascinating, and they'd spent many days sitting in the front pew and staring at it. They had finally figured out that the massive, majestic figure near the top—the one who looked both angry and compassionate—was supposed to be Jesus. Kinseth was comforted by that.

The rest of the painting, though, had been a mass of naked bodies flying through the air, some being torn apart by warring parties of what might have been angels or some other creature. Some of the people were rising up toward Jesus. Others appeared to be fighting against the overwhelming pull of evil that dragged them down to the bottom of the painting.

No one looked very happy in this painting. Not even the ones going up.

Kinseth had marveled at the way the painting seemed so alive, even with its obvious omissions and holes to be filled in later. Most of those holes had been filled in over the last few years. But there had been one omission that always stirred Kinseth's curiosity. At the bottom right corner of the painting there had been a hole for as long as they could remember. Someone had started painting in that spot once and then erased everything there and left it blank for years.

Now Kinseth couldn't take their eyes off that corner. Now that corner held the image of a man. Kinseth knew the face when they'd first seen it on the book at the bookstore. It was the face of the prisoner, the one who had needed a friend.

Now that face was out of the book, had somehow been taken off the prisoner even. Now it was painstakingly attached to the wall, as part of the scary beautiful thing.

It was the same face but not the same expression. There was a meanness to it, a hardness that covered up a sadness.

Kinseth could barely force themselves to look at the rest of the image. But they couldn't *not* look at it either. Twisting around the powerfully built torso of the naked man was a fat, muscular serpent wrapped in two tight coils. Kinseth crossed their legs involuntarily and shuddered. Was this really an appropriate picture to paint on the wall of a church? They didn't think so, but they had also learned from their book that this mass of naked, suffering humanity had been painted on a famous church in Italy hundreds of years ago. Now someone had repainted most of it here, in this abandoned place.

Kinseth felt pity for the prisoner on the wall. What he must have suffered. They wondered if the prisoner were dead now and thought about going to visit him again. If that key to the hospital-room door was still under the patient's pillow, they would go visit again, they decided. Just once more at least.

Then they heard a sound from the hallway in back. Footsteps coming from the room where the trapdoor was hidden. Kinseth were ready for this, as it had happened before. They quickly dropped to the floor and rolled backward, underneath the pews, curling into a small ball and facing their head toward the front. From beneath the pew, they had just enough of a line of sight to see the lower half of the artist who sometimes came in here.

The artist was singing when he entered, an out-of-tune melody that had something to do with apple cores and hearts in love. It made no sense to Kinseth, but they were untroubled. Many things made no sense to them.

The artist stopped in front of the scary beautiful thing and let out a sigh. "Almost, my lovely," he said aloud. "Almost done."

He walked over to the bottom right corner of the painting, and it appeared to Kinseth that he was caressing the new face that now adorned that part of the wall. "Minos, lord of the damned," he whispered admiringly. "All unpretty things belong to you, my friend. They belong to you."

The artist staggered backward a step and appeared to be hearing something that wasn't there. In a moment he joined in the imagined noise, emitting a wailing sound that so frightened Kinseth that they began edging backward under the pews, backward toward the main doors of the small auditorium, carefully dragging the precious art book with them. They weren't sure how they would sneak out the doors without being noticed, but they felt certain it would be better to be near the doors while the artist was in the room.

The artist let out a cry that was either pain or pleasure and dropped to one knee. Then, like a stack of bricks falling over, the artist tumbled to his side and was silent. Kinseth waited. A moment later the artist moaned and slapped at the floor, as if he were having a mild seizure.

Kinseth edged all the way to the back pew, then decided to take advantage of the fact that the artist was moaning and reaching toward the painting on the wall. They slipped quietly out of the auditorium and pushed out the front doors of the church.

They ran home then, ran all the way without stopping. And all the while one thought raced through their mind: *All unpretty things belong to Minos.*

– – –

When Number 26 came to his senses, the first thing he noticed was sunlight streaming through the windows of the church sanctuary. He lay crumpled by the altar, and slowly he focused on the painting above him. He had seen it gloriously before, he and Minos sparring in eternal union. He had smelled the fires of hell—the very fires he had painted at the bottom of the altar wall—felt their heat on his face, heard the crackling of the flames as they mixed with the cackles of the demons who swarmed hungrily around the doomed souls being herded into eternal damnation. It had been terrifyingly glorious until the noxious aromas of hell had finally overcome his senses and sent him into unconsciousness.

He looked above to the other figures in the massive painting, a work that had taken him month upon month to complete. Painstaking research, constant reference to live models. Yes, they had served him well, he thought, grinning. Their suffering was not for naught. Herein they lived again in his reproduction of Michelangelo's finest work. Yes, yes. From top to bottom the Master would be well pleased with his labor. There was little left to be done, a nuance here, a quick fix there. In days they would be ready for their ceremony of dedication.

Number 26 sat up wearily on the floor and again took note of the sunlight streaming in through the windows. He had a nagging feeling that this was important, that he was forgetting something and the sunlight was trying hard to remind him what it was.

My mind isn't functioning well, he said to himself. *I can't even remember the last time I ate something.*

He stood unsteadily and breathed deeply of the musty air that filled the old church. He considered briefly trying to find Number 61. A small dose of some kind of pick-me-up would certainly help erase the weariness he now felt.

His mind itched, and he turned to looked upward at the light in the windows. Then it came flooding back to him. Today was an important day, with important work to do. He might already be late for the task at hand.

He wiped the side of his mouth with a sleeve and pushed aside thoughts of any helpful medicines from Number 61. He needed a clear mind for the work ahead. A clear mind and a clean body. He would have to shower and groom. He expected that 39 had already prepared the necessary tools, but he would still need to hurry in order to keep his team on schedule. He turned and staggered down the hallway back toward the choir room and the trapdoor hidden there.

Yes, today was going to be an important day.

He was glad that he hadn't missed it.

FRIDAY, OCTOBER 3, LATE AFTERNOON

T. W. Collins opened his office door, feeling the familiar thrill that came with nailing down a sweet contract for a favorite client.

"Well?" Becky said expectantly. "That was a one-hour-and-forty-five-minute conference call. Does that mean good news for Rivera Frenz or bad news for our favorite up-and-coming pitcher?"

T.W. laced his fingers and cracked his knuckles, palms out, in an exaggerated gesture of success. "Ah, Becky," he said, "you know me. What do you think happened?"

A look of disappointment fell across Becky's face. "Oh well," she said sympathetically. "Don't take it too hard. There's still the Diamondbacks. Maybe they'll pick up an option on the kid."

T.W. looked for something to throw at his assistant, found nothing, and sent her an offended pout instead. "Oh, you wound me," he said. "If you cut me, do I not bleed?"

Becky laughed. "So what is it really?"

"Six years, option for seventh. They wouldn't give us asking price, but they did give us more than our bottom-dollar price. Riv's gonna be quite happy—and quite rich. And he's going straight to the majors as a relief pitcher. The Phillies brass say they want his strong young arm in the pitching rotation as soon as possible, especially after seeing the way he's performed in the Japanese leagues."

"It's a done deal then?"

"Verbal agreement. They're going to fax over the formal offer in an hour or so. But we got all the details hammered out. It's a good deal."

"Well, good for you, T.W. Does that mean I get a raise?"

T.W. rolled his eyes. "It means you can still work here at your current salary. Unless, of course, you insult the boss again."

"Hey, I thought I was the boss. Says so in my job description, I'm sure."

T.W. laughed in spite of himself. He was feeling great. His commission on this new contract would add a tidy sum to his bank account. His sister seemed back to her normal, cheerful self. The police hadn't found that Conklin bomber yet, but the guy had disappeared and no longer seemed to be in contact with Hummingbird. Things were finally returning back to normal, and normal was good for T.W.

He plopped down onto the reception-area couch and put his feet on the magazine-laden coffee table. "You know, I've got to wait around for that fax to come," he said, "but if you want to take off early today and get a head start on the weekend—"

He stopped short when he realized there was a green military-style cloth jacket hanging on the coat rack by the door. "Hey, Beck," he said. "Where'd that coat come from?"

Becky seemed to notice it for the first time. "Oh, that. Guy came in while you were in conference. Said he wanted to talk to you about representing his nephew or something. I told him you were unavailable and he should make an appointment, but he said he'd wait. After about five minutes he said he'd come back another time. He must have forgotten his coat when he left." She cocked her head and then went outside to pull a flyer off the glass. T.W.'s eyes flicked from his assistant, flyer in hand, to the jacket, alarm bells ringing in his brain.

He stood and, with a trembling hand, reached out and opened up the green jacket that hung nearby. Inside it, sewn lumpily into the lining, were two small packs of something. And flashing red numbers through a hole in an inside pocket—a timer. It didn't appear to be counting down—yet, but T.W. decided now was not the time to take chances.

"Hey, T.W.," Becky said as she came back into the office. "It's the strangest thing. Did you see that flyer on our door? It's one of your yellow pages advertisements. But somebody has written something across the front of it."

"Unpretty," T.W. said in unison with his assistant. She gave him a startled look, apparently unsure of how her boss knew what was on the ad.

"C'mon, Beck," he said. "We're done here for the day."

"Uh, let me get my purse—"

"No time for that."

He grabbed Becky by the shoulder and forced her back to the door. They both stumbled out of the office and into the street.

— — —

Jonathan Shelby opened his eyes and remembered where he was. The humming of hospital machinery was now familiar and, in its own way, comforting. He was still exhausted, but he could tell he was on the slow road to recovery. If only the dreams would cease . . .

"Aurora?" He spoke his wife's name because he still didn't have the energy to sit up and see if she was in the room.

"I sent her home," a man's voice responded. "She needed rest. I told her I'd sit with you for a while and that she should try to get a few hours' sleep."

"Father Robinson," Jonathan said with relief. "I can't tell you how good it is to hear your voice again."

Ready's face strayed into Jonathan's vision, a paternal smile pasted on it. "It's good to see you in control of your faculties again."

"Wow," Jonathan said after a moment. "I must have been in really serious shape for you to make a personal appearance." He studied him. "Or is it because of who took me? Did they know who I was? About . . . the Order?"

Ready met his gaze. "I don't know. You were there. What do you remember? When they tortured you, drugged you, what did they say? What did they ask?"

"In other words, did I cave? Did I give away our secrets?"

"Did you?"

Jonathan stared into his brown eyes a moment and then looked to the wall. "The man said a lot. But I don't think he knew me as an enemy. He was more interested in using me, studying me."

"For what purpose?"

"He never said. But he mentioned Minos. It has Michelangelus Movement written all over it."

"We knew they were here, that they had taken others. The cost . . . to you, to Aurora, will count for something, my friend, I promise. It will help us get closer, perhaps even capture them."

They shared a long look, and then Jonathan said, "I'm addicted, Ready. I have to go through detox. And even then I'm not sure if I'll be . . . right."

Ready loosed a soft laugh. "You? Nah. You're too ornery to let something like kidnapping or drugs undo you. You're tough, man. And God is with you. He was with you through these last terrible days. He'll be with you as you move forward. Nah, you're tough. It was Aurora I was worried about. She's fragile, that one."

Now it was Jonathan's turn to laugh. "Yeah. Fragile like a brick wall," he said with admiration. "She's the strong one in our family."

Ready patted his friend on the arm. "You're right. Don't know what she saw in you," he joked. "You're just lucky you met her first. Otherwise who knows? I might not be a priest anymore."

Jonathan smiled again. "Well, I don't know what she saw in me," he said in response, "but I'm not arguing."

"Me either," Ready said. "You two belong together."

There was another period of silence between the two men, but this time neither one felt compelled to fill it. Ready sat on the bed, listening to the quiet. Jonathan lay in the bed, reveling in it.

Finally Jonathan spoke again. "They tell you what they did to me?"

Ready nodded, his face growing passive, his eyes tightening with compassion.

"I don't remember most of it," Jonathan continued. "Just snatches of things. A word here, like Minos. An image there. And to tell you the truth, I don't want to remember it. I know you want me to, Ready, the Order needs me to . . . but I just want to forget. Is that okay? To want to forget everything and anything that happened to me?"

Ready didn't respond, choosing instead simply to listen.

"I suppose someday I'll have to deal with it all," Jonathan said. "But not now. Not yet." He sighed. "Right now I only want to rest. And forget."

Ready patted Jonathan's arm again. Jonathan recognized something in his friend and spiritual mentor's expression.

"You're praying for me right now, aren't you?"

Ready's face softened into the grin of a child caught with his hand in the cookie jar. He nodded and shrugged.

"Don't stop, Ready. Don't ever stop praying for me."

Ready give a single nod that told Jonathan he would always have someone praying for him—and that he always had.

Jonathan sighed again. "They said I should have died," he said. "That there was such a high concentration of different drugs in my system that I should have had a major heart attack or a stroke or lung failure. That I should have at least had some kind of lasting brain damage."

Ready said nothing, listening. And praying.

"I guess in spite of everything someone up there was watching out for me. Why is it still so hard for me to believe, after all I've seen?"

"God is always hard to believe," Ready said. "That's why we trust him. And you, my friend, have been on the front lines of the battle. In such a place he's harder to see, harder to believe, because the enemy is so clear. But it's in just such a place where he shines brightest."

Jonathan closed his eyes and let Father Robinson's words sink in. After a moment he felt Ready rise from the bed and heard him return to a seat nearby.

It was good to have Ready in the room, praying. It gave Jonathan a feeling of safety he hadn't been expecting when he woke up, but he liked it. He felt his heartbeat ticking at an even, moderate pace. Enjoyed breathing deeply and without strain. After a moment he felt an unusual impression that God wanted something of him, wanted him to do something to make the world a better place . . . something of his old call that had led him to the Order.

He tried to do as Ready had taught him, focusing his thoughts on Jesus Christ, letting that image of God flood his consciousness until he felt calm. After a moment his mind began to wander back to the earliest moments of his abduction. He didn't like that train of thought, and so he deliberately refocused his energies on the image of Christ. He knew his man-made image wasn't accurate, but he liked picturing Jesus sitting in a chair next to him, as if they were about to begin a conversation about life or art or the latest movie they'd both seen. In his mind Christ reached out and touched his hand.

It's a promise of strength, he thought suddenly.

Then the hand of Christ reached up and touched his head. Jonathan's mind inexplicably wandered back to the kidnapping. He caught his breath, faintly reliving the moment when he had woken up inside the trunk of a car. The images blurred and danced, but they still moved forward. He felt the familiar panic closing in.

Strength, his mind said. He gritted his teeth and let the memory continue.

The next thing he remembered was being dragged out of the trunk of the car by two large, faceless men. They heaved him up onto the porch of a house. Jonathan froze his memory there. A basic suburban house. He tried to remember the colors of the house, the general shape, but every time he tried to focus in on that part of the memory, the house disappeared into the fog.

He experienced a moment of clarity on the porch. For the first time he remembered this clearly. There was a moment, there on the porch, when he'd tried to escape. They caught him, of course. Jabbed something into his neck and dragged him to the door of the house. He knew the memory would fade from there, but something caught the corner of his vision. He concentrated on it.

He could almost hear the Jonathan Shelby from two weeks ago passing a message to him today.

Remember this, the old Jonathan was saying. *Memorize it. No matter what happens. The police will want to know this later. If there is a later. Dear Jesus, help me remember this . . .*

The memory faded into darkness. Nothing. No real memory of anything until he woke up and saw Aurora's beautiful face hovering over his hospital bed. He replayed the moment on the porch in his mind. Standing in front of the door of a nondescript suburban house that would become his prison. He stared at it, willing the memory into view.

He opened his eyes.

"Sixteen sixty-nine," he said out loud.

"Did you say something, Jonathan?" Ready was quickly standing beside the bed again.

"Sixteen sixty-nine," he said again. Inwardly he smiled. Sometimes it was possible to make the world a better place, even when lying helpless in a hospital bed.

"What's that, Jonathan?"

"The number on the house. The place where they kept me. I remember it. It was sixteen sixty-nine."

Ready leaned in close, searching Jonathan's eyes. "You're sure?"

"I'm sure, Ready. The house number was sixteen sixty-nine. I don't know the street or even what the house looked like. But I know the number. I told myself to memorize it. The house number was sixteen sixty-nine."

Ready patted him on the shoulder as he stood. "You've done well. I know it was hard, going there, remembering."

"Yeah, whatever. Get outta here. Leave a note for Aurora and go. I'll never get any sleep with you squirming around in that chair forever. And you have a lead to chase."

Ready wrote the note, patted his friend once more on the arm, and said, "I am praying."

"I know," Jonathan said. "Don't quit."

— — —

Number 61 heard someone climbing the stairs two at a time. She turned the corner of the kitchen just in time to see 39 appear at the top of the staircase. His face was flushed and annoyed, his eyes narrowed.

"He forgot to start the timer," 39 said in disgust.

"What?"

"Number twenty-six. He delivered the note. He dropped the jacket without arousing suspicion. And he walked away clean. But he forgot to start the timer on the detonator."

"Oh no."

"Right. It's all over the police radio right now. They've sent a bomb squad to that lawyer's office to defuse the C-4 we sewed into the lining of the jacket."

"I tried to tell him that it was too soon to use the same method again. That if we needed to get rid of the lawyer we should do it differently."

"I know. But when he's made up his mind, all you can do is obey. Especially if those two goons of his are nearby." An unpleasant memory in the chair of 26's studio flashed past 39's consciousness. He deliberately set it aside.

"Serial forgetfulness is one of the symptoms of his addiction."

"I know."

"With that note and an intact bomber jacket in police custody," she said, "it's only a matter of time before they trace the suppliers and then the suppliers are traced back to us."

"I know."

"How long do you think it'll take them?"

"Hard to tell. If they're good, twenty-four to forty-eight hours. If they're average, a few days more."

"Don't suppose we could hope for police ineptitude?" She allowed herself a small smile. A police fumble had saved them in Salem.

"Not likely," he said. "Not this time. What we have to do now is damage control."

She nodded. "Where's he now?"

"You know Johann. After planting a bomb he usually stays away until after dark, just in case someone tries to follow him."

"That's good, at least. What about Forty-four and Forty-eight?"

"They're still hiding out with the girl. They won't bring her back here until after dark as well."

"The girl . . . what is it about her? She has no resemblance to the painting. And his fascination with her led us to this whole new fiasco with the lawyer. His choices are endangering our mission."

He went to the window and stared out through the curtains. "The drugs are taking over. He's unclear in his thinking, direction. Given this pace, we'll soon be compromised."

There was a moment of silence, then 61 said, "What are your orders, sir?"

"I think it's time for Plan B."

She nodded.

"You're dismissed," he said formally.

"Thank you, sir," she responded. She hurried downstairs to her supply room. She had a lot to do in a little amount of time.

— — —

Buck arrived late to the scene of the latest threat but was pleased to see the bomb squad had isolated the explosive-laden jacket and appeared confident in their ability to disarm the C-4. He saw T. W. Collins standing with a woman and a few uniformed police officers a safe distance away from the bomb-squad activity and made his way over to speak to the sports attorney.

T.W. greeted him as a friend, though not a close one. "Detective," he said.

"Mr. Collins." Buck nodded back.

"My sister is gone," he said, clearly agitated. "The shop is closed. Her assistant too. She's never closed during the day."

"Whoa, calm down," Buck said. "I'm sure one of our guys took them to a safe location, with the bomb and all."

"Can you find out who it was? Where she is? She's not answering her cell phone."

"Sure, sure. I'm telling you, she's probably at the police station right now."

"Thank you, Detective."

Buck nodded toward the woman with T.W. and extended his hand. "Buck Barnes," he said by way of introduction.

T.W. turned quickly. "Of course. I'm sorry. Detective Barnes, this is my assistant, Rebecca Proctor. Becky, this is Detective Barnes."

"Call me Buck," he said reflexively. "Everybody else does." Then he added, "Well, everyone except Mr. Collins."

"Nice to meet you, Detective Barnes," the assistant said. Buck had to grin at her show of loyalty. "Now can you check on Hummingbird?"

"Did either of you see anything? Before you noticed the jacket?" Buck asked, as he dialed the police station on his cell and listened to it ring.

A look of dawning realization passed over T.W.'s face. "Yes," he said suddenly. "I'm sorry, Detective. I think we're still a little shell-shocked by the fact that a bomb was planted in my office.

But yes, my assistant here saw the man who left the jacket. Becky, can you describe him for Detective Barnes?"

"Yes, I think so," she started.

"A full description might not be necessary," Barnes said. "Just tell me if he looked something like this." He held out the suspect sketch that Hummingbird Collins had done previously.

"Yes," she said immediately. "That's him. That's the man who came into our office earlier. Who is he?"

"I don't know yet," Buck said grimly. "But I intend to find out."

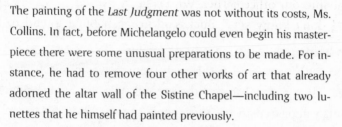

TEN

The painting of the *Last Judgment* was not without its costs, Ms. Collins. In fact, before Michelangelo could even begin his masterpiece there were some unusual preparations to be made. For instance, he had to remove four other works of art that already adorned the altar wall of the Sistine Chapel—including two lunettes that he himself had painted previously.

Interesting, isn't it? That the master artist had to destroy his own works in order to create something truly beautiful?

I've had to do that myself from time to time, Ms. Collins. Sometimes it has been my own work, sometimes it's been the work of others. But destruction is a small price to pay when something stands in the way of beauty, is it not?

EXCERPT FROM THE MICHELANGELUS RECORDINGS,
TAPE 3,
TRANSCRIBED BY H. J. COLLINS

— — —

FRIDAY, OCTOBER 3, LATE NIGHT

Kinseth Roberts had promised Elaina they'd be *ready* for bed by 11:00 P.M., but they hadn't promised to be *in* bed by that time, so Kinseth didn't feel at all guilty about being awake and watching out their window, even though it was now close to midnight. All of the lights were out in their room, but they still had the telescope peering out. Robby and Kenny both wanted to look at the stars. Seth didn't care one way or another, so they all spent some time staring into the telescope while it pointed upward toward the moon.

After a while they heard the sound of a car engine on the street. Seth was immediately interested and forced them all to turn the telescope downward, pointing across the cul-de-sac at 1669 Kirby Court. Two men got out of the car. One of them opened the trunk and reached in. When he stood up again he was holding the limp form of a woman.

Kinseth wondered if this new woman was a guest or a prisoner. They guessed it was the second, because at one point the woman appeared to try to struggle out of the man's grasp, but she was obviously too weak to do more than give token resistance. Kinseth wondered if they were going to stab the girl in the neck like they had that last prisoner. They didn't have to, though, because she didn't struggle very long.

Kinseth thought something looked familiar about the woman. They tried very carefully to aim the telescope at her face and increased the power to zoom in on her features a bit.

It's the lady from before, Kenny said.

What lady? said Robby.

Don't be an idiot, Seth said. *You know what lady.*

I don't want it to be that lady. Robby pouted. *She was nice to us.*

Nobody wants *it to be that lady,* said Kenny, *but it's her anyway.*

The two men and the limp woman stood on the front porch and waited. They didn't stand there very long this time. Another man opened the door to the house after only a minute or two of waiting, and they all went inside. A few minutes later one of the men came back outside and drove away in the car. If this was like the times before, that man would come walking back on foot within the next fifteen minutes or so.

Kinseth felt a confusion of emotions, and it made them feel dizzy and a little nauseated. They put aside the telescope and went to lie in bed. Kinseth tried to remember the faces in the painting on their new book. But try as they might, they couldn't remember a face that matched the one of the nice lady. If the face didn't match, then why would she be a prisoner over there? Didn't they find matching faces of all the other prisoners?

Kinseth didn't like thinking about this and decided they needed to go to sleep and think about it tomorrow. Just as they were drifting off to sleep, Kinseth heard a voice whispering.

All unpretty things belong to Minos, the lord of the damned.

SATURDAY, OCTOBER 4, MORNING

The fax rolled in during the wee hours of Saturday morning. Detective Barnes had never been one to avoid work on weekends, and after the bomb scare last night and with Hummingbird's disappearance, he figured it was only appropriate to continue working today as well. After all, there was a madman out there killing people in this city. *In my city,* he said to himself.

T. W. Collins was asleep in the lobby of the police station, pledging to remain there until they could tell him where his sister was.

Seeing the hope in his eyes at Buck's approach, the detective shook his head. "No one reported seeing her during the evacuation yesterday. One cop even said he thought the bookstore was already closed, but he couldn't be sure. Maybe she left on her own? Got scared and went into hiding?"

"No," T.W. said. "She would have contacted me."

"Have you checked with Ready Robinson? Maybe he found out something, took her away to protect her."

Frustration seeped to the surface in T.W.'s voice. "Can't get in touch with him. Don't know why that guy has to live such an obscure life. It's a pain for anyone who needs to find him."

"I think he likes it that way."

"Or he's in the same trouble that Hummingbird is in, and you and I are just sitting here yammering instead of doing everything we can to find them."

"Relax, Counselor," Buck said. "Ready Robinson is due to call me at ten o'clock today. We'll know more in a few hours."

T.W. clenched his jaw. "Detective, I heard what happened to your friend, that other detective who works with you."

Barnes nodded.

"I don't want that to happen to my sister."

"We'll do everything we can to make sure that doesn't happen, Counselor." Buck finally glanced down at the fax that was waiting for him. "Mr. Collins," he said without taking his eyes off the paper, "you'll probably want to see this. Care to step into my office?"

— — —

Ready Robinson had to admit that sometimes the bureaucrats got it right.

During one of the periodic "budget crises" that politicians publicized during election years, some cost-cutting councilmen with a background in accounting and package delivery attacked the city's zoning and construction codes. They decided that from that point on, no homes within the same zip code could use the exact same house numbers, regardless of what street they were on. Some residents grumbled at first about having odd intervals of house numbers on their streets (say, for instance, a four-number interval between this house and that house but then a sixteen-digit jump between the second house and a third). And some grumbled that their house numbers were too long (say, five digits rather than only three). But the opposition was weak and shallow and quickly died out as more and more construction companies erected more and more houses on more and more streets under the revised numbering guidelines. And everyone was happier when postal and city service workers were able to do their work more accurately.

And today Ready Robinson was especially grateful for those bean-counting bureaucrats. Because Ready could look at a map of a four-square-mile area of the city located within its unique zip code, and with a few hours of mind-numbing work, he could isolate a single, distinct house within that zip code using only the house number as an indicator of where it was.

After leaving Jonathan Shelby's room yesterday, Ready had spent most of the evening poring over maps and digging up listings of the individual house numbers of all of the homes within the four square miles he'd previously marked out from the traffic videos that Galway had sent him. It had been tedious work, but in the end, late last night he had finally identified and confirmed that only one house in that entire area held the number 1669. It was in a little cul-de-sac that backed up to a greenbelt that ran through the southeastern part of the city.

Kirby Court.

Ready had never been there, and he had been tempted to go check out the place last night before finally deciding that he would have better success scouting the location during daylight hours. And before admitting that he was really very tired anyway.

He had finally allowed himself to drop off to sleep close to midnight and then had arisen as usual at 4:30 in the morning. He'd had a feeling of unexpected burden during his prayers this morning, but they had never resolved into a specific name or a specific course of action. He had waited beside his bed until around 8:30 A.M. before finally feeling a sense that it was time to get the day started. A quick breakfast of juice and toast, and he was out, heading over to 1669 Kirby Court. He had parked his car a half-mile away and walked toward the address on foot. He didn't want to take a chance that anyone at the house might recognize a car that had also been outside Hummingbird Collins's apartment in recent days.

It was unseasonably warm for an October morning, and Ready walked with his coat open, enjoying the sunshine that mixed with the cool morning air. He checked his watch and noted that he was scheduled to call Detective Barnes in about forty minutes. That should give him enough time to reconnoiter around the house on Kirby and get some hard information to use to obtain search and arrest warrants.

Ready rounded the corner and found himself staring into a typical American cul-de-sac. Well-kept houses, trimmed lawns, raked leaves, and even a few white picket fences. Basement windows. Some homes even had large wraparound porches. He could see swings, slides, an occasional trampoline or above-ground pool in some of the backyards.

One would never expect such a neighborhood to hide a mass murderer. But Ready had already learned the hard way—too many times—that looks could be deceiving.

They were eighteen, maybe twenty miles from North Downtown. Whoever had bombed the gallery and abducted Jonathan Shelby from near there had gone out of his way to target that location. He was a planner, this one, someone who approached his crimes with forethought. Ready grimaced; it was easier to trip up an opponent shooting from the hip than one who was anticipating and defending against your next move.

Ready watched the neighborhood for several minutes, but nothing changed within its confines. He was just about to circle around and see what he could find in the greenbelt behind the cul-de-sac when the door at 1629 Kirby Court opened, and a severely disfigured young man walked out.

Ready forced himself not to look away, though he was careful to remain mostly hidden by a row of bushes around the outer edges of the first house on the street. Ready wasn't sure what had caused the disfigurement, but he felt an unanticipated compassion for the young man.

The scarred one walked to a patio table and chairs set up on the wraparound porch. He was carrying a small box in one hand and a large book in the other. He set both down on the patio table, then opened the box and poured out the contents.

Ready checked his watch again. It was getting close to 10:00. But something about the young man made Ready terribly curious. Detective Barnes could wait for his phone call.

Ready Robinson took a deep breath, stepped out from behind the row of bushes, and walked toward the young man sitting on the porch at 1629 Kirby Court.

T.W. Collins waited impatiently at the front doors of the public library. Through the windows he could see the librarians moving around in a leisurely way, getting themselves organized before opening up to the public at 10:00 A.M. He wanted to pound on the glass, shout that he was in a desperate hurry, on police business, and that it was only five minutes before 10:00 anyway, and couldn't they simply open up a little early, just this once? But he decided that patience would win him more in this situation than impatience would, so he simply stood at the door and passed the time with the few other early birds who couldn't wait to get into the library on a Saturday morning.

He looked again at the copy of the fax Detective Barnes had given him an hour ago. It was from the Buonarroti Accademia of Fine Art in Rome.

Dear Detective Barnes,

This letter is in response to your recently faxed request and the sketch you sent with it.

To answer your question, yes, the person in the sketch does appear to have been one of our students some years ago. I have checked the school identification records, and the man in your sketch bears a strong resemblance to a Mr. Johann Smidt. I can only assume it is the same person.

Mr. Smidt graduated from our university almost thirteen years ago, earning the prestigious Michelangelus Certification as well as an award of merit for his final project. For that project, Mr. Smidt created a detailed reproduction of eight specific scenes from Michelangelo's famous painting the Last Judgment. As I recall, they were some of the finest works of art produced by students in our school, both before and since.

Regretfully, Mr. Smidt did not leave any contact information for himself when he left the Accademia, and so I am not able to offer you anything in that regard. The best I could discern from speaking to a few of his old professors was that Mr. Smidt had been planning to return to his hometown in the United States where he intended to join his father in the family business. I hope

that this information is helpful for you, Detective. If we
at the Buonarroti Accademia may be of further assistance
to you, please don't hesitate to let us know.
                    Sincerely,
                    Dean Agostino Magliano de' Marsi
                    Buonarroti Accademia of Fine Art

"We finally have a name to go with our face," Detective
Barnes had said, showing T.W. the fax. "And a few clues to the
personality of our madman."

"Johann Smidt. Not a very common name, is it?"

"No, and that's going to work in our favor."

"So what do we do now, Detective?"

Buck Barnes had given him a quizzical look. "*We*, Mr. Collins?"

T.W. knew where this was going. The negotiator in him had
come to the fore. "Listen, Detective." He had paused, then tried
a different approach. "Buck," he said, "I know you have a job to
do."

"Absolutely."

"And I appreciate that you have kept me in the loop on this."
A short nod.

"Buck, you and I both know that I'm not going to sit at home
twiddling my thumbs while I wait for you to tell me that my
sister has been rescued. Or worse."

"What are you asking for, Mr. Collins?"

"Look, it's Saturday. My guess is that most of the people you
would turn to for research help aren't even here today and that
they'll be hard to drag back to work on the weekend anyway."

Detective Barnes had sighed.

"I'm sitting in your office right now, ready to do just about
anything to help track down this killer before he has a chance to

harm my sister. I'm a professional at ferreting out and organizing information—it's a natural part of my job. I'm a native of Lehigh, West Virginia, born and raised here, so I know its unique history and out-of-the-way locations. And I'm offering my time to you free of charge. That's got to be a bargain for taxpayers, right?"

Detective Barnes had looked thoughtful for a moment, then said, "All right, Mr. Collins." A pause. "T.W."

He had stared a moment at the fax from Dean Magliano de' Marsi. "If we assume that the hometown referred to in this letter is our very own Lehigh, West Virginia," Detective Barnes had said, "then our first goal is to match this name, Johann Smidt, with a name in some kind of city record—an electric bill, a property tax statement, a library card, anything. If we can do that, then we can attach it to an address, a phone number, a work location, something that we can physically go to and investigate. The letter also mentions a father but doesn't name him. If we can find the father, we might also be able to find the son that way."

"Can you access city records for things like electric bills and such?"

"I can do that. It will take me a little time to get the proper authorizations and passwords into the proper databases, but even on a Saturday I should be able to get into searching mode within an hour or so."

"Okay. How about if I hit the library and start digging through the *Lehigh Chronicle* archives for any record of the name Smidt over the past fifty years?"

"That's a good place to start. And it keeps you safely out of sight for the time being."

T.W. had stood. "I'm on my way."

"T.W.," Detective Barnes had said, "promise me you won't go off half cocked into some impetuous rescue attempt or something stupid like that."

T.W. had hesitated.

"I'm willing to work with you, Counselor," Barnes had said. "But if I do that, then you have to be willing to work with me."

"Right," T.W. had said finally. "I understand. I'll call you as soon as I find out anything."

Barnes had nodded, satisfied. "I'm going to take you as a man of your word, T.W. And I'll call you as soon as I have any new information as well."

T.W. had shaken the detective's hand and headed out the door to the library complex.

Of course, that had been more than half an hour ago, and he was still waiting for the blasted library to open its doors. He resisted yet another urge to pound on the glass and then was pleasantly surprised to see a plump librarian with a smiling face walking over to unlock the front door.

———

Ready Robinson walked up the sidewalk toward the house at 1629 Kirby Court. If the young man noticed him, he didn't show it. Ready paused at the steps leading up to the porch, uncertain. It seemed a little presumptuous just to walk onto the young man's porch and start a conversation. But he was still not close enough to talk to the boy without shouting. Finally Ready made a decision, crossing into the brownish grass and walking alongside the porch until he was—albeit on the other side of the railing—only a few feet away from the young man.

He saw now that the young man was playing with a box of small, brightly colored plastic toys. They were action figures of cowboys, Indians, firefighters, soldiers, and the like. And the large book on the patio table, resting facedown, was some kind of art book, judging by the impressive painting that covered its back jacket. Ready was not high enough to make out a clear image of the painting, but it looked familiar, though he wasn't sure why. Maybe it was something he'd studied in seminary?

Ready also saw, close up, the damage on the face of the young man. Almost the whole left side of his face was ravaged. It looked as though someone had tried plastic surgery and it had helped a little but still left marks and discoloration where skin grafts lined the large red scar that traveled over one eye and down his left cheek. Ready also realized after a moment that the eyeball in the left socket was fake. From a distance this wasn't as obvious, but close up it gave the young man a startling look.

At first Ready had to admit he was repulsed by the boy's face. It was, well, harsh to look at. But again, as before, he quickly felt a new, almost supernatural compassion for the person who wore these damaged features.

He waited a moment and then another, but the young man said nothing. He didn't even acknowledge that Ready was there, standing in his front yard. Finally Ready spoke. "Hello," he said.

"We're not supposed to talk to strangers," the young man said matter-of-factly.

Ready hesitated. "That's a good rule," he said. "How about if I introduce myself so we're not strangers anymore?"

The boy said nothing.

"My name is Charles Robinson," he said. "But most people call me Ready."

The boy said nothing.

"May I ask what your name is?"

The young man looked up and gave Ready a serious look. There was something of confusion in his good eye for a moment, but in the end he still said nothing.

Ready realized he was getting nowhere. He glanced at the

patio table and saw again the box that held the plastic toys. Scrawled in marker across the top of the box he read "Kinseth's toys."

"Is your name Kinseth?"

The young man looked up again, then gave a short nod. "We're not supposed to talk to strangers," he said again. "Even strangers who know our name."

Ready was a little bit thrown off by the boy's use of plural pronouns. Was there something here he was missing?

"Right," Ready said. "I understand." He turned and faced the street, wondering what his next move should be. Out of habit, he stuffed his hands into his pockets and realized he'd left something in his right-hand pocket when he'd last worn these pants, the first night at the hospital with Jonathan and Aurora Shelby.

He turned back toward the young man, who was now studiously ignoring him. He took a moment to study the toys the boy was playing with and then made a decision. He pulled the item out of his back pocket and placed it on the railing of the porch.

The young man stopped ignoring him and reached out for the bent and dirtied plastic cowboy on the railing. He cocked his head and gave Ready a quizzical look.

"Are you a friend?" he asked.

"I like to think so," Ready responded.

"We gave this to a friend."

Lightning bolts went off in Ready's head. So this boy had actually seen Jonathan Shelby during the time he was kidnapped.

"He is a friend of mine."

"Is he the devil?"

Ready, again, was caught off guard. "No," he said. "He's not."

"Is he Minos?"

Ready shook his head. "No. His name is Jonathan. He's a good man. His wife's name is Aurora."

"If he's a good man, then why is he in hell?"

"I'm sorry, Kinseth," he said. "I don't know what you are talking about."

The young man picked up the art book off the patio table and shoved it forward. He put a thumb down on the bottom right-hand corner of the painting on the back cover of the book. It took Ready a moment to place the painting, but then he realized it was the *Last Judgment*, one of the last paintings by Michelangelo Buonarroti. He leaned in, trying to make out the image in the painting that the boy was pointing to.

"You can come up here," Kinseth said. "You can see it better up here."

Ready thanked him and quickly ascended the steps. He sat down at the table next to the young man. When he did, he realized that the boy wasn't simply playing with his plastic toys. He was arranging them, re-creating the *Last Judgment* out of cowboys and firefighters on the table.

Kinseth shoved the book toward Ready and placed a finger again on the bottom right corner of the painting. The image was small, but Ready had to agree that the figure that had been painted as Minos did resemble his friend Jonathan Shelby. And in the painting Minos was definitely on the shores of hell.

"That's not Jonathan," Ready said after a minute. "That's just someone who looks like my friend."

The young man nodded. "We didn't think so. All unpretty things belong to Minos. But the friend didn't look unpretty to us."

Lightning bolts again went off in Ready's head. *Did he just say "unpretty"?*

"He was a good singer. We liked hearing him sing."

Ready wanted to tread carefully now, but he had to know. "When did you hear him sing?"

"When he was a prisoner."

"Was he"—Ready hesitated—"was he your prisoner?"

The boy almost laughed. "No. He was their prisoner." He motioned toward the house across the cul-de-sac, toward 1669 Kirby Court.

There was a moment of silence between them.

"He was their prisoner?" Ready asked quietly.

"Uh-huh," Kinseth responded. "Like that nice lady is now."

— — —

Buck Barnes ran another search in the public records database, this time in the telephone logs. Again there was no entry associated with the name Johann Smidt.

"Looks like I'm going to have to do this the hard way," he muttered.

It had been relatively easy to gain access into the city property and utilities databases. A call here, which (since it was Saturday, of course) meant a referral there and another call, but soon enough he had tracked down the right Web portal address and matched it with the right security password. Suddenly he had the vast records of the city of Lehigh, West Virginia, at his fingertips. Well, at least the records of the city from the past twenty-one years.

For now, at least, twenty-one years should be enough time to cover what he needed. If Dean Magliano de' Marsi's information was correct, Johann Smidt likely returned to this happy little burg twelve or thirteen years ago. And if he owned property, used electricity, or even filed for a driver's license, Buck Barnes should have been able to find him.

It was after 10:30 A.M. before Detective Barnes realized

that his daily phone call from Ready Robinson hadn't come yet. That was a concern. But Ready Robinson was about as easy to track down as, well, Johann Smidt, so Detective Barnes decided to assume that Ready would take care of himself. And that the best way to use his time right now was to track down the Conklin bomber, not to spend it worrying about a former football player with hermetic tendencies and a secret priesthood.

Detective Barnes paged back on his computer until he had returned to the county assessor's database of property tax payments. This time, instead of searching for Johann Smidt, he simply typed in the name Smidt. Out of more than three hundred thousand people in Lehigh, there were only forty-four with that name in the property tax records. More than he'd expected but definitely better odds than one in three hundred thousand.

Next he applied a zip code to the search results. That narrowed it to eight potentials. *Now we're getting somewhere,* he thought.

Detective Barnes hit the print button in his computer and made notes to himself on a piece of scratch paper. He would have to get search warrants for all eight houses. And he would have to assume that whichever one of these was the hideout of Johann Smidt, it would be a dangerous place simply to walk in through the front door.

He mulled over his options. Should he try to hit all eight homes simultaneously in a big show of force and hope to catch Smidt unaware in one of them? Or should he target each house individually, quietly tackling them one by one until they found their suspect? Buck was trying to figure out a way to better his odds and narrow his choices when the phone on his desk rang.

"Barnes," he said into the receiver.

"Buck, it's T. W. Collins. I think I may have found something." He spoke in a hushed voice, obviously dodging the local librarian. "I started doing systematic searches through the public announcement sections of the newspapers archived in the library's databases."

"Funerals, weddings, anniversaries?" Barnes said. "That kind of thing?"

"Right," T.W. said. "I searched one year's worth of announcements at a time, checking any that had the name Smidt anywhere in them. I started with this year's archives and then went to last year's, the year before, and so on."

"Get to the point, Counselor."

"It's not a lot, but about thirty-three years ago there was a birth announcement in the paper. Herman and Martha Smidt proudly announced the birth of their firstborn son."

"Johann?"

"Yep. No middle name. Just Johann Smidt. What makes that even more compelling is that it's the only time—the *only* time— that the name Johann Smidt appears in our paper in the last thirty-three years. And believe me, there are more Smidts in this city than I would have ever expected, and they all seem to have lots of kids."

"Excellent. Very helpful. Herman and Martha Smidt. That's something we can work with."

"One more thing, Buck. About five years after the birth announcement, there's an obituary for one Martha Smidt. Doesn't say much, not even how she died. Just says she passed away and was survived by her husband and son. No names on the husband or son, but my guess is that they are Herman and Johann, and by that time the father was already trying to cover his tracks in the public records."

"Hold on a second, T.W.," Detective Barnes said. "I want to check something."

He pulled up the printout of the eight Smidt houses he had targeted. "We got him, Counselor," he said after a moment. "Or at least we're getting close to him."

"What do you mean?"

"I've got a list of eight property tax records in my hand," he said. "All the properties are owned by someone named Smidt, and all are within the zip code we have targeted as the location of the Conklin bomber."

"And?"

"One of them was purchased a little more than twelve years ago, about the same time the whole neighborhood was being built by the contractor. No mortgage lien holder listed; apparently it was paid in full with cash up front. And the property taxes have always been paid to the penny, and on time, year in and year out. The owner listed on the tax file is one Herman A. Smidt."

"You think that's it then? You think that's the place where Johann Smidt is hiding out? At dear old Dad's house?"

"I think it might be. And if it's not, maybe Daddy can at least give us a clue to where his son really is."

"You're a miracle worker, Buck."

"It's all about teamwork, Counselor."

"Okay, give me the address. I'll meet you there right away."

"Now, wait a minute, T.W. Remember your promise."

"Buck, we know where it is. Let's go check it out."

"Half cocked is not the way we'll go," Barnes said. "Give me forty-five minutes to get us the right warrants and to assemble a SWAT team. We'll hit this place in the next hour or so, and when we do, we won't let anybody slip away. Understand?"

T.W. let out a soft sigh. "I understand, Buck. I guess there's a reason you're a police officer and I'm just a sports lawyer."

"You did good, T.W. Finding that father's name. That was

good police work. Now we need to be patient so we don't waste it."

"Right. What would you like me to do next?"

"Meet me back here at the station. If you're a good boy," he said with a smile in his voice, "maybe I'll let you ride along when we go to the bad guy's house."

"I'll see you shortly."

Buck immediately dialed another number. "Judge Santos?" he said when the line picked up. "I need you to authorize a couple of very important warrants."

ELEVEN

In the end it was Michelangelo's own student who betrayed him. Daniele da Volterra had studied under the master for years. One might have even called him a friend of Michelangelo. Until, of course, he betrayed the great artist.

Pope Paul IV took offense at the nudity in the *Last Judgment* and commanded Michelangelo to change it. The artist, of course, refused. So the pope went to a weaker man. Daniele da Volterra did not refuse, accepting a profitable commission to paint draperies around the exposed genitalia of the most prominent nudes. For mere money the student was willing to commit an unpretty forgery on his master's work of genius.

That's why, my dear Ms. Collins, my father worked so hard to make sure that money would never need to be a temptation for one such as me. And having access to a fortune, I must admit, has certainly been a convenient circumstance. That way I can, like Michelangelo Buonarroti, concentrate solely on my work in the world.

EXCERPT FROM THE MICHELANGELUS RECORDINGS,
TAPE 4,
TRANSCRIBED BY H. J. COLLINS

— — —

SATURDAY, OCTOBER 4, EARLY AFTERNOON

When Hummingbird Collins opened her eyes, she felt an immediate cramp in her neck. Her head, she realized, had been hanging loosely on her shoulder while she slept, leaving her muscles stiff and aching. The cobwebs cleared from her mind as she realized that she was securely chained to a large metal chair.

She swallowed back the cry in her throat and tried to make sense out of her current situation. She was in a darkened room. But it wasn't pitch black. The walls and floor of the room were bare. No, wait. In the middle of each wall, near the top, there were dark, boxlike things bolted in. Security cameras maybe? She was handcuffed, hands and feet, to the chair.

And someone was watching her from the shadows.

"I see you," she said, trying to take the tremble out of her voice.

"I knew you had good eyes, Ms. Collins."

Hummingbird felt a chill run through her. It was the same voice she'd heard on the microcassettes that had been taped to her door.

"Brace yourself," the voice said.

Hummingbird tensed and caught her breath. Was he going to torture her now? The figure unfurled from the spot where it had been leaning against the wall, reached over, and flicked the light switch. The brightness temporarily disoriented Hummingbird, but after a moment her eyes adjusted.

"What do you want with me?"

The man looked bemused. "You are not the first person to ask me that question," he said with a friendly air. "To be honest, I'm not sure myself."

"Where am I?"

"In my studio. This is where I create my greatest works of art."

Hummingbird surveyed the room again. She was right about the boxlike things. They were cameras bolted into the walls. But other than the cameras, the room was bare, with concrete floors and walls. Hummingbird didn't see how this could be an artist's studio. "You drugged me. And my coworker. Why?"

The man shrugged. "We needed to get your coworker out of the way, and killing her seemed a waste. You we needed to make cooperative."

"So what do you want with me?"

"I told you, Ms. Collins, I'm not sure. Usually I only bring models back to my studio, and while you are certainly not unattractive, I can't use you for my current project. Perhaps you are simply an indulgence. Everyone needs an indulgence from time to time, right, Ms. Collins?"

Hummingbird felt her spine shiver at being called a madman's indulgence. Visions of what his indulgences might require made her feel temporary terror. Then she heard a voice in her mind.

It's okay to be afraid, honey. T.W.'s voice rumbled comfortingly between her ears. *Just don't let being afraid be the thing that stops you from being brave.*

Hummingbird steeled herself and sat up straight in the chair. "Let me out of here," she demanded firmly. "I want to go home."

The man looked bemused again. "Surely you know that you can't go home, Ms. Collins." He studied her for a long moment. "No screaming? At every turn you continue to impress me."

Hummingbird felt her desperation rising. "Who are you?" she said finally.

"Around here," he said, "names are unimportant. I call you by your surname out of respect for you. But as we get to know each other I think you'll find that names will be unnecessary. Maybe, if you become enlightened, you will adopt a different sort of title entirely."

Hummingbird said nothing, and the man responded in kind. Then Hummingbird thought of Jonathan Shelby and realized, gratefully, that unlike Shelby, she was still clothed. Did that mean she might be spared the treatment he had received?

"You are an artist too. I saw your sketches, that day in the store."

Hummingbird nodded tightly, unsure where this conversation was going.

"I would like you to see my current project sometime," he said, almost as if they were just meeting at a dinner party. "But it is not yet time."

"You must let me go," Hummingbird pleaded. "You must. I didn't talk to the police. I didn't. Why would you take me now? I did what you asked me to do."

The man walked over to Hummingbird and knelt before her, patting her hand comfortingly. "I know you didn't talk to the police," he said. "Not even to that nasty detective who kept bad-gering you. We monitored your calls and contacts. You've been a very good girl."

"Then why not let me go?"

"Because, obviously," the man said, "now you are a bigger threat than ever to us. And . . . you intrigue me. I see potential in you."

"But . . . but I trusted you. What you said."

He laughed, but not unkindly. "Ms. Collins, even I wouldn't trust a killer."

Hummingbird felt hope draining from her spirit. She closed her eyes and began reciting to herself. *The Lord is my shepherd, I shall not want . . .*

"You don't have to see such darkness from me, Ms. Collins. There is a choice ahead for you." He rose and looked down at her. "I enjoyed our walk the other day, Ms. Collins. I couldn't help but feel that you enjoyed it too."

Yea though I walk through the valley of the shadow of death, I will fear no evil . . .

"In fact, I told my father about it."

For you are with me . . .

"This does not have to end in death. I can show you life like you've never known before. A future . . . only an artist could truly appreciate. I'd like for you to meet my father, Ms. Collins. Would you like to meet him right now?"

— — —

Number 61 paced nervously in the kitchen of the house at 1669 Kirby Court. Her bag was stuffed and waiting on a chair. She knew that 44 and 48 were downstairs—backup in case the boss needed them. But she wasn't sure where to find Number 39, and that worried her. If he were still in the tech/observation room, he might not be able to leave until after 26 was finished with his new toy in the studio, and that might be too late.

She sighed with relief when she saw 39 appear in the doorway of the kitchen.

"How are . . . things?" she asked tentatively.

"Going according to plan," he said with apparent calm. He produced a small computer component that 61 recognized as an external hard drive. "Everything important is in here," he said quietly. "If anyone were to search the hard drives on the computers downstairs, they'd find a few half-edited, pirated movies from the Orient, a raft of downloaded music charged to nonexistent accounts and customers, and every variation of FreeCell available on the Internet."

"Nothing else?"

"Nope. I've been covering my tracks for twelve years, just in case this kind of thing was necessary. Always pays off in the end. They'll never be able to trace anything on those computers, because there's nothing for them to trace on those computers. It's all in here." He pointed to the external hard drive. "And in here." He pointed to his own head.

She nodded and picked up her bag. "How did you get past the two goons?"

He gave her a puzzled look. "I'm their superior officer," he said with a shrug. "I just told them to move out of the way."

"Right. Of course." She paused. "We, the Movement, do not need them?"

"They've been corrupted by Twenty-six. It is best to leave them behind. They can serve as sacrificial lambs to the authorities," he said, little concern in his voice. "If they maintain silence, we shall reclaim them in time."

"And if they don't?"

"You know the answer to that as well as I. Did you get the supplies you needed?"

"Yes. I left everything else. The drugs and the C-4 are common knowledge already, and replaceable, so I left them. Everything else is in this bag." She gestured toward the small duffel bag in the chair.

"And the cocktail?"

She reached inside the bag and pulled out a full syringe with a covered needle on the end. "It's all in here."

"Is it enough this time?"

She allowed herself a wry grin. "You want to test it?"

He returned her grin. "No. I've seen what that combination can do."

She pushed the syringe back into her backpack.

"So there's only one thing left."

She shook her head. "Already done. I took care of it earlier this morning." Her grin became fierce. "And believe me, it was a pleasure."

He nodded his approval. "Very good," he said. "Then it's time to hurry up and wait."

Number 61 felt butterflies in her stomach. Was she nervous or excited, she wondered. She thought about it for a moment, then made a decision.

Excited. Definitely excited.

━ ━ ━

Kinseth were finally starting to feel as though they could trust Mr. Ready Robinson. They had been talking for almost two hours now. Mr. Ready had been very interested to know more about that nice lady who was a prisoner at the house across the cul-de-sac, but Kinseth were already worried that they might have said too much, so no matter what questions Mr. Ready asked about the prisoner, Kinseth refused to respond. Once, when Mr. Ready seemed about to raise his voice, Kinseth simply closed their eyes and started humming. Mr. Ready seemed to understand, finally, that Kinseth weren't going to say any more about the nice lady.

Kinseth's visitor had started to leave, and they were going to let him, but then Mr. Ready turned back and sat down again. They had talked a lot after that, about the pictures in Kinseth's book, about toys, about Elaina, about a lot of things.

"How old are you, Kinseth?" Mr. Ready had asked.

Kinseth had shrugged. It had been a long time since they had thought about that.

After a while, they had stopped talking, but Kinseth were comfortable with that. Mr. Ready seemed comfortable with it too. Then Mr. Ready had said, "May I?" and pointed to the box of toys. Kinseth had nodded, and so they'd arranged the toys on the patio table. Mr. Ready had picked up fairly quickly that they were trying to copy the painting onto the table, using only the plastic toys. It made for some interesting clumps of cowboys and such, but it didn't have to be perfect.

Kinseth felt their belly starting to grumble when Mr. Ready finally leaned back in his chair and stopped working. Kinseth leaned back as well and looked at the man. His face was calm, staring at Kinseth with both patience and compassion. They decided to try an experiment. They looked at Mr. Ready and then quickly flashed a smile. Mr. Ready looked a little confused but didn't respond. Had he known it was a smile? Or did he only see the grimace that so many other people saw when Kinseth smiled?

They decided to try again, holding the smile a little longer this time. There was a beat in the silence, and then Mr. Ready's face relaxed into a smile as well. A warm, comfortable smile that seemed as if it was used to coming out.

Kinseth let their own smile linger a minute longer, then pointed to the cowboys and said, "Do you want to do more?"

"No, thank you," Mr. Ready said.

"We like this picture." They pointed back to the book.

"Me too."

"But it scares us a little."

"Me too."

"We like him best." They pointed to the figure of Christ in the upper quadrants of the painting. "He seems most real."

Mr. Ready nodded thoughtfully. "He is."

"We think we belong with him."

"You do."

"But unpretty things belong to Minos. To the devil."

Mr. Ready cocked his head in uncertainty.

"Are we unpretty, Mr. Ready?"

It seemed at first that Mr. Ready was going to say no, that he was going to say a lot of things. But finally he just pointed to the figure of Christ on the back of the book.

"Why don't you ask him?" he said.

Kinseth thought about that for a minute. "Is she unpretty?" they asked finally.

"Who?"

"That nice lady from the bookstore. The one who gave us this book."

Mr. Ready looked worried. "No. She's not."

"What's her name?"

"Hummingbird. Hummingbird Collins."

"Is she a friend?"

"Yes."

"She doesn't look like anyone in the picture."

"Why is that important, Kinseth?"

They shrugged. "Because they always look like somebody in the picture. That's why he takes them. So he can put them on the wall."

Mr. Ready seemed to be fighting confusion.

"Have you seen this painting before?" Kinseth asked.

Mr. Ready shook his head. "Not in person, no. But I hope to visit it someday, if I ever get to Rome."

"Do you want to see it?"

"You mean the real painting, on the altar wall of the chapel?"

Kinseth nodded.

"How?"

"We can show it to you," they said. "We left a stick in the door last time we were there."

"Where?"

Kinseth gestured toward the greenbelt. "It's over there. In the old, empty church. Want to see it?"

Mr. Ready looked surprised. He stood up, then sat back down. "Yes, Kinseth. If you want to show it to me. I would love to see it. And we need to talk about the lady, Hummingbird. Is she in the church too?"

"Help us put our toys away first," they said. "We will show you then."

— — —

Buck welcomed the brief moment of rest. For the time being, the phone was silent, the computer hummed contentedly on the desk, and T. W. Collins sat absorbed in his own thoughts across the room. Barnes slid back in his chair and let out a deep breath.

"Everything is set in motion," he said. "They are calling in the SWAT team, and once they're ready, we'll take a few officers of our own and head out."

T.W. nodded his approval, anxious to get moving but showing remarkable restraint, considering the circumstances. Buck almost hated what he had to say next.

"I've thought more about it, and I want you to stay here when we make the raid."

T.W.'s gaze grew steely.

"It's for your own protection. You're a civilian and a liability. And it's unorthodox for you to be present when we drop in on Johann Smidt."

"You can't keep me away, Buck. Short of arresting me, that is. It's not as if you're going to be able to hide a convoy of police vehicles. If you don't take me, I'll go on my own."

Buck weighed the options. He could arrest him. That would

keep T.W. safe and out of the way, but it would also undermine the growing trust the two had worked together to build this day. And knowing that the guy in front of him was a lawyer, it would also likely result in a lawsuit.

But taking him would be a risk, one that he doubted Captain Philips would approve. Of course, what the Cap didn't know wouldn't hurt him.

"One condition."

"I'm listening."

"You promise to stay in my car, parked a safe distance from the scene, for the whole time. Until we get your sister safely out of that house. No matter what."

"I can live with that. Though I reserve the right to bail if the threat extends and I feel my life is endangered in the car."

"Always the negotiator, aren't we, Counselor?"

"You started this." T.W. paused. "So am I in or what?"

"You're in. Just remember, you stay in my car."

T.W. nodded and looked away. Buck felt the smile on his face even after it was gone. This was shaping up to be a good day after all.

— — —

Hummingbird Collins didn't respond. She didn't know how to respond. What do you say when an insane mass murderer asks if you want to meet his daddy? Fortunately the man wasn't really expecting an answer. He appeared to be used to having people do whatever he said, and Hummingbird was no exception.

"He's looking forward to meeting you," he said. "I told him all about you."

Hummingbird watched in disbelief as the man removed a set of keys, unlocked the handcuffs on her hands, then knelt down to unlock the ones on her feet. She waited, heart beating wildly, as he worked the lock on the second foot. She could feel adrenaline rushing into her bloodstream.

It was now or never, she decided.

As soon as the lock came off the second foot, Hummingbird lifted her knee hard, catching the madman square in the chin. He rocked backward. She sprang out of the chair and raced to the door of the studio, turned the knob, wondering if it would be locked, if her captor was right behind her, ready to grab her arm. It was open! Natural light drew her forward, and she pushed off the ball of her foot, hearing the man behind her, perilously close.

She didn't get far. Hummingbird ran directly into a very large man. Two very large men, to be exact. They barely budged when she crashed into them, almost as if they had been expecting her and were prepared to stop her. One of them shoved hard with his shoulder, knocking Hummingbird, breathless, into the wall. The other clamped steely fingers around her neck, raising her until she stood on tiptoes simply to breathe.

A second later the man released his grip, and Hummingbird leaned down, gasping for breath. But she had no reprieve. Another grabbed a handful of her hair and yanked her backward into the studio room. It was the madman, dragging her back to the chair. In a flash one hand was cuffed again, then the second. She tried to kick at the man, but a swift backhand across her cheekbone stilled her struggle with pain that felt like a miniature explosion underneath her left eye socket. She gasped for breath and felt hot tears streaming down her face.

"Let me go!" she screamed. "You have to let me go!"

"Ah, the screams at last. You disappoint me, Ms. Collins." Another blow, this time on her right cheekbone, made her bite her tongue, both literally and figuratively.

In the gasping silence that followed, she heard the man speak again, deadly calm returned to his tone. "You can't go yet. You still haven't met my father."

He turned to the two men who now filled the doorway. "I can handle it from here," he said. They nodded and stepped away from the opening. "Wait," the man called. "Tell Sixty-one to bring me a sedative."

One of the men shuffled uncomfortably back into the doorway. "Number Sixty-one isn't in the house at present, sir."

The madman looked surprised and angry. "Well, where is she?"

The large man in the doorway kept his gaze focused toward the floor. "We're not sure, sir. She didn't tell us she was leaving. Perhaps she's getting more supplies for Number Three?"

The madman nodded slowly, accepting the explanation. Then he spoke to the room in general. "Thirty-nine," he said, "where is Number Sixty-one?" It took a moment for Hummingbird to realize he was speaking toward one of the surveillance cameras on the wall. There was no answer. The madman did not look happy. He turned to the large man in the doorway. "Forty-four?" he said.

The large man also looked surprised. "I'm not sure, sir. He was here not long ago. Maybe he's in the barracks? Or maybe he took Sixty-one on a special errand?"

The madman's face flushed red, then seemed to calm itself. "You two," he said to the doorway, "get upstairs and find them." He turned toward Hummingbird and gave her a grim look. "I'll make sure that Ms. Collins is more compliant from now on." He held out a hand toward the doorway. One of the large men took one step into the room and passed something unseen from his pocket to the madman's hand. Then he was gone.

The man turned to Hummingbird. "I admire your spirit," he

said to her calmly. "But unfortunately I can't have you acting up in my father's presence."

He walked to Hummingbird's right side and, with a quick snapping movement, cracked his fist across her wrist and bent the fingers of her hand painfully down over the edge of the chair's armrest. Hummingbird was paralyzed with fear and pain. Her eyes grew wide as she watched, almost in slow motion, as the man revealed a switchblade in his other hand. With surgical precision and speed, he unleashed the blade and jabbed it directly into the center of Hummingbird's palm until the tip of the knife actually tapped against the hard metal surface below her hand. Hot agony traveled up her arm and into her brain. The pain was so unexpected and so intense that Hummingbird forgot to breathe, forgot to scream, forgot to do anything but sit trembling in the chair.

Just as quickly as the man had inserted the knife, he pulled it out of the wound, letting it drip blood momentarily into her palm and onto her arm. Hummingbird reflexively closed her fist and felt the moistness greasing her palm with red, stinging ooze.

The man stepped away and pulled a cloth from a pocket. Hummingbird was writhing now, wild with pain. He wiped the blade on the cloth and casually addressed his captive.

"You are an artist, I know," he said calmly. "So I was careful to wound in a place that would heal without damaging nerve endings in your fingers. It would be a shame to have to end your artistic career in case you embrace enlightenment."

Inexplicably Hummingbird felt herself begin to hiccup.

"I trust I've made my point, Ms. Collins?"

She nodded, head bobbing almost uncontrollably as she tried to suppress the pain that flooded her mind.

"Good," he said. "Then we'd better do something about that mess."

He stepped close again and took hold of Hummingbird's fingers. She dared not resist. He placed her hand flat on the arm of the chair and folded the cloth over the wound. He lifted her hand and folded the rest of the cloth over the back of her hand where the knife had poked through. Once he was satisfied that he'd covered both sides, he tied the ends and squeezed Hummingbird's palm. She let out a short cry and then choked it back. She could see that even though he was hurting her, applying pressure to the wound was the appropriate way to stop the bleeding. After a minute or two he released her hand.

"Ms. Collins," he said, "I am tempted to unhook your left hand so that you can use it to continue applying pressure on this wound." He gave her what could only be described as a flirtatious smile. "But I'm not sure I can trust you."

Hummingbird said nothing. She didn't know what to say.

"Can I trust you, Ms. Collins?"

She nodded her head slowly, and the madman unlocked the handcuff on her left hand. She immediately grabbed her right palm and pressed, gritting her teeth through the pain.

"You're going to kill me, aren't you?"

"Honestly, Ms. Collins, I haven't decided yet. There is a lot that remains to be seen."

Cold reason now flooded through Hummingbird. So that was it. She'd made her escape attempt. She'd failed. She'd been punished for it. And sooner or later, no matter what she tried, she was going to do something that was going to be catalyst enough for this madman to take her life. Knowing that there was no hope actually gave Hummingbird a new sense of calm.

I'm ready to die, she thought. *But I won't go alone.*

The madman seemed unconcerned with time or even with conversation. "I do so love the music," he said under his breath. Hummingbird had no idea what he was talking about, as there was complete silence in the house around them. After a while she realized that he was listening to something she couldn't hear. And that he was waiting.

She felt the blood in her right hand stiffening, beginning to clot. She released the hand from her left and gripped the cloth. It was damp and wet but appeared to be doing its job to staunch the flow of blood. Finally she spoke.

"Okay," she said. "I'm ready to meet your father."

TWELVE

One aspect of the *Last Judgment* troubles me, however. Sitting at Christ's feet, on his left side, is the representation of Saint Bartholomew. This Christian martyr was actually flayed alive with knives until he was dead, dead, dead. Michelangelo has painted him with an upward gaze toward the judging Messiah, and in his hands Bartholomew holds two things. His right hand proffers a knife that was ostensibly used to kill him. His left hand holds the sagging, macabre, full outer skin of the martyred saint, complete with fingers, toes, hair, and face.

Of course, I am undisturbed by the presence of the macabre. This is a normal part of art. What I find unexpected is the face that is painted on the drooping skin of the martyr.

You see, it is Michelangelo's.

A distorted self-portrait of sorts that the artist included in his masterpiece. I have been unable to discern exactly why the great Buonarroti would have painted himself in this degrading position. In my line of work that unusual choice by the Master could have difficult implications.

EXCERPT FROM THE MICHELANGELUS RECORDINGS,
TAPE 4,
TRANSCRIBED BY H. J. COLLINS

— — —

SATURDAY, OCTOBER 4, AFTERNOON

Ready Robinson followed the young man through the maze of pathways and across the greenbelt behind the cul-de-sac at Kirby Court. It wasn't long until he saw the church that Kinseth was talking about, a small Baptist church that looked as if it had been empty for several years.

They walked to the front door of the building, and Ready saw Kinseth almost clap with glee when he discovered his precious stick still held open the door to the church.

"In here," the young man said, motioning for Ready to follow him. "There's no electricity, but light still comes in through windows."

Ready said nothing and followed the young man through the door. It was bothering him that Kinseth knew something about Hummingbird, about her captivity, and that he couldn't bring the information out of the boy. Kinseth obviously had found a way into and out of that house at 1669 Kirby Court, and Ready wanted to know what it was. But everything within him told him that patience was the key, that waiting on this boy was key.

Waiting was sometimes the most proactive thing a person could do. So he would wait, he would continue to earn the young man's confidence, and when the time was right, the needed information about Hummingbird would come. He felt a gentle assurance about it, a peace that could only come from God. So he followed Kinseth.

The young man led him into the sanctuary and then stopped at the back pew, motioning ahead toward the altar.

Ready was awestruck.

There, filling the entire wall from floor to ceiling, was Michelangelo's *Last Judgment*, the picture he had just studied in Kinseth's book. There were gaps here and there, and even a few figures that had been given bodies but no faces. But there was no mistaking the fact that nearly all of the intricate, artistic masterpiece had been painstakingly re-created on the wall of this hidden little church.

Ready stepped slowly down the center aisle and toward the altar. "Who did this, Kinseth?" he asked quietly. "Who painted this?"

"The bad man."

Ready stopped and turned back to face his companion. "Who?"

"The bad man. The one who hurts people."

"What's his name?"

Kinseth shrugged.

Ready continued walking toward the altar wall. Kinseth fell into step behind him. Up close the artwork was even more impressive, with tiniest details imprinted into every image on the wall. Ready recognized his friend Jonathan Shelby in the figure of Minos painted in the bottom right-hand corner. He studied it for several minutes, fascinated. The artist had painted with such realism that Ready could even make out the individual hairs that spiked out of Jonathan's goat-eared head.

"Why?" Ready asked. "Why does he do this?"

Kinseth shrugged again. "He's sick," the boy said. "Sometimes he hurts himself while he's painting."

Ready faced his new friend again. "You've seen him working on this?"

Kinseth nodded.

"Has he ever seen you?"

Kinseth shook his head.

"How long has he been doing this?"

Kinseth shrugged. "We don't know," he said.

Ready turned back to the painting. One could spend days

studying the intricacies of the artwork here. But Ready didn't have days. He had no time at all, really. He prayed for help in knowing what to do.

After a moment he focused on one particular figure in the composition. It appeared to be a man with short brown hair, a look of horror on his face. One hand covered his left eye, and his right arm was wrapped in self-embrace around his torso. He was nude, although the genitalia were indistinct, suggesting that perhaps this form could be seen as either man or woman. A demon wrapped around the legs, obviously dragging the soul down to its damnation. A second serpentlike demon peered from behind, sinking its venomous teeth deeply into the figure's left thigh.

Ready stared at the mesmerizing figure, and a slow dawning of realization gripped his consciousness. The figure may have been a man or a woman, but regardless of the gender, the face was Corona Sanchez, the schoolteacher who'd been kidnapped and killed a few years before. Ready stared into the horror painted on Corona's face and knew it was real. The woman had suffered unimaginably, and the monster of 1669 Kirby Court had captured her suffering just so he could include it in the lines and colors of this hidden painting. That same monster now had Hummingbird.

Ready turned away from the masterpiece. If he continued looking at it, he knew, he'd begin to recognize the faces of other people whose disappearances had been in the news. Men. Women. Even children. Bile rose in his throat.

He turned toward Kinseth and found the boy standing near him. Ready said nothing but sent him a beseeching look.

The boy stared at him, understanding. "She's not in the painting," Kinseth said with a strained hopefulness in his voice. "That nice lady? She's not in the painting."

"He's going to hurt her anyway, Kinseth. Maybe he already has."

The young man's lip trembled. "She was nice to us."

"She's a special person, Kinseth."

"A friend?"

"A friend."

It seemed as if there was an argument taking place inside the boy's head. Ready could only stand helplessly by, waiting. Finally the young man spoke.

"We know a way into the house."

Ready nodded.

"But sometimes they're watching. When they're watching we have to be very secret."

Ready nodded again.

"The people in there are not nice. They are"—he paused—"they are *unpretty.*"

Ready waited.

"We can take you into the house," Kinseth said softly. "If you want to go. We can take you to the nice lady."

"Yes, Kinseth," Ready said just as softly. "I definitely want to go."

— — —

Detective Barnes pulled into a tidy suburban development and after a couple of turns pulled to a stop behind a SWAT truck. "The SWAT team is almost into position," he said over his shoulder to T.W. "They're sealing off any potential escape routes from the house—without being seen. And they'll need to set up for a fast, forced entry into the house in case it appears the hostage's life is in danger."

"Hostage. Is that what we're calling my sister now?"

Detective Barnes tipped his head in deference. "In case Hummingbird appears to be in immediate danger." He paused. "After SWAT gives us their all clear, we send in the fire engine."

"What? We don't have time! We have to get to Hummingbird now!"

"Look, T.W., I know that Hummingbird is your number one concern, but this house we're raiding sits nestled in a nice little suburban neighborhood, in a block full of ordinary houses, filled with families and kids living their normal lives. Think of the Conklin gallery. Each person in each of the houses on that block is somebody's son or daughter, somebody's brother or sister, somebody's mama or daddy. You understand."

T.W. felt immediately chagrined. Of course. They were dealing with killers here, murderers who had hidden themselves for years right next door to dozens of innocent people. But how was the fire department supposed to protect them?

"You've seen Smidt's calling card, right in your office. If something like that C-4 goes off in that little cul-de-sac, there's no telling what kind of damage it could do. So we've got to get those nice, ordinary neighbors out of harm's way before we attempt to storm the castle, so to speak."

"I understand. But why the firetruck?"

"Watch and see." Right then the massive engine, lights flashing, passed them and rolled into the cul-de-sac, then parked haphazardly.

"Ahh, nice," T.W. said, leaning forward. The engine conveniently blocked any exit from the cul-de-sac. "Easier to catch a crook on foot than in a car."

"Exactly." He paused a moment, watching. "There. You see? Our virtuous firefighters have taken out several complicated-looking instruments and are waving them around in the air with concerned looks on their faces. Looks to me like we have some sort of gas leak in the area. Does it look that way to you?"

T.W. grinned at his sarcasm and watched as the firefighters split up and started knocking on doors of the houses in the cul-de-sac, temporarily evacuating the entire block. "You'll get them all to safety before you move in on Smidt."

"That's the plan."

"What if somebody comes out of the house at the sixteen sixty-nine address? Won't that mess up the plan?"

Detective Barnes shook his head. "Not at all," he said. "In fact, if that happens we've kind of hit the jackpot, haven't we? We infiltrate the house through the front door our first suspect has kindly left wide open. Then we go into stealth mode, securing the house room by room until everyone is taken down."

"And if they don't come out?

"Then we decide whether we want to try to contact the occupants of the house to see if we can talk them out and avoid incident. Or if we want to tear-gas the place and go charging in full throttle."

"All right. I understand the plan. I'm ready."

"One more thing. You stay in the car the whole time. Remember your promise."

"I understand."

"You should be able at least to see what's going on from where I park and to listen to the activity on the radio. I'll even be with you until it's time to enter the house. But unless your life is somehow unexpectedly in danger, you stay put. Got it?"

"Got it, Buck. I promise."

"Okay then," Detective Barnes said as he turned the key to start up the Malibu to pull a little closer. "Let's go catch us a madman."

- - -

Hummingbird Collins said nothing as the madman carefully loosed her from the restraints. He stepped back and gave her an appraising look.

"I think Dad's going to like you," he said approvingly.

She waited for his permission, then stood. He crossed behind her and took her right hand, seemingly unaware of the fresh throbbing he caused by gripping the wound. She thought at first he was going to make her walk out holding his hand like a little girlfriend in some happy couple, but he quickly disabused her of that notion by twisting her arm into a submission pose behind her back. Then he shoved, indicating that she should walk forward. He pressed his thumb into her wrist and pulled upward just enough to let Hummingbird know he could easily dislocate her shoulder, could possibly break her arm, if she tried to run away. With his fingers he applied pressure on her wound.

"I thought you trusted me now," she said, panting against the pain. "Is this really necessary?"

"Some things don't have to be necessary," he said casually. Was he humming?

She stole a glimpse at her captor's face. He seemed completely calm, enraptured almost. His pupils were normal, but his eyes flitted about, as if they were following some captivating story being played out in the room—a story that only he could see.

Hummingbird let him lead her out through the door of the "studio" and into a short basement hallway. She saw three other doors and a set of stairs leading up to the main level. The madman pushed her toward the stairs, and a flicker of hope lit inside her. At least she knew there'd be an exit on the main floor. The flicker died, though, when the madman stopped in front of the door closest to the stairs.

"Knock first," he said. "It's impolite to go in unannounced."

Hummingbird raised her free arm warily and tapped twice on the door.

No one responded.

"Here's hoping he's in a good mood," the man said, as if they had just been invited in. He was positively giddy, it seemed. He produced a key with his right hand and unlocked the door.

They pushed their way inside, and Hummingbird was surprised to find a complete hospital room set up in there. Equipment beeped and hummed, sterile fluorescent lights glowed, and a man lay unmoving on what looked like a top-of-the-line medical bed.

She felt relief when the madman finally released her arm, until she turned to face him and saw that he was closing, and locking, the door to the room. The lock, she saw, wasn't simply a push button or latch but actually a key-entry-only doorknob, and the madman was now tucking the key comfortably into his pants pocket.

"Now, Ms. Collins," the madman said formally, "I'm pleased to introduce you to my father."

Hummingbird took her first good look at the older man in the hospital bed and suppressed a gasp. His skin was deathly pale. He was connected to various medical devices that snaked from his body like worms and caterpillars. An IV bag, partially filled and draining fluid into a vein, hung by his head. A catheter bag hung by the side of the bed. A heart monitor, a brain monitor, and another monitor that Hummingbird didn't recognize were also attached to the man. A mechanical ventilator hissed and sighed through a tube that inserted itself into a tracheal opening on the man's neck, causing his chest to rise and fall slightly with each new gust of oxygen. The man's eyes were open but blank, staring at the ceiling above.

"She's just a little nervous," the madman said to the unmoving form in the bed. "She's not always this quiet." He turned to her. "Tell him a little about yourself, Ms. Collins." He leaned close to her ear and whispered, "Tell him about your work as an artist. He's very interested in that kind of thing, and it'll make a good first impression."

The madman took a step back, an intoxicating smile on his face. He was proud, she decided. Proud to show her off to his father and proud for her to meet his father. She felt mounting pressure to say something, but her mind was still processing the absurdity of the situation; her mouth remained closed.

Is he serious?

The madman frowned now. "Tell him about yourself, Ms. Collins. It's rude not to speak to a person after you've just been introduced."

Her eyes wandered from the madman to the bed-ridden one and back again. How should she respond to this insane demand? At last she could keep her thoughts no longer to herself.

"This man is dead," she said dully.

Hummingbird was unprepared for the thundering backhand that dropped her to the floor.

— — —

Ready Robinson followed the young man past the dilapidated altar to a door on the west end of the altar area. Kinseth seemed to know this place well; he walked with a confidence and assurance that were betrayed only by the gentle trembling of his fingers.

He stopped on the other side of the door, and Ready followed the boy's lead. They listened to the silence just long enough to judge that no one else was in the hallway, then they walked steadily down the corridor until Kinseth stopped again, near an open door. Kinseth stood beside the entrance, trying to peer in while not being seen by anybody who might be in the room. Ready did the same. It looked empty. After a moment Kinseth took a cautious step forward, then another, stealthily entering the room.

Ready realized this must have been some kind of music room. It was wide and long, with sound-dampening panels on the walls and a decaying piano in the corner. At the back of the room were stacks of expandable—well, at one time they must have been expandable—risers of the sort that a choir might stand on while performing. He watched with curiosity as the young man headed directly toward the risers.

"Kinseth," he said softly. The boy stopped and turned at the sound of his voice. "Kinseth, I think we should go back to the street, back to Kirby Court. We need to go back to the house where Hummingbird is being kept so you can show me how to get into it."

The young man looked confused. He started to say something but then seemed unsure. "We need to go this way," he said finally. Then he stood, staring at Ready, waiting.

Ready looked at the aged surroundings of the abandoned choir room and sighed. This was starting to look like a very big dead end and a waste of valuable time. He sighed again and reached into his pocket to retrieve his cell phone. This call was long overdue anyway, and perhaps it was time to get the police more intimately involved.

He dialed the number for the direct line to Buck Barnes's office and waited. After the fourth ring the call dumped into voice mail. Ready hung up in frustration. What to do now? Call back to the switchboard and ask them to page Barnes? Try to break into the house himself? He slipped the cell back into his pocket and glanced back at Kinseth. The boy was still waiting, staring.

"Kinseth, where are you taking me?"

The young man inexplicably nodded toward the risers.

Ready knelt on the floor. "There's nothing there, Kinseth."

A confused look crossed through Kinseth's face. "We're taking you to the nice lady," he said.

Ready felt his patience wearing thin. "We who? Who's going with us?"

Now it seemed that Kinseth was getting edgy. "We are. Us." He patted his own chest. "And you."

"And who is us, Kinseth? Are you working with the bad man? Are you a friend to the man who is holding Hummingbird? Is this some kind of trap?"

Kinseth shook his head feverishly. "Us," he said emphatically. "We are . . ."

"What?" Ready said. "Who?"

"We are . . ." The young man closed his eyes, raising his fingers to his temples as though feeling a sudden pain. "We are . . . Kinseth," he said. "But . . . it hurts sometimes to be all Kinseth. We can't manage it all at once. But we want to help you. To help the nice lady."

Ready stood and moved to the young man, immediately regretting his previous impatience. "It's okay, Kinseth," he said soothingly, gripping the young man's shoulders compassionately. "I'm sorry. I understand. It's just that I am so worried about my friend."

The boy nodded and opened his eyes. His one good eye stared quizzically at Ready's face.

"Okay," Ready said with an air of resignation. "How do we sneak into that house?"

Kinseth nodded again toward the risers.

Ready said, "Lead the way, my friend."

Then he watched in surprise as the young man squeezed into

a space behind the risers, knelt down, and pressed a spot on the wall. He was even more startled when a trapdoor, about four feet high, opened in the wall and fell away with a hydraulic hum, leaving an opening into a dimly lighted tunnel that apparently ran underground.

— — —

In the deserted sanctuary of the Baptist church, silence ruled for several minutes after Ready and Kinseth exited through the platform door. Then came a shuffling sound, and a voice in the tiny balcony spoke softly into the emptiness.

"That could be a problem."

— — —

Hummingbird Collins tasted blood where her teeth had cut her tongue. *That man has got to stop hitting me,* she thought fiercely.

That man, meanwhile, was screaming at her. "You will not speak such things about my father! You will show respect in this room!"

She started to rise from the floor, but the screaming man swatted her to the ground again.

"You are a worthless whore! An ungrateful daughter of dogs! Have you no reason? Have you no insight? Have you no mind to discern the art of life? To think I thought you might . . ."

Hummingbird decided it was wisest to curl up into a ball on the floor, because every time she showed any sign of life, the madman hit her again. Then suddenly he was lifting her up roughly by the hair, forcing his face centimeters from hers, strafing her eyes with his hot breath.

"My father is not dead. I won't let him die. I won't. And you will recognize that truth, or you will die, right here, right now. I will kill you with my bare hands. Do you understand, Ms. Collins? Do you understand?"

Hummingbird wanted to nod her head, but the fierce grip with which he held her head left her unable to do more than whisper, "Yes, yes. I understand. I'm sorry. I'm sorry. I must have been mistaken."

The madman dropped her, and she fell back into a crouch against the wall. She stared at him, looking intently into his eyes to try to catch a hint of what his next move would be. *Yep,* she said to herself. *He would kill me.* She let out a deep sigh and felt her jaw tighten. *And that's really starting to get on my nerves.*

Then, just as quickly as he had exploded, the madman turned passive once more. "I think, Ms. Collins," he said formally, "that you owe my father, not me, the apology."

Hummingbird looked wildly from the madman to the dead man. The machinery that intertwined his flesh hissed and whirred and beeped and hummed. She watched the ventilator push air into the dead man's lungs and press it back out again. She stood up warily, trying to keep distance between herself and the madman.

"Yes, sir," she said ingratiatingly. She stepped toward the dead man, careful not to turn her back on the living one. "Of course," she continued. "How rude of me. I'm so sorry." She found herself next to the man in the bed. She took in a deep breath. "Please forgive me, sir," she said to the dead man, "for what I'm about to do."

She leaped around the edge of the bed until she was standing between the wall and the dead man's left shoulder. In the same movement she leaned over and clasped the ventilator tube in her left hand, gripping it right at the point where it inserted itself through the tracheal opening in the man's neck.

A look of sincere horror entered the madman's face. He started toward Hummingbird.

"Don't." She said it like a swear word, spitting the command out through clenched teeth. "Take one step closer, and I'll rip this tube right out of your father. How long do you think it would take him to die then?"

If the situation had not been so serious, Hummingbird might have laughed at those words. After all, how do you kill a dead man? But her captor thought he was still alive, and that was enough.

The madman froze. There was silence between them as both considered the new possibilities of the current situation. He took a step backward. Hummingbird felt herself relax just a bit, felt the trembling in her hand. He took another step back, and Hummingbird's eyes flew wide in alarm.

"Don't," she said again. "Stay away from that door."

He seemed to have regained his composure. "Consider what you're doing, Ms. Collins," he said. "One word from me, and my soldiers will be in here faster than you can think." His words were calm, but his eyes, nervously flicking to the door, betrayed him.

Hummingbird's mind raced. "But before you can call those thugs, you have to unlock that door. And then there's the sixty seconds or so it'll take for them to get in here. They're upstairs now, right? And then there will be those precious minutes while you try to pry the breathing tube from my hands, hoping that I won't somehow tear it or poke holes into it. And then, when you finally have the tube again, how long will it take you to reinsert it? And what will you do about the blood that fills the hole in your daddy's neck?"

The madman was silent, stunned.

"How long do you think the brain can last without oxygen?"

His face grew grim. "Not long enough," he muttered. "But no matter what happens, you will never get out of here. Once you pull that tube, I have no reason to keep you alive anymore. If my father dies, you definitely die."

"There's no way you would let me live. Because I will never become one of you, never buy into whatever madness has captured you."

The man gave a glaring nod of acknowledgment, and Hummingbird realized she hadn't really thought this all the way through.

"So," Hummingbird said, feeling her heart race but doing her best to project the calm of a seasoned killer. "What do we do now?"

"It appears, Ms. Collins, that we are at an impasse."

— — —

Elaina Roberts heard the rumbling engine outside her bedroom window and wondered what kind of monster truck had moved into their neighborhood while she'd been sleeping. She rolled over onto her back and glowered at the ceiling. She had to get off this night shift at the hospital. Oh, sure, the extra money was nice, but the constant schedule of staying up all night and then sleeping half the day was wearing her out. Fortunately Kinseth had adapted to it well, though. He seemed content entertaining himself for most of the day and then sleeping through the night while she was away.

She wondered where her little brother was at this moment. She hoped he was in the house, but she also knew that he liked to go exploring on days when the weather was nice, trekking through the greenbelt for hours on end.

She heard a commotion beginning outside the window and a squeal of high-powered brakes in the cul-de-sac. She glanced over at the clock by her bedside and felt like whining. She'd hoped to get at least another hour's sleep, maybe even two hours.

But she was wide awake now and curious about all the noise outside.

She sighed and got out of bed, wrapping her ratty old housecoat around her. The sun was shining through the curtains in her room; it appeared to be a nice fall day. She wondered again why she'd never put foil in the windows of her bedroom to block the daytime sun. That was a trick that a lot of day sleepers used to help convince the body's internal clock that it was okay to sleep past noon. But it had never been high on Elaina's priority list. She found that the best sleep usually followed a good, hard night's work, and no curtain or foil in a window was a substitute for that. Besides, she liked being able to crack an old-fashioned curtain and peek out into the street below without having to peel away a layer of foil first.

She looked into the cul-de-sac and was surprised to see a very large, very red firetruck parked conspicuously at the entrance to her street.

"Kinseth?" she hollered as she grabbed some clothes from the dirty laundry basket. "Kinseth, you in here, baby?"

THIRTEEN

Michelangelo Buonarroti once said that a beautiful thing never gives so much pain as does failing to hear and see it.

I find it interesting that he would say that, for I too have discovered how closely beauty and pain are intertwined.

EXCERPT FROM THE MICHELANGELUS RECORDINGS,
TAPE 2,
TRANSCRIBED BY H. J. COLLINS

— — —

SATURDAY, OCTOBER 4, AFTERNOON

"Such beauty, Ms. Collins. It hurts me to see you pass it by."

Hummingbird Collins stared at the madman across from her and made a mental list of her options in the current situation. The items on that list were depressingly few. "Why don't you sit down," she ordered finally, figuring that at least then she could look down on him. There might be some psychological benefit to that.

The madman pulled the visitor's chair to him, then made a show of also removing the switchblade from his pants pocket before he sat down. He did not unsheathe the blade, but he did rest the knife conspicuously on his right thigh, within easy grasping distance.

"The power of suggestion is an interesting force, Ms. Collins," he said into the ensuing silence. "For instance, you suggested that I sit down, and now here I am. Sitting down. Interesting, don't you think?"

Something about the man's voice had changed. It was calmer, almost soothing. It took on a chocolate quality—bittersweet but chocolate nonetheless. What was he doing?

"Perhaps we should both try to relax, Ms. Collins," he said in the syrupy voice. "Rest is always a better alternative than violence, isn't it?"

Hummingbird felt a shudder of fatigue run through her bones. These past hours—however many they may have been—had been a long, emotionally and physically draining experience. Now she wished that she had been the one to sit down. But she refused to release her grip on the dead man's breathing tube, as that seemed to be the only thing keeping the killer at bay.

"Let go of the tube, Ms. Collins," he was cooing. "You're not a murderer, and he's a defenseless old man."

"No." She said it quickly.

The madman caught her gaze and looked deeply into her eyes. "It seems that your hand is cramping up. Isn't that painful?"

Hummingbird felt the muscles in her hand spasm and realized he was right. A sudden uncertainty fluttered through her brain. How long would she be able to hold this tube in her sweaty, straining, cramping palm?

"Besides," he was saying, "I've decided that I prejudged you unfairly. Of course I'm not going to hurt you. I would never hurt a lovely young woman like yourself. My father wouldn't approve."

"Never hurt me?" she said sarcastically, feeling the swelling that was taking place under her eye and licking dried blood off the corner of her mouth. "You'll excuse me if my recent experience with you seems to indicate otherwise."

The madman only glowered in response.

— — —

Ready closed the gap between himself and the trapdoor and saw Kinseth agilely descending a short stepladder inside the tunnel. The floor of the tunnel was about three feet down from the opening into the choir room, which Ready quickly calculated to mean a seven-foot ceiling. Whoever had created this tunnel had intended it to be used by full-grown adults. It was entirely encased in concrete—floor, walls, ceiling. Low-watt fluorescent tubes illuminated the underground hallway at intervals of about thirty feet, leaving a progression of shallow pools of light that faded and then reappeared as one walked down the hall.

Ready eased himself into the tunnel and looked down the row of lights. The column sloped downward almost immediately, apparently descending farther in order to be completely concealed underground. It also banked into a lazy curve some distance away, and by Ready's best guess, that meant it traveled underneath the greenbelt that he and Kinseth had just crossed in order to enter the church.

The young man waited for Ready to step out of the way, then he reached for a button. Immediately a faint hydraulic hum sounded, and the trapdoor shifted out, then up, and back into position to cover the opening into the choir room.

"Where does this tunnel lead, Kinseth?"

"The hospital," Kinseth responded matter-of-factly.

Ready wanted to ask for an explanation of that off-the-wall answer but decided he'd pressed the boy enough already. It was time to trust him. To trust a friend.

"Lead on," he said after a moment.

Kinseth gave a happy grimace and started confidently down the corridor. Ready took a breath, shrugged, and followed.

— — —

Elaina Roberts opened her front door in time to see a firefighter ascending the steps of her porch.

"What's going on?" she called out to the woman in full fire-fighting gear.

"Nothing to worry about, ma'am," the firefighter said with a friendly drawl. "We've had reports of a natural-gas leak in the area. We're not registering anything on our instruments yet but want to have the gas company check it out before we leave. In situations like this, it's department procedure to evacuate anyone in the area, just as a precaution. We're asking all residents to go wait behind that firetruck over there."

"I see," Elaina said. "How long do you think it will take to check out everything?"

"The gas company tells us they should have everything wrapped up within the hour. Is there anyone else in the house with you, ma'am?"

Elaina bit down on her lip. "No," she said, "but my younger brother—he's not home right now, and he could come home at any minute."

"Okay," the firefighter said. "I'll inform the others and tell them to keep an eye out for him. What does he look like?"

"He's, well, he's a mentally challenged young man. He's only nineteen. He was in an accident seven years ago, see, and . . . well, he's got a large red scar that runs across the left side of his face." The firefighter nodded, impassive. "And he's easily confused. He may not understand what's going on. He usually plays out in the greenbelt behind the cul-de-sac. I'll just go find him and—"

The woman was more forceful now. "No," she said. "I'm sorry, ma'am, but I can't let you in that area. The gas company has asked us to restrict anyone from going into the greenbelt."

Elaina felt a maternal apprehension overtaking her. "Well, if that's where the gas leak is, then I've got to get my brother out of there. He won't understand—"

"Please remain calm, ma'am." The firefighter was standing next to her now, hand on Elaina's shoulder, gently directing her toward the big red truck at the end of the cul-de-sac. "We've got people back there. If your brother's in that area, our people will find him and bring him safely to you. I promise."

"But—"

"No." The woman's voice carried firm authority. "You need to go wait behind that firetruck right now, ma'am. Please."

Elaina allowed herself to be steered in the direction of the small crowd that was now gathering behind the big red machine, hearing the buzz of conversation that was going on all around it. But her mind was elsewhere, worrying for the one person she had left in her life, the one person she could honestly say she would die for.

"Kinseth, baby," she whispered, "wherever you are, I hope you're safe."

Hummingbird adjusted her grip on the breathing tube and wondered what to do next. It was obvious that this little standoff wasn't going to last forever, and as long as the madman with the knife stood between her and the exit, she was almost helpless. Add to that the fact that there were two large goons somewhere outside, ready to recapture her at a moment's notice, and she began to give into despair.

Time was what she needed. Time to think, to work out a way of escape.

"What's your father's name?" she asked quickly, trying to

keep the madman talking. He certainly was not the shy and silent type. Maybe if she could get him talking he would unwittingly reveal a clue that she could use to get out of this place.

"As I've told you, we don't need names in this house," the man said evenly.

Hummingbird searched for another question, something to keep the man from getting out of that chair and slicing at her with his knife.

"What happened to him? Why is he in this condition?"

"My father had a debilitating stroke two years ago. It could have killed him. But it didn't. I wouldn't let him die. He's been living here ever since."

Now she was genuinely curious. "What do you mean, you wouldn't let him die?"

The madman gave her a quizzical look. "I mean I wouldn't let him die. Some suggested that we take him off the life-support machines and let him pass on. But I wouldn't let that happen. Not to him. Not yet."

Hummingbird frantically tried to think of something new to say, but nothing came to mind. She was relieved when the madman spoke again.

"Do you believe in an afterlife, Ms. Collins?"

"Yes. Of course," she said.

"I don't. And my father doesn't either. If there were such thing as a loving God, he would never have allowed my father or me to do some of the things we've done. But I must confess something to you. When my father was moments away from death, I had what you might call a shadow of a doubt."

"You doubted your disbelief?"

"Please, Ms. Collins. Surely even you know that unbelief is a kind of belief all its own. Yes, I doubted my belief in disbelief. Not with certainty, not by any means. I still don't believe in God or in heaven or hell or any kind of afterlife. But . . ." His voice trailed off.

"But what?"

"Well, Ms. Collins, at the last moment when my father was almost gone, one inescapable question kept running through my mind: What if I'm wrong? What if there is life after death, after all? I couldn't let him die then, could I, Ms. Collins? Because if there is an afterlife, it won't be a pleasant one for my father. Better to keep him here, in this place, on these life-giving machines, until I can firmly erase that shadow of doubt."

"I see," Hummingbird said. She felt a trickle of sweat roll down her forehead. She couldn't hold this position much longer. And now she knew why he had exploded and attacked her earlier when she'd said his father was dead. That was, in effect, saying his father was rotting in hell.

I'm trapped, she thought feverishly. *And there's no telling what this madman will do when he realizes his father is, in fact, already dead.* She adjusted her grip on the breathing tube once more.

The man stood up suddenly, switchblade now comfortably in his right hand.

"I've been watching you, Ms. Collins," he said. "You're getting tired. And the reality of your situation is beginning to settle in, isn't it?"

"Sit down," Hummingbird hissed.

The man ignored her command. "You are at the disadvantage, Ms. Collins," he said calmly. "I've been resting comfortably in that chair, regaining my strength and my wits. You've been standing in that awkward position for some time now. Your right hand is useless. Your left is cramping and stiff. The muscles in your shoulder and back are stinging. And you know there's no way you're getting out of here alive, no matter what you do."

Hummingbird wanted to argue with him, but everything he'd said was true.

"Release the tube," he said quietly. "Let go, and I promise I'll make your death swift and painless. Not at all like it was for Corona Sanchez or Abram Erskine. And your death won't be futile; there will be purpose in it."

"You're insane," she said desperately.

"I'm an artist."

Hummingbird didn't respond except to adjust her grip on the ventilator tube again.

"Something on your mind, Ms. Collins?"

Memories of her childhood came flooding back, of happy days banging a tambourine next to her mama in the church pews, of a boy stealing a kiss in the back row of the bus on a youth-group trip, of praying for T.W. not to get hurt while he played football in college—but never missing a game. Of the comfort that came when she heard her mama reading aloud words of hope and anger and love and sorrow that threaded through King David's poetry in the Psalms.

"I will lift up my eyes to the mountains," she said finally, re-membering words from one of Mama's favorite Psalms. "From whence shall my help come? My help comes from the Lord who made heaven and earth."

"There is no God to help you now, Ms. Collins."

She was determined not to show weakness, not to do any-thing to please this maggot who had beaten her, who had threat-ened her. Even so, she couldn't stop the tears from coming. She glared at him through the wet streaks that stained her cheeks. "My help comes from the Lord," she said with gritty defiance, "who made heaven and earth."

No one was more surprised than Hummingbird when, at just that moment, the large metal cabinet by the back wall made a creaking sound and slowly moved in an arc toward her. A hidden passageway. But who had arrived?

— — —

T.W. Collins sat in the Chevy Malibu and had to admit he was impressed. So far, at least, the plan was working.

Detective Barnes had kept his promise and parked the car across the street from the entrance to the cul-de-sac, leaving it at an angle that allowed T.W. to see past the large firetruck and keep a clear view of the house at 1669 Kirby Court.

You in there, Humm? he wondered. He didn't know if he should hope that she was or was not.

Detective Barnes sat in the driver's seat of the Malibu, quietly directing traffic through the police radio in the car. Most communications were short: *move here, stay there, give me a status update,* that kind of thing. Close to thirty people already milled around behind the firetruck, but no one had come out of the house at 1669 yet. The firefighters had done their jobs. The neighbors had arrived in an orderly fashion. Several were grumbling about the inconvenience, but most were simply passing the time chatting as if it was an impromptu block party.

Another group of residents was ushered to the waiting area. That left only one more house besides the target residence.

"Detective Barnes," a voice crackled on the radio, "one of the women says her younger brother is missing."

Barnes swore.

"He's a nineteen-year-old Caucasian male. Has a scar on his face and is mentally disabled. The sister says she thinks he's in the greenbelt behind the cul-de-sac."

"Nothing back here but us monkeys," another voice interrupted. "Want me to break off and give a quick look around?"

"No," Barnes said quickly. "Stay with your SWAT assignment. We're almost ready to approach the house. But send word immediately if you see someone matching the kid's description."

"Roger."

"Okay, Justins, you in position with the firetruck?"

"Roger, boss."

"Good. Take the residents and lead them around the corner and out of sight. Have some of the firefighters help you. We need to let the SWAT officers move into position in the front and also need to get the snipers up on the roofs without causing undue—" Detective Barnes swore again.

One of the residents standing on the edge of the crowd was pointing.

"Move 'em, Justins! Go!" Barnes snarled. "And Hanes, pull that high-powered rifle of yours back into the bushes."

"Sorry, boss. Had an itch." The gun disappeared, but it was too late. Murmurs of concern were waving through the gathered residents. An plainclothes officer was now showing a badge to the residents and urging them to move quickly around the corner. The firefighters were helping, but now the crowd was starting to panic.

"Oh, blast it, Hanes," Detective Barnes said. "I thought they taught you better in the SWAT forces."

Another voice cut in. "They do, Detective. And we'll make sure Sergeant Hanes learns the lesson again when this is all over."

"Might as well move into position on the porch, Hanes," Detective Barnes said. "Looks like we're running out of time. Cortez, back him up."

"Roger."

"Roger."

Two forms appeared on the front lawn of the house at 1669 Kirby Court. One crept stealthily up the stairs and onto the porch, careful to avoid any line of sights from the windows or doors. A second figure crouched in place at the foot of the stairs, just on the left.

"Snipers in position," Barnes ordered.

"Roger."

"Roger."

T.W. watched in awe as a figure rose silently on the roof of a house two doors down from 1669. He assumed a second sniper was doing the same thing on a different house, but he couldn't see that one.

"Detective," a voice said.

"What is it, Hanes?"

"There's no doorknob on this front door."

Barnes was definitely losing patience. "You need a doorknob to bust into that house, Hanes?"

"Negative, sir."

"Then stay on task."

"Roger."

Detective Barnes sighed and set down his radio transmitter.

"Now what?" T.W. asked cautiously.

"Now we have to make that decision we talked about earlier."

T.W. suddenly wished he was more comfortable praying.

— — —

Ready Robinson leaped through the opening in the tunnel wall and was only mildly surprised to discover an entire hospital room set up in there.

A quick survey of the room revealed that what he'd heard going on here was almost correct. Hummingbird was definitely being threatened by a man who said he was going to kill her. What he didn't expect was to see a man lying in a hospital bed, hooked up to more machines than Ready could name. He also didn't like that fact that the threatening man was brandishing a knife of some kind.

"Somebody asking for help?" he said. It was goofy, he knew. But at that moment he felt just a little bit like a superhero.

"Ready, oh, thank God!" Hummingbird said.

The madman took in the new development with disgust on his face. He looked past Ready's shoulder. "You," he said to the wall behind him. "You're the unpretty one from across the street."

Kinseth stepped behind Ready, an instinctive plea for protection. But he said nothing.

"So you found the tunnel," the madman said to Kinseth. "Which gives me two reasons to dispose of you." The madman now took a good look at Ready. "You, on the other hand," he said thoughtfully, "you have a face I can use." He flicked open the blade on his knife.

"Put it away," Hummingbird commanded. "Put it away, or I'll kill your father before you can move." She tightened her grip on . . . on what? A breathing tube of some sort.

The madman hesitated, then lowered his knife.

Ready gave Hummingbird a quick look, noting the makeshift bandage on her right hand. Her face was bruised and blue from apparent blows. Her lip was cracked and bloody. And she'd been crying. Righteous fury surged through him. But killing a defenseless patient? In front of his son? Surely there was another way. "Hummingbird . . ."

"Ready," she said, never taking her hand off the tube, "we have to get out of here." She looked meaningfully at him, her eyes pleading for him to understand the situation.

Ready followed her gaze to a monitor of some sort—wait, it was a brain-scan monitor. And it registered no activity whatsoever.

Ready followed the machinery around and saw a heart monitor. The volume had been turned down, but the visual was a flat line. He looked back at Hummingbird and saw the muscles in her palm twitching. She was holding on to the tracheal tube of a ventilator machine that still pumped air in and out of the patient's lungs.

Why would Hummingbird threaten to kill a dead man?

He looked back at the madman and saw a gleam of hatred in his eyes but also concern for the dead man. Ready understood and knew, deep within, what had to be done.

"Right," he said to Hummingbird. He walked over to the bed in two quick strides, grabbed the upper portion of the breathing tube with one hand, and gently peeled off Hummingbird's fingers with his other hand.

"You," he said to the madman, "probably know already that Hummingbird is no killer." He let a fierce grin cross his face, the same grin he had used when he earned his nickname playing defense for the Philadelphia Eagles decades before. "But me, on the other hand, there's no telling what I might do. I belong to those who have long hunted people like you, people who prey upon the innocent."

The gambit worked. The madman seethed, but Ready could see that he was also wary of this new threat to his father.

"Kinseth," Ready said firmly, "take Hummingbird back through the tunnel, and go get help. Call the police and tell them to break down the blasted door to this house if they have to. I'll keep Mr. Happy Knife here."

"You don't know what—" the madman started.

"Kinseth," Ready said, calmly interrupting him.

The boy nodded and took Hummingbird's hand. She started to follow, then hesitated. "Ready?" she asked.

"Go, Humm. Go now. Your brother's probably worried sick about you."

A moment later Ready Robinson and the madman were the only living people in the hospital bedroom hidden away in the basement at 1669 Kirby Court.

The madman raised his switchblade again. "That," he said, "was likely your last mistake."

— — —

Number 48 hung up his cell phone and tapped his fingers on the kitchen table. "Still no answer on either Thirty-nine or Sixty-one's cell."

Number 44 looked pained. "How are we supposed to find those two?" he complained. "The boss knows they come and go as they please. They could be anywhere."

"Yeah," 48 commiserated. "But with all due respect, sir, I don't want to be the one to tell him that."

Number 44 nodded absently. Suddenly a small red light began blinking in a corner.

"Somebody's on the porch," 48 said.

"Good," said 44. "Maybe it's them. Go down and check the surveillance monitor. I'll wait here for the all clear."

"Yes, sir."

Number 48 descended the steps into the basement and wasn't surprised to see that the door to the hospital room was closed. He wondered briefly what the boss was doing with that new girl in there, then walked past the hospital room to the tech room. He checked the monitor that displayed the front porch and saw nothing. A red light was still flashing in the corner of this room too, though, so he studied it for a moment longer.

"Probably a cat," he muttered at last. He reached over and hit a button that stopped the light from flashing. In the monitor, he saw 44 opening the door. But instead of shutting it again after he saw that no one was there, 44 stepped out onto the porch, swinging the door behind him. He had a curious expression on his face.

Then 48 saw three things happen at once.

First, a black blur flashed across the porch, tackling 44 and sending him sprawling hard onto the ground.

Second, the front door to the house completed its lazy swing, clicking shut behind the place where 44 had been standing and automatically locking.

Third, a new figure, albeit smaller, raced up the steps of the house and dived for the front door, barely missing the moment when she could have blocked it from closing and locking her— and her teammates—outside.

Number 48 stared open-mouthed into the monitor, and it took at least a full ten seconds before what had just happened fully registered. "SWAT? Here?" he muttered.

The scuffle on the porch was embarrassingly brief. After all, 44 prided himself on hand-to-hand combat, and he was not a small man. But the first SWAT officer had caught him completely off guard and had him handcuffed and subdued before he knew what had hit him.

Number 48 felt his armpits beginning to perspire. Numbers 39 and 61 were missing. Had they sold out the boss to the authorities? And the rest of them along with him?

He watched in dumbfounded disbelief as the SWAT officers dragged 44 down the steps and disappeared out of the range of the camera's lens.

It wasn't time for standing and thinking; it was time for action. He turned to the door and raced down the little hallway to the hospital-room door. He rammed on it, yelling, "Number 26! Sir! We've been compromised!"

- - -

Ready Robinson felt a surprising calm as he stared down the killer with the knife, both of them ignoring the pounding on the door. Neither man spoke, but the madman glared at Ready and toyed with the switchblade in his hand, alternately flicking it open and snapping it shut.

Ready took a moment to assess the situation of the old man on the ventilator. He knew that he would never deliberately kill a defenseless man in a hospital bed, but he also knew that the madman didn't know that, and this was an advantage that Ready had to exploit, at least for the moment. How long this stalemate could last, however, was anybody's guess. He hoped it would be at least long enough for Hummingbird and Kinseth to get safely away and maybe long enough for the police to infiltrate the house. The pounding at the door gave him hope that help had already arrived. Somehow Buck had discovered this place.

Ready was no doctor, but he had seen his share of hospitals and even a corpse or two in a hospital bed. He dared to look again at the machinery humming around him and at the patient in the bed. The brain scan showed absolutely no activity. Ready knew that a heart could continue to beat after full brain death but never for more than twenty-four to forty-eight hours. Sometimes not even that long. The man's skin was cool to the touch and deathly pale but still retained a faint pink tint that made Ready assume he had not been dead for long. Maybe a few hours at most.

Then he noticed the IV bag. There was the typical line from the bag into the patient's arm, but someone had cinched the tube near the top, meaning that no liquid actually flowed from the bag into the dead man's arm. Ready saw a second line snaking out of the bag, carefully positioned so a person standing at the foot of the bed couldn't see it. This line followed the metal of the IV stand down, then over to the bed, where it was inconspicuously inserted into the carotid artery of the man's neck. Someone had intended for this line to be hidden from view, but this was the one that was actually draining into the patient. Ready smelled the faint aroma of formaldehyde and suddenly thought he recognized the fluid in the IV bag. The thin, pale orange liquid was certainly not a nutrient solution for a living patient.

Ready turned back to the madman, who was now watching Ready with curious interest more than overwhelming hostility.

Ready looked at him, calculating in his head to determine if Hummingbird and Kinseth had had enough time to get through the tunnel and into the Baptist church and praying for direction. Then he stared the madman directly in the eyes and pointedly released his grip on the breathing tube of the patient.

"What are you doing?" the madman asked evenly.

"I think it's time we are honest with each other," Ready replied. "I'm not going to kill your father."

The madman still looked suspicious. "It's likely I will still kill you," he said. "But why have you decided not to hurt him?"

Ready took in a deep breath. This was going to be risky. "You strike me as an intelligent man." The madman said nothing. "Are you the artist behind that painting in the Baptist church?"

"Yes," the man said. "I've been working on it for years."

"It's stunning," Ready said in all honesty. "And I think someone who can see what's in that painting should also be able to see what's right in front of his face."

"What do you mean?" The corners of the madman's eyes narrowed.

Ready took a chance and stepped slightly away from the bed and the dead man on it. The madman took a step forward in response.

"I'm not going to hurt your father," Ready said.

"You mentioned that already."

"I'm not going to hurt him because someone else has beaten me to it."

The madman's nostrils flared, and his eyes widened just a bit. Ready tried to remain calm, serene. He didn't want to agitate the killer more than was necessary.

"You had better explain yourself," the madman said through gritted teeth.

"See for yourself," Ready said evenly. "Brain activity doesn't register at all." He gestured toward the monitor.

"The machine is broken. That whore must have kicked it."

"There's a flat line on the heart monitor."

"No. Even when the brain scan is low, there's always . . ." His eyes seemed to focus for the first time on the heart monitor and the steady green line that illuminated the screen.

"And"—Ready hoped this didn't cause the madman to explode—"someone has replaced your father's IV bag with a bag of embalming fluid."

He reached over and gently turned the IV stand to reveal the second tube that was draining fluid into the old man's neck.

The madman said nothing, but the look on his face said it all.

Immense, unexpectedly total loss.

His mouth dropped open slightly, his jaws lifting and parting as though he wanted to say something but couldn't. The knife slid from his fingers and clattered unnoticed onto the floor. The madman took another step toward the bed, then another, until he was standing next to the dead man and seeing—apparently for the first time—that his father was irrevocably deceased.

In that moment Ready saw an opportunity. The madman seemed to have forgotten that he was in the room, consumed as he was by the new knowledge of his father's death.

"Who . . ." the madman whispered. "When . . ."

Ready took a quiet step toward the doorway into the tunnel.

The madman didn't seem to notice, so he took another, then another, until he stood only inches away from the opening in the wall.

The madman reached out with a tentative hand and touched the skin of his father's arm, recoiling quickly at the coldness of the body.

Ready didn't wait any longer. He backed into the tunnel, then turned and ran toward the church on the other side. He wondered if Hummingbird and Kinseth had made it to safety already and how long it would take before he could join them. Then, when he was about fifteen yards down the dimly lit underground hallway, he heard the madman's wail—a long, mournful cry. It was the sound of an animal experiencing a devastating loss.

Ready almost felt sorry for him at that moment.

Almost.

FOURTEEN

Even during his own time, they called Michelangelo "Il Divino"—
the Divine One. They may not call me that in my lifetime, but
they will call me that. Because, you see, Ms. Collins, though I
blush to admit it, I am an even greater artist than Il Divino himself. And I look forward to the day when I can show you why.

EXCERPT FROM THE MICHELANGELUS RECORDINGS,
TAPE 4,
TRANSCRIBED BY H. J. COLLINS

— — —

Number 48 heard the cry emanating from the hospital room and
immediately stepped away from the door. The boss sometimes
had frightening hallucinations—the result of that drug that 61
fed him so often—and there was no telling what he might do
when the flashbacks hit. He'd been known to punish his own soldiers in the studio.

But 48 wasn't about to risk having to endure what 39 had endured. Interrupting the boss during his time with Number 3 was
never a good idea. Interrupting him with bad news now, in this
emotional state, seemed like suicide.

He stood stymied in the little basement hallway, considering
his situation.

The boss was inaccessible, which might be for the best.

Number 44 had been apprehended by the police, right on
their own front porch.

Numbers 61 and 39 were missing. Either they were traitors to the cause, or the police had already taken them into custody too.

That left only 48 to defend the house.

He went upstairs, crawling when he got to the top floor. He inched his way over to a window and tried to peek outside without moving the curtain. He couldn't see everything, but he did see a big red fire engine filling the entrance to the cul-de-sac and a crowd of people moving slowly out of sight behind it. Number 48 was nowhere to be seen. The SWAT team had probably swept him away, handcuffed, to a police cruiser hidden around the corner. The rest of the street seemed deserted, but given how quickly those two SWAT officers had appeared out of nowhere on his front porch, he didn't trust the seemingly vacant neighborhood outside.

He thought of the tunnel. They'd always planned for the underground exit that led to the Baptist church to be the escape route if they ever needed to abandon the house. The old man had paid almost as much as the price of the house in order to have the builders put that thing in—and even more to make sure they kept it a secret when they built it, disguising it as an underground waterway for supposed special plumbing that they were adding to the house. Then they'd spread a little more money around to make sure nobody ever bought the church. After all, if a Realtor discouraged any interested parties, they could honestly say they'd had no firm offers. Number 48 thought they should have just bought the church themselves, but Number 3 had been very careful. He didn't want anyone connecting the ownership of that church to the house at 1669 Kirby Court. He felt it was better simply to keep it empty by less obvious means.

Now, 48 thought, he could really use that tunnel and its access to the church on the other side of the greenbelt.

He crawled back across the floor and descended the steps to the basement. There was no noise on the other side of the door to the hospital room. He wondered if the boss's panic had passed, if it was safe to go in there now. He reached haltingly toward the door and tried the knob. Still locked as usual, and he had never had access to a key. He wondered briefly if he could knock it down but decided against it. After all, he and 44 had installed this metal-reinforced door and frame themselves. It would probably take a jackhammer to knock the thing down. Besides, the boss would likely view that as some kind of violation of his father's privacy. Again, the image of 39 in the studio chair flashed in his mind. The boss was not generally a forgiving person.

He decided to risk calling out to the boss again. "Number 26?"

Silence was the only response.

He tried knocking again.

Nothing.

He felt his blood pressure rising. He heard the faint clicking of the red light in the tech room down the hall. He ran to look at the monitor.

Someone was on the front porch again.

A moment later he saw the yellow light flicker next to the red one.

Someone was on the back porch too.

This was getting serious.

He paced a moment in the room, wondering what his next move should be. He wasn't used to this kind of role. Usually everybody else told him what to do. He was comfortable with that. When someone else did the thinking, all he had to do was act. That was the way it was supposed to be, the way they'd trained him. Now he was supposed to turn away single-handedly a team of SWAT officers and who knew what else from their formerly supersecret safe house?

He allowed his pacing to take him out of the tech room and into the supply room. He saw something on the corner table and suddenly had an idea.

— — —

T.W. Collins watched as Buck Barnes spat on the ground and returned to the Chevy Malibu in disgust.

"Problem?" T.W. said when the detective slid back into the driver's seat.

"Nothing's ever easy in this business, T.W.," he said shortly.

"Got that guy on the porch, though," he said optimistically. "That was a good thing."

"Yeah." Detective Barnes grumbled. "But Cortez didn't make it to the door fast enough to keep it open. One more second and she would've been in there, and this whole thing would be over by now."

"Did you get any information out of the guy?"

"Nope, he's not talking. Didn't even ask for a lawyer. Just leaned back in the backseat of the police cruiser over there, closed his eyes, and appears to be trying to go to sleep."

"Detective Barnes." A voice broke in over the radio.

"Go."

"Cortez here. We're back in position. Orders?"

"Wait for my command," he said. "Hummel, status report at the back of the house?"

"Ready and eager, boss," a voice said. "Just give the word, and we'll do the rest."

Detective Barnes put the mouthpiece of the radio into his lap. "Well, T.W.," he said. "Looks like it's time for that decision we talked about earlier. What do you think we should do?"

"If we go in, Hummingbird might get hurt, right?"

Barnes nodded.

"What about your SWAT officers?"

"They knew the risks when they joined up."

T.W. hesitated. He'd been so ready to go in, guns blazing, earlier. Why was he wavering now? Hummingbird was probably in that house, and if they didn't get her out soon, there was no telling what would happen to her.

The trouble was, if they went in full force right now, there was no telling what would happen to her then either. Had they already killed her when they saw that first guy get captured by the SWAT team? Would they kill her when they heard the teargas canisters break the windows? When the doors were busted down?

"I think," T.W. said, "that this is a decision you'd better make, Buck. I've seen you in action now, and I think I'm learning to trust you. Even with Hummingbird's life."

Detective Barnes nodded his acknowledgment and didn't hesitate. "All units," he began, "prepare for—"

"Detective Barnes." A new voice keyed into the conversation, cutting off Barnes's order. T.W. didn't recognize it, but Buck apparently did.

"Sunny? Kinda busy right now."

"Sorry, Buck," the voice said sweetly. "But I've got a nine-one-one dispatcher on the line here, and she says she's desperate to get hold of you."

"Put her on the radio," Detective Barnes said.

A second later another voice crackled on the radio. "Is this the officer in charge of the operation at Kirby Court?"

Barnes appeared to be trying hard to suppress growing anxiety and impatience. "Ten-four. We're kind of in the middle of something right now, operator."

"I understand, sir," the voice said. "But I've got a man on my line here demanding to talk to you. He says to tell you he's inside the house at 1669 Kirby Court. He says to tell you to tell your people to pull back from the house. And he says to tell you that he's got a bomb."

Detective Barnes appeared to be going through a list of his favorite curse words. Then he picked two and spat them into the air before responding to the dispatcher. When he clicked on the mouthpiece again, his voice was all business.

"Forward his call to my cell phone."

— — —

Ready Robinson heard only silence behind him when he finally reached the short stepladder that led to the trapdoor in the church choir room. He was glad to see that Hummingbird and Kinseth had left it open—it meant that they'd gotten this far at least. He quickly ascended the ladder and ducked his head under the doorway into the room. He had to squeeze to fit between the wall and the stacks of risers, but the tight fit was the last thing on his mind. Once inside the choir room, he turned and searched the wall until he found the disguised button that Kinseth had pushed to get the trapdoor to open. He pressed the button and was relieved to hear the hydraulics kick in and to see the trapdoor swing out and then back into position, covering the hole in the wall. He had to admit, the fit was perfect, and it blended in very nicely with the rest of the wall. If Kinseth hadn't shown him it was there, he likely would never have seen it on his own.

He slipped out from behind the risers and wasted no time heading for the door. He jogged down the hall, made a wrong turn, backtracked, and finally burst through the stage door at the front of the sanctuary. Hummingbird and Kinseth were waiting for him there, standing at the place where the center aisle spilled out into the front area of the church. Ready deliberately avoided looking at the monstrous painting on the wall behind the altar and focused on his friends instead.

Hummingbird looked battered but defiant. Kinseth's eyes were slightly widened, and he stood partially behind Hummingbird, looking out around her.

"Okay," Ready said breathlessly as he moved to the center aisle. "Let's get out of here. You two should have already been long gone anyway. There's no telling when that psychopath is going to reappear."

"Johann Smidt is an artistic genius," a voice said. A cold voice. And one that didn't belong to either Hummingbird or Kinseth.

Ready turned his head toward the back of the church and finally saw why Hummingbird and Kinseth weren't already gone, why they'd stopped here. A man stood near the end of the aisle. His hair was short, brown, and tucked under a green knit cap. He carried a backpack lazily in one hand, and in his other hand was the dark shape of a handgun. On his right was a woman, close in height to the man. She had a lean, muscular frame and wore her dark hair straight, cut short around the edges of her face. She too carried a backpack, but Ready didn't see a weapon in her hands.

"Ready," Hummingbird said casually, as if all the pressure of her recent experience had left her incapable of new fear. "This lady here was a visitor to my bookstore recently. And now she and this nice man seem to object to us leaving the church so soon."

The man stepped toward them. "Of course, you are right to some extent," the man drawled. "Johann Smidt is something of a psychopath. Still, one learns to overlook the little character flaws when in the presence of greatness." He stopped about halfway up the aisle and took a good, hard look at the people he held captive.

"You know," he said, "we were only planning on having to deal with one of you." He gestured toward Hummingbird. "You. We only had to dispose of your body once Johann was done with you and then make our way out of this town. Imagine our surprise when your two heroes came sauntering in here earlier." Now he waved toward Kinseth and Ready. "You have complicated what was already a complex plan."

Ready looked past the man, down the aisle, at the woman. She stood still back there, waiting, watching.

"Do you two work for him?"

The woman turned away. The man let a lazy gaze fall on Ready. "We did. We've had . . . a parting of the ways."

Ready nodded. "Which one of you killed his father?"

Hummingbird whipped her face toward Ready, clearly wondering why he taunted them, but he refused to meet her gaze. If they were going to get out of this, they were going to have to talk their way out, and Ready knew they'd have to venture deeper toward danger to escape.

"We should kill them all," the man said softly. "We can't take the chance."

The woman never looked at her companion. "Yes," she said, "but three bodies are much harder to dispose of than just one."

"We'll make two trips."

"A risk."

"It's a bigger risk not to."

"Well," the woman said, "we don't have to make a decision yet. For now, we just wait as planned."

Ready felt a little relief in hearing that their deaths were not to be immediate but still knew he had to do something before the killers had a chance to reconsider. He tried to piece together the clues before him. These two had killed the old man but had apparently intended that the old man continue to seem alive. That would indicate that the patient in the hospital room back there had been in a coma for some time. Long enough that his son had become accustomed to seeing him that way.

"Why did you expect Hummingbird to come here?" Ready asked suddenly.

The man shrugged and rolled his eyes, as if the answer were obvious and he had no intention of wasting his time telling it, but his cold eyes rested on Hummingbird.

"They thought that he would bring me in here," Hummingbird said, staring from one to the other. "He was going to force me to a point of decision—'enlightenment' is how he referred to it—or he would force me to 'serve' in some other fashion. They were going to watch while he killed me, right here on the altar of this church. As part of some grisly dedication service."

"You are not one of us. We could see it right away. Johann was deluded."

"But your blood would have added to the beauty behind you," the man said. "It still may. It would be the final act of this play, a fitting end, given the subject matter. But it has to be Johann who sees it through. Anything else would be . . . unpretty."

"What about Johann?" Hummingbird asked. "He will just let you walk away from him? After you've killed his father?"

"He is a ticking bomb," said the woman, eyeing her fingernails. "And I'll soon light another fuse." She gave Hummingbird a sad smile. "He's a drug addict, you know. Another victim of the drug scene that haunts this town. Tragic."

Ready felt like kicking something. This was why he had been prepared. To fight this enemy. Here. Now. *Help me, Lord. Help us! Show me!* "So what do we do now?" he asked their captors.

"Like we said earlier," the man answered. "We wait."

— — —

Number 48 heard a click in the earpiece of his cell phone. Then a voice was speaking in his ear.

"This is Detective Barnes," the voice said. "To whom am I speaking?"

"Names are unimportant," 48 said. "Are you the person in charge of this assault on my home?"

"Perhaps you'd be willing to let us come in and chat about that."

"That's unlikely."

"You called me, sir. You have something to say?"

"Tell your people to move away from the house."

"Why should I?"

"Because we planted C-4 charges under the porches at both the front and back doors, and I now have my thumb hovering over the detonation button." A bluff, sure. But 48 was betting that this Detective Barnes guy wouldn't want to take the chance. He heard Barnes speaking in the background.

"All units, pull back. Possible explosives in the area outside the house." There was a muffling sound. Number 48 couldn't be sure, but he thought the detective had also called for bomb squad backup. Smart. They could check the veracity of his bombs-in-the-porches bluff while Barnes kept him talking on the phone.

"Okay," Barnes said into the telephone. "My people are backing out."

Number 48 watched a figure back down the steps of the front porch. He switched the monitor to the camera in the back but saw nothing. He flipped the switch and shut off the red and yellow flashing lights, then waited. If someone was back there, the yellow light would flicker back on. When it stayed dark, he let out a breath. He'd bought himself a few moments at least.

"So what do you want, Mr. No Name?"

Number 48 hesitated. What did he want? A car out of here? Too easy to follow, too easy to sabotage. A helicopter? Too dramatic. Also too easy to follow.

"I want to walk out of here. By myself. Just walk away. Then you and your people can have whatever's left in this house—people and property."

"Look," Barnes was saying now, "surely you know how this will turn out. Why not make it easy on yourself? Come out now, hands behind your head, and we'll all go downtown and talk it over. After all, your buddy out here—the guy we nabbed earlier—he's saying all kinds of nasty things about you. Surely not all of them can be true."

Number 48 almost laughed. He would have laughed if he hadn't been so nervous. Number 44 was well trained in reverse interrogation. He knew how to give the minimal amount of information to a questioner while soaking up the maximal amount of information about his enemy at the same time. He guessed that 44 was, at this moment, seated somewhere pretending to be asleep. Self-hypnosis was what it really was. Number 39 had tried to teach it to them both; 44 had shown a natural ability for it, but 48 had never been truly successful.

"When I walk out of this house," 48 said firmly, "I'm walking away from you and all your people, or I'm taking you all with me."

There was a conspicuous silence, then one word. "Fine."

— — —

Ready Robinson was accustomed to waiting, confident that his God had brought him here, to this place, now, for this. So he decided to do that to which he was accustomed.

He didn't bother to ask permission; he simply slipped down

onto his knees, relaxed his posture and his thinking, and began.

Today, he prayed, *I will serve Jesus Christ with all my heart, soul, and mind, to the honor of God the Father, by the grace of God the Son, through the power of God's own Holy Spirit.*

He heard a faint noise to his right and took notice that Hummingbird had followed his lead. She too was on her knees, whispering quiet words through bruised lips. He strained to listen, and it registered somewhere in the back of his mind that Hummingbird was reciting something from the Psalms. He smiled.

Just like her mother, he thought.

"Where can I go from Your Spirit?" Hummingbird's whispers flowed like breath through the air. "Or where can I flee from Your presence?" she said in muted tones. "If I ascend into heaven, You are there; if I make my bed in hell, behold, You are there."

She paused as if trying to remember a line, then, "If I take the wings of the morning, and dwell in the uttermost parts of the sea, even there Your hand shall lead me." Another pause. A soft sigh. "And Your right hand shall hold me . . ."

Ready let his mind drift away from Hummingbird and back to his vows.

Today, I will pursue a life of obscurity, he continued, *hiding myself behind the veil of anonymity whenever and wherever possible, to the honor of God the Father, by the grace of God the Son, through the power of God's own Holy Spirit.*

Today, within the limitations of my obscurity, I will incarnate my life in the life of my chosen city, understanding, interacting, and influencing it as God gives me opportunity, to the honor of God the Father, by the grace of God the Son, through the power of God's own Holy Spirit.

Today I will offer myself as a loyal and living sacrifice to my Lord, to my friends . . .

He paused a moment, then reworded his vow. *I will offer myself as a loyal and living sacrifice to my Lord, to Hummingbird Collins, and to Kinseth Roberts, to the honor of God the Father, by the grace of God the Son, through the power of God's own Holy Spirit.*

He heard the gentle rustling of minutes passing slowly by, felt an uncommon stillness that was welcomed as a friend behind his shuttered eyes.

May the Lord Jesus Christ bless and enable me to keep these, my vows, today and every day. Amen.

Ready paused to breathe after reciting his vows.

Waiting.

— — —

Detective Barnes heard T. W. Collins yelp when he clicked shut the cover of his cell phone.

"Buck!" The lawyer's voice was alarmed. "What do you think you're doing? Are you sure it's wise to let him walk?"

Barnes didn't answer. Instead, he clicked on the mouthpiece of the police radio. "Sunny," he said quickly, "you still there?"

"Go, Buck," a bright voice replied.

"If that maniac inside the house calls back, just have the nine-one-one operator patch him right through to me."

"Ten-four, Buck."

The silence that ensued was profound. Detective Barnes could tell that T.W. wanted to say something, but he was also giving the detective the benefit of the doubt in this situation.

"Sniper One," Barnes said after a few minutes. "Report."

"No visible activity, Detective."

"Sniper Two?"

"No shot yet, Buck. But I thought I saw movement at the front window earlier. I'll let you know if anything new shows up."

"Roger."

He tapped his cell phone nervously. Maybe it had been a mistake to hang up on this guy. It had been a risk, but it had also seemed like the right thing to do at that moment.

"Buck?" T.W.'s voice was tentative. When Barnes didn't respond, the lawyer simply leaned back in his seat and watched the house.

Suddenly, out of the corner of his eye, he saw a figure running past the firetruck and into the cul-de-sac, toward the officers.

"Bogey! Bogey!" Officer Justins was shouting into the radio. "Only turned my back for a second, and she took off."

Barnes used three of his favorite swear words this time and added a distinctly unflattering commentary about Justins's family tree to boot.

"Cortez!" he shouted into the radio. The SWAT officer didn't respond on the radio, but a dark figure appeared as if from nowhere and met the bogey in the middle of the street. Barnes had expected her to level the running woman but saw her instead pull up when the woman came running directly toward the SWAT officer.

The running woman stopped short when she reached Cortez, gesticulating and apparently trying to communicate some information that was important to her.

"Cortez?" Detective Barnes radioed. "Get that woman out of the street."

Again Cortez didn't respond on radio, but she did begin gently ushering the woman back toward the fire engine.

"Cortez." Barnes was getting angry now. "Report."

"One second, Detective," was Cortez's clipped reply.

Barnes turned to say something to T.W., then stopped himself when the man just shrugged and gave him a "Beats me" look of sympathy.

256   SHARON   CARTER   ROGERS

The radio crackled on a moment later. "Buck?" It was Cortez's voice.

"Go."

"That's the lady whose younger brother is missing." There was some background noise. "Yes, ma'am." Cortez was apparently speaking to the woman again. "Yes, ma'am. Yes, I'll tell them. Now please, we need you to return to the rest of the residents. Every moment you are out here limits our ability to find—"

The voice in the background grew louder. "—tried to tell that jerk with the police badge, but he just kept—" The running woman's voice faded away as Cortez finally got her to return to the crowd of neighborhood folks.

Cortez's voice resumed. "Okay, Buck," she said. "That was the woman whose younger brother is missing. Her name is Roberts. She said that you should know that there's a sick man in that house."

"What?"

"She said her brother had mentioned meeting the residents of the house. She said she'd only seen four people coming in and out of the place but that her younger brother also mentioned that there was a 'patient' in a hospital bed in there. From her brother's description she gathered the patient was a comatose man. She thought we might want to know that before we stormed in. She says if we go in with tear gas, it could kill that sick man in there."

"Roger." Barnes sighed. "That's good information to know. It also means tear gas has just been taken out of our arsenal."

"Roger that, Buck. Don't want to kill a helpless man down there."

Buck couldn't think of any new curse words, so he reused an earlier one. "Justins," he growled, "anybody else over there tries to get your attention, you give it. And you relay any pertinent information to me right away. Got it?"

"Yes, sir," a meek voice sounded over the radio.

"We almost went in, Justins. And if we had, that man's death would have been on your hands."

"Yes, sir. Sorry, sir."

"Oh, and Buck—" It was Cortez.

"Go."

"Ms. Roberts respectfully requests that we not shoot her little brother if it turns out he's in the house."

"Roger. Nobody shoots the mentally challenged young man. Affirmed." Detective Barnes sighed. Then he spoke again into the radio. "Sunny," he said, "I think it's time to get Captain Philips out here. He's the best negotiator—" The sound of a cell phone ringing interrupted the detective's order. "Belay that," he said quickly. "Looks like Mr. No Name is ready to talk again. Hold your breath, people. Here goes nothing."

He flipped open his phone and spoke into the mouthpiece. "Detective Barnes. To whom am I speaking?"

The man ignored his taunt. "I'm coming out, Detective," the man said. "But I don't think you're going to be happy about it."

FIFTEEN

Looking at the *Last Judgment*, one immediately sees that Michelangelo delineated four layers in this chilling masterpiece. At the top of the painting are two lunettes that appear to represent heaven. In these lunettes angels swirl and cling to the icons of Christ's passion.

The next layer is a sea of humanity, with the Christ figure himself in the middle. All eyes are turned toward Jesus, responding somehow to some great command or expression of power.

Next down is the battle for souls, where the redeemed are being dragged upward and the cursed pulled down to the bottom level.

At this bottom level we find the River Styx, the gates of hell, Minos the lord of the damned, snakes and demons feasting on the carnage, and a writhing, gasping mass of people suddenly aware of their eternal condemnation. It is in this place that Michelangelo gives us our only real glimpse of a mysterious and hungry—always hungry—hell.

I don't know about you, Ms. Collins, but I have always found this bottom level of hell to be the most exciting part of the master's work.

EXCERPT FROM THE MICHELANGELUS RECORDINGS,
TAPE 6,
TRANSCRIBED BY H. J. COLLINS

The sanctuary was silent—so quiet that Ready falsely hoped for one brief moment that they were finally alone. But opening his eyes dispelled that notion completely. Everything was as it had been. He was still kneeling to the right of the center aisle, between the altar and the front pew. At the front of the center aisle Hummingbird Collins also was kneeling. Her eyes were still closed, but she had stopped whispering psalms into the silence. Standing next to her and looking uncomfortable was Kinseth.

Down the center aisle, of course, were the two killers, the man and the woman whose gun and presence kept them from making a final escape. The man leaned casually against the end of the pew; the woman sat across the aisle from him at the edge of her pew.

Ready looked at the man and didn't see the same monster he'd seen in Johann Smidt. Smidt had been insane. This man was simply evil.

The man's voice finally broke the silence. "So which one are you today?"

Ready wasn't sure whom he was talking to until he saw Kinseth's head bob up in response to the question. The man with the gun lazily detached himself from the pew and walked a few steps toward Kinseth.

"Which one today?"

Kinseth didn't respond, but Ready noticed his eyes flickering as though he were trying to think hard through the answer to the question.

"Robby maybe?"

"Which one is that?" said the woman.

"The kid."

She nodded. "Which one is the rebellious snot? I hate that one."

"Seth. Are you Seth today, boy? It fits your actions."

Kinseth still said nothing. But he was obviously feeling tension. His breathing became labored, and Ready noticed his left hand trembling.

"Leave him alone." It was Hummingbird. She stood and faced her captors with a courage that Ready had to admire.

The man ignored her, intent on playing his little game.

"Or are you Kenny, that awkward teenager who just wants a date with my lovely companion here?" He gestured back toward the woman, who grimaced and turned away.

"His name is Kinseth," Ready said, choosing to remain on his knees. "Kinseth Roberts." He looked at the boy until he caught his gaze and then locked onto it, willing courage into the young man's soul. "And he is a *friend*."

Kinseth flushed and favored Ready with a grimace. Ready smiled back, steady, unmoving.

"How precious," muttered the woman in the back.

The man simply chuckled and returned to his lazy recline against the end of the middle pew. He gazed back at Ready, studying him with interest. "You have a good face," he said finally. "Under other circumstances Johann would have been very interested in you."

The woman stood and walked over to the man. She spoke in low tones, but her voice echoed around the auditorium anyway. "Listen," she said, "I've been thinking. Why don't we just go? He's helpless without us, about to die. He shows all the signs. And these people know too little about us to be a threat. They think we killed the old man but have no proof. If we kill them, the cops, probably the FBI, will be on us, and that may compromise our mission. Once we're gone no one will ever find us. Let's just disappear."

The man looked thoughtful. "I don't trust that one, though," he said, waving his gun toward Ready.

"Fine," she said. "Him we kill."

"No!" Hummingbird shouted.

The man raised an eyebrow. "You'd rather it be him?" He pointed the gun at Kinseth.

"No." Hummingbird was more subdued now.

Ready felt it was time to say something, to defuse the confrontation between Hummingbird and the captors before someone lost patience and someone else got hurt. He opened his mouth to speak, not sure what he would say but hoping that words would come anyway.

He never got anything out, because at that exact moment a missile hit him between the shoulder blades, snapping his neck and head painfully backward and knocking him into a sagging heap on the floor below the altar.

— — —

Number 48 adjusted his wardrobe and spoke into the cell phone. "I'm opening the door, Detective. Tell your snipers to hold their fire. I'm wearing a jacket packed with enough C-4 explosive to make the Conklin bombing look like a Sunday morning firecracker."

Number 48 heard a muffling of the receiver on the other end of his phone but still made out the gist of the detective's rapid-fire orders commanding snipers to hold their fire and telling ground personnel to put some distance between themselves and the house at 1669 Kirby Court. He gave everyone a moment to respond to the detective's orders, then he opened wide the front door to the house, careful to stand back and away from the opening before him.

"Okay," Barnes was saying in the earpiece. "No one is going to fire a shot."

Number 48 picked up the spare bomb jacket he'd loaded,

walked through the doorframe, and paused. On the street he saw the red firetruck and several police personnel crouching behind cars and other protective structures around the cul-de-sac. A quick look to the roofs revealed one, no, two snipers with rifles at the ready.

Number 48 spoke into his cell phone. "As you can see, I'm not bluffing."

"All I see is you wearing an ugly green jacket and holding a second one in your hand."

"This second one is for you. Proof that I mean business."

"What do you mean?"

Number 48 gently placed the spare jacket on the porch outside the door. "I'm going to close this door," he said. "When I do, you can send one—only one!—officer up to the porch to get this spare jacket. It's identical to the one that took out the Conklin Art Gallery. Take it to your bomb squad, and they'll verify the explosive sewn into its lining. And remember, this jacket I'm wearing has more than double the amount of C-4 in it, and I've got plenty more where that came from."

He stepped back from the opening and closed the door. After a moment the red light flicked on, and he knew someone had picked up the jacket. He waited. In due time he heard Detective Barnes on the cell phone again.

"Okay, you've made your point," the detective snarled.

"Right, Detective," 48 said. "And now we do things my way."

"What's your way, Mr. No Name?"

"Like I said before. I walk out of here. Nobody follows me. I disappear, never to be found again."

Kinseth had wanted to say something, to warn Mr. Ready about the madman who came rushing out of the stage door behind him, but everything had happened so fast that they hadn't even had a chance to blink.

The artist had hit Mr. Ready—hard—right in the middle of the back. Now Ready was dazed and lying in a heap on the floor beneath the altar. The artist was swinging at him—hard—kicking him while he groaned, kicking until Mr. Ready seemed almost paralyzed by it all.

They heard the nice lady, Hummingbird, gasp behind them. They felt as if they should do something, but they didn't know what to do. The artist scared them—all of them. They wanted to run away, but the bad man and the bad lady were in the way. And besides, Mr. Ready was a *friend*.

Kinseth ran to Mr. Ready. "Stop it! Stop it!" they shouted. But the madman just shoved them out of the way, hitting them hard across the bridge of their nose. Kinseth thought their nose might be bleeding, but they weren't sure.

The artist was shouting now. Some strange words that sounded like a foreign language, mixed in with some bad words that Elaina had said were never supposed to be spoken by gentlemen, calling Ready bad names. Then he rolled Ready onto his back and crouched over him with a knee on his chest and another knee on Ready's left arm. Ready's right arm was trapped painfully behind his back.

The big black man gazed up at his captor, dazed, hurting.

Then Kinseth saw the artist pull a knife—a switchblade—out of his pocket. He flipped open the knife and started grinning. His eyes were wild, like the eyes Kinseth had seen painted on Minos in the wall behind them.

"You," the man was saying, "have a face I can use. But I've no reason to keep the rest of you."

Then, to Kinseth's horror, the man made a swift cut along the left side of Ready's face, slicing open the skin between his ear and the bottom of his jaw. Kinseth felt paralyzed.

The artist, the madman, was going to cut Ready's face off his body.

Kinseth felt flashes of fear and remembered what it was like to feel the skin of their face flapping open after the car wreck. They wanted to cover their good eye, to block out the whole scene playing out in front of them. But they couldn't. Their eye wouldn't close, and their body wouldn't move.

Mr. Ready choked in surprise at the wound, tried to struggle, but couldn't escape the madman's grasp. The man raised his knife again and prepared to slash another time, to cut underneath Ready's chin. He would slit Ready's throat in the process, but the madman didn't seem to care. All he wanted was the face.

Kinseth blinked, and then Hummingbird was rushing the madman with an unexpected ferocity. She wasn't shouting, wasn't yelling. Just attacking.

She aimed her left shoulder and hit the artist with all the momentum she could muster. The rest of her body crashed into him, and they both went tumbling over Ready and into the altar. Kinseth heard a crack as the madman's head hit the ivory arm rail on the altar and broke the rail into pieces. Hummingbird wearily moved away, gasping for breath.

The madman didn't move.

Kinseth saw blood flowing from the wound on Ready's face and watched as he struggled to rise. And Kinseth knew what to do.

They ran to their friend, gently pushed him back to the ground. "Lie still," they ordered. "Help is on the way." They didn't know that for sure, of course. But that's what Elaina had said to them after the accident, and it had made them feel better.

Ready's eyes got a glassy look, but he was trying to grin. "That was some tackle," he slurred. "Humm should try out for the Eagles."

Kinseth grimaced in response to Ready's attempted smile. "Lie still," they said again. "Help is on the way."

Then Kinseth carefully but quickly rubbed away any dirt or dust from their hands. They reached down and, with their left hand, pressed on Ready's cheek. With their right hand they pulled up Ready's sagging left ear. When the cheek and the ear touched once again, they held the wound together with their bare hands, applying pressure to the skin and praying for God to make the bleeding stop long enough for help to come.

Ready closed his eyes. "Thank you, Kinseth," he whispered through gritted teeth. "Thank you, friend."

Kinseth wasn't sure why they were crying. "Lie still," they said again. "Help is on the way."

— — —

Buck Barnes looked toward T. W. Collins and squinted. T.W. realized that for all his bravado, the detective was seriously worried.

"Buck?" he said.

The detective covered the mouthpiece on his cell phone. "We've got another problem," he said.

"You mean besides the fact that we've got a killer holed up and he's threatening to blow us all to kingdom come?"

Detective Barnes nodded grimly. "He's ready to abandon the house."

T.W. was confused. "That's a good thing, isn't it, Buck? That's what we want, right?"

"Think about it, T.W. If he wants to walk away from that house, what is he leaving behind?"

T.W. processed the thought. If the killer was intent on leaving, it could mean he was simply trying to cut his losses and escape. Then T.W. realized what Buck was thinking. The killer was coming out alone. He hadn't threatened any hostages, hadn't used a hostage as a bargaining chip, hadn't used a hostage as a shield, nothing. That meant there was either no one left in the house . . . or there was no one left alive. It also meant Johann Smidt wasn't in the house—at least not alive. If he were, they'd be dealing with him now, not this No Name guy. And this No Name guy wouldn't be abandoning his boss and running away.

"We have a problem, Buck."

"Yeah, now you're seeing it," Barnes said grimly.

T.W. noticed a man in a business suit headed toward their car. Detective Barnes immediately perked up, opened his car door, and stood to meet the man. T.W. listened in to their conversation.

"Captain Philips," Barnes was saying, "glad to have you here. Have you been briefed on the situation?"

"Yes, Buck," Captain Philips said. "They tapped me in on your cell-phone line. I've been listening to both your cell conversations and the police radio."

"Well, I'll tell you, Cap, I'm a little concerned about this one. If what the bomb squad is telling me is true, this thing could blow up big. No pun intended."

"You're doing fine, Buck. Just keep the perp talking."

"Captain," Barnes said, "I think it's time that a seasoned negotiator take over. I—" He hesitated. "I'm not sure I'm the best person for this job."

"Nonsense," Philips said. "Get into the car. Get the suspect back on the phone. See if you can get him outside. That's step one. We'll worry about step two when the time comes."

Detective Barnes seemed to be wrestling with the captain's order, but he finally agreed.

"And don't worry," Philips said. "I'll be right here with you. Now let's get to work."

Captain Philips reached for the back door to the sedan and let himself into the backseat. Detective Barnes slid back into the driver's seat.

"Who's this?" Captain Philips asked when he saw T.W. in the passenger seat.

"Temporary deputy," Detective Barnes said without hesitation. "I pressed him into service for the duration."

"One of those, huh?" Captain Philips said knowingly. "Fine. Your name?"

"Uh, T. W. Collins. Uh, sir."

The captain nodded, then turned his attention back to Barnes. "Funny, Buck," he said. "I seem to have heard that name before."

"Temporary deputy, Cap. Legal advisory capacity and all that stuff."

"That's your story?"

"And you know the rest, Cap."

"Get the suspect on the phone. I have dinner reservations I don't want to miss."

"He's still there. Got him on hold."

"Good job."

T.W. immediately admired the way Captain Philips seemed to put Detective Barnes both at ease and at the ready. The detective quickly switched his cell to the speaker-phone setting to allow Captain Philips to hear the conversation without using his cell. T.W. was glad about that as well. Up to this point he'd had to strain to make out the conversation through the overactive speaker in the earpiece of Barnes's cell.

"Okay, Mr. No Name," Barnes said into the phone. "We're considering your . . . proposal. But first we need to know who you're leaving behind in the house."

"Nobody."

"You're the only one in the house?"

There was a moment's delay. Then, "I'm in the house alone."

"What about Hummingbird Collins?"

"Not here."

"Johann Smidt?"

"Don't know who that is."

Barnes looked puzzled by that statement, but he kept the curiosity out of his voice. He paused, thinking.

Captain Philips scribbled something on a notepad and thrust it toward Barnes. T.W. caught a glimpse of the pad and read the words, "Private, not a general."

"Okay," Barnes said after a moment. "Here's how this is going to work. You come out. You leave the front door open. You stop at the bottom of the driveway while my people enter the house. When they give the all clear that you haven't booby-trapped the house or hidden some hostages in there, then"—he paused for a breath—"then I let you walk away. You get a fifteen-minute head start. Fifteen minutes, that's it. Then the chase is on. Those are my terms, take it or leave it, soldier."

The decision time on the other end of the phone was remarkably brief. "I'm opening the door."

Captain Philips leaned over the seat and grabbed the mouthpiece on the radio. "All units," he said, "this is Captain Chester Philips. Hold your fire, but stay in position. SWAT, prepare to enter the house at the front door. Wait for my signal. Acknowledge."

Several voices on the radio gave terse acknowledgments of the captain's orders. A moment later the front door to the house opened.

— — —

Hummingbird felt slightly dazed and sore all over. But she'd stopped the madman, at least for the moment. He lay beside her in a crumpled heap, unconscious. Hummingbird tried to clear the cobwebs from her mind and stand, but before she could, the other woman shoved her aside and knelt next to the madman.

"Well?" It was the man with the gun. He was still standing about halfway down the center aisle, and he was talking to his companion who now inspected the fallen artist.

"Mild head trauma. He'll probably have a concussion, but he'll come around shortly."

The man gave a mirthless smile. "The great Johann Smidt, finally taken down by one of his own captives."

"Orders?" It was the woman.

"Proceed as planned."

The woman produced a large needle and syringe, and Hummingbird immediately started crawling backward to put some distance between herself and the woman with the needle. However, the woman paid no attention to Hummingbird and instead inserted the needle with expert precision into the arm of the unconscious man, carefully draining the liquid into his vein until the syringe was empty. Then she stood.

"What about them?" she said. She didn't need to point to Hummingbird and the others; it was obvious whom she meant. "There will be no culmination with Johann in such a state," the woman said. "And we need no one tracking us down. They'll blame Johann and the others for the bombings. We can fade away."

The gunman cocked his head to one side, considering. "Congratulations, children," he said casually. "Today you get to live."

He pocketed the gun and motioned to the woman. She jogged down the center aisle, grabbing her backpack as she passed the middle pew. The two of them hurried toward the exit without looking back. Then they were gone.

Hummingbird felt a grateful surge that was immediately diminished when she finally got a good look at Ready and Kinseth. The young man was still pressing Ready's flesh together, trying to slow the bleeding.

"We've got to get out of here," she said to no one in particular. "Got to get Ready to a doctor."

She remembered then that Ready probably would have a cell phone somewhere on him. She rushed over and began searching her friend's pockets.

"He's lying still," Kinseth said to her. "Help is on the way."

Hummingbird found the cell, or what was left of it, tucked into Ready's back left pocket. It was cracked in half and broken into unusable pieces, with wires and little metal parts sprinkled all over. Apparently it had been kicked a few times when the madman had been beating him.

Hummingbird heard a groan and saw Smidt's arm twitch out of the corner of her eye.

Have to do something, she thought frantically. *Have to get Ready out of here.*

She inspected the wound on the side of Ready's face. There was a lot of blood. It covered Kinseth's hands and formed a shallow pool in the carpet. But she was encouraged to see that Kinseth's efforts were having an effect. The side of Ready's face was still wet and oozing, but the flow of blood seemed to have slowed.

He needs a bandage, she thought. Then her eyes caught sight of the madman's switchblade, still opened, on the floor between Ready and the altar. She grabbed it without thinking, trying to ignore the stickiness of the blood on the blade. She jabbed the knife into the cloth on the shoulder of her shirt, gouging a deep tear into the fabric. It was enough to allow her to rip it the rest of the way and tear off the sleeve. She quickly turned it inside out, folded it into a makeshift compress, and put a hand on Kinseth's shoulder.

"You did well, Kinseth," she said kindly. The young man nodded. "Now let's use this."

She showed the makeshift bandage to the boy. He gave her a grateful look and carefully removed his hands from the side of Ready's face. Hummingbird pressed the compress onto the wound and was pleased to see that it covered the entire area that was bleeding. After it was in place, Kinseth put his hands carefully back onto the bandage, still intent on stopping the bleeding.

"Ready," Hummingbird said softly. "Ready, we've got to get out of here."

There was no response.

Buck Barnes watched the front door open at the house at 1669 Kirby Court and wondered just what he was going to do next. He was glad Captain Philips was here, though. That tough old bird had lived through dozens of situations like this. It was he who had put into words what had been only a nagging concept floating around the back of Barnes's brain until that point.

Private, not a general.

That was an important observation, and Barnes felt a little

stupid for not catching on earlier. This would-be bomber was a private in Johann Smidt's little army of crime. He was used to taking orders, used to having the course of action spelled out for him by a superior. Subconsciously he was still longing for Johann Smidt to stand behind him and tell him what to do, but apparently this private had been left to make do on his own. Now he was trying to ad-lib his way out of a stressful situation. But that was against his natural instincts—and that provided an opening for Detective Barnes. If the general was gone—in this case, Johann Smidt—then maybe, just maybe, Detective Barnes could bluff his way into becoming the new general, at least long enough to take down the suspect.

Barnes tested this theory in the way he gave his instructions for exit of the house. He'd laid down the orders like a commanding officer and dared the private not to comply. It had worked, and now the bomber was leaving the house, walking slowly down the driveway.

He was wearing an oversized military-style green jacket. Wires extended out of the right vest pocket and attached to what appeared to be a detonating device that the bomber held in his right hand. In his left hand he held a cell phone up to his ear.

Detective Barnes heard a voice crackle on the radio. "I have a clean shot." It was one of the snipers. "Request authorization to take the suspect out."

Barnes stifled a curse. The sniper didn't know that his words could be heard in the background through Barnes's own cell phone. The bomber stopped and raised his detonator high.

"Tell your snipers to stand down. Stand down!" he shouted toward two rooftops. "Stand down, or I blow us all to kingdom come right now!"

Captain Philips was immediately on the radio. "Stand down!

Stand down! Sniper One, Sniper Two, lower your weapons and back away until you are out of sight. Go! Go!"

Barnes spoke quickly into the cell. "Just relax, soldier," he said. "Look, both snipers are moving out. See, you're safe, soldier."

The bomber said nothing, but he slowly lowered his arm. After confirming that both snipers were no longer in sight, he continued descending the driveway until he stood at the edge of the street.

"SWAT, you may enter the front of the house," Captain Philips said. "Proceed with caution. Officers at the back of the house, hold your positions."

Four heavily armed and uniformed SWAT officers quickly appeared and then disappeared into the house.

A moment later their voices started reporting in.

"Living room, clear."

"Kitchen, clear."

"Preparing to enter the basement."

"I've kept my end of the bargain, Detective," the bomber said. "And now I'm walking away."

Barnes hadn't expected the bomber to attempt to move so quickly, but the man was already crossing the cul-de-sac, heading away from the firetruck and toward two houses on the opposite side.

"No, not yet, soldier," Barnes ordered. "We're not done here yet. No hostages, no booby-traps, then you go. That was our deal."

In response the bomber simply closed his cell phone and threw it high in the air.

Barnes looked grim. "You a betting man, T.W.?"

The lawyer looked surprised by the question. "No, not really," he said. "In my line of work betting on sports can get you into a lot of trouble."

"Well," Barnes said, "sometimes I like to gamble. And right now feels like one of those times."

In one quick move the detective bounded out of his Chevy Malibu and started running behind the firetruck, taking an angle that would let him cut off the bomber just before he reached the other side of the street.

SIXTEEN

A heart of flaming sulfur, flesh of tow,

Bones of dry wood, a soul without a guide

To curb the fiery will, the ruffling pride

Of fierce desires that from the passions flow;

A sightless mind that weak and lame doth go

Mid snare and pitfalls scattered far and wide

What wonder if the first chance brand

Applied to fuel massed like this should make it glow?

Add beauteous art, which brought with us from heaven,

Will conquer nature; so divine a power

Belongs to him who strives with every nerve.

If I was made for art, from childhood given

A prey for burning beauty to devour,

I blame the mistress I was born to serve.

A SONNET OF MICHELANGELO,
EXCERPT FROM THE MICHELANGELUS RECORDINGS,
TAPE 6,
TRANSCRIBED BY H. J. COLLINS

———

Ready Robinson felt dizzy and lightheaded, felt like passing out, actually. Then he blinked his eyes, saw Hummingbird and Kinseth leaning over him with worried expressions, and wondered if he *had* passed out.

The left side of his face stung with unreal pain, and Kinseth's hands pushing insistently beside his ear weren't helping it feel any better.

Ready blinked again, and suddenly his memory of what had just happened came rushing back. He tried to sit up, felt seriously dizzy, and lay back on the floor again.

"—me, Ready?" Hummingbird was saying something. "Ready, can you hear me? We've got to get out of here. Before—before that madman comes to."

Ready blinked once more, and his head stopped spinning. "Yes, Humm," he said. "Right. Gotta get out of here. I understand." He reached up and gently touched Kinseth's hand. "Kinseth," he said kindly, "it's okay now. Here, let me."

The young man nodded gravely and released the pressure on Ready's makeshift bandage. *Where did that come from?* Ready wondered absently. Then he saw Hummingbird's torn shirtsleeve and put it together in his mind. Ready used his left hand to hold the bandage in place and rolled precariously to his right, supporting his weight with his right arm.

"Whoa," he said, feeling the lightheadedness that accompanied that move.

"Ready." Hummingbird's voice was strained. "Ready, you have to walk. I know you've lost a lot of blood, and you're probably feeling kind of weak. But you have to walk because I can't carry you."

"I'm okay, Humm," he lied. "Just give me a minute to get my bearings."

"Ready, we may not have a minute."

Ready wanted to nod his head, but the movement threatened to increase his pain, so he just said, "Let's go then." He wobbled to his feet and felt like passing out again. Hummingbird quickly slid under his right arm, steadying him with her strength.

"Good thing I never took steroids," he mused. "Otherwise I'd be too big for you to hold up like this."

Hummingbird snorted. "Even when he's bleeding to death, the great Ready Robinson can't resist making jokes."

Ready wanted to smile, but it hurt, so he didn't. "Hey, just because you're facing down a psychopathic killer doesn't mean you can't enjoy yourself."

With Hummingbird on one side and Kinseth on the other, Ready steadied himself and looked toward the end of the center aisle at the exit doors. "We seem to be free of certain people with guns," he said.

"They left," Hummingbird said. "They said they could kill us, but they didn't have time to dispose of our bodies."

"Thank God for right schedules."

"Him, on the other hand." Hummingbird gestured toward the unconscious madman at the altar. "He's still got time for us. Which is why we need to get out of here before he wakes up."

As if on cue, the madman groaned again and flopped over onto his back.

"Right," Ready said. "Well, we're not waiting on me." He took a wobbly step toward the exit, then another, felt his dizziness lessening, and soon was walking at a reasonably fast pace down the aisle, Hummingbird under one arm and Kinseth standing close to the other, apparently ready to catch him if he fell. He squeezed Hummingbird. "Thanks, Humm," he said. "And by the way, that was a great tackle. Textbook. Head up, shoulder down, hit, wrap him up. Textbook."

"Ready," she said with a small smile, "anybody ever tell you that you talk too much when you're delirious?"

"I'm not delirious," he said indignantly. "Just a little light-headed is all. I'm fine." Then he looked down at her still-bandaged right hand. "Hey," he said, "we need to get *you* to a doctor."

Hummingbird just rolled her eyes.

Buck Barnes had run two-thirds of the way across the street when he decided that he needed to cut back on fast food and start making use of the workout facilities down at the station. But his angle was good, and in just a moment's time he was standing between the bomber and the houses toward which the bomber had been headed.

"Back off!" the man in the C-4 jacket shouted, raising the detonator in front of him. "Your boss promised me a fifteen-minute head start!"

Buck held up his hands. "Detective Barnes," he said with just a catch of breathlessness in his voice. "At your service."

"What are you doing?" the bomber said angrily. "I let your people into the house. Now let me pass, or this whole block goes up in flames."

"I can't let you go, Mr. No Name," Barnes said simply. "But you knew that already, didn't you?"

The bomber's face grew tight.

"And I don't want you to kill yourself either. Is this really how you want to go out? As a pathetic suicide bomber?"

"You're not giving me a lot of choices, are you, Detective?"

"Sure I am," Barnes said. "I'm giving you a chance to go out with honor. As a man."

"There is no honor in surrender."

"But there can be in defeat. Every soldier loses a battle somewhere along the way. That doesn't mean he should simply fold up and die. It means he fought bravely, fought hard, but somebody else's soldier just came out on top that day."

"Let me pass, Detective."

"Think about it, soldier. Why are you the only one left here?"

There was a split second of hesitation. "I don't know."

"Well, we know that one of your comrades has already been captured. Should he die because he didn't make it out?"

"No."

"Then why should you have to die? And where's your boss? What happened to him?"

"I don't know. Maybe you've got him too."

Detective Barnes shook his head. "Nope. We don't know where he is either. You know what I think? I think he saw us coming. I think he knew we were close to raiding this house. I think he sold you out, left you here to face us while he ran away with his tail between his legs."

The bomber said nothing, but his face looked grim. Detective Barnes took another chance. "That sounds about like him, doesn't it? When it comes down to it, you sacrificed everything for him. And he never thought about anybody but himself."

The bomber looked nervously around the cul-de-sac. Two of the SWAT officers had exited the house and were now standing at the ready at the top of the driveway. Detective Barnes didn't look up, but he really hoped that the snipers were staying out of sight. He held out his hand.

"It's over, soldier," he said, trying his best to sound like an army general consoling his troops after a fierce battle lost. "You fought well. Now live to fight again."

The bomber took a step backward and adjusted the detonator in his hand. "You promised me fifteen minutes," he hissed.

"Your boss promised you more than that," Barnes said quickly. "At least with me you get to live."

The bomber stared at Buck, and there was a moment of silent decision making. "Do you believe in an afterlife, Detective?"

Barnes didn't like the direction this conversation was taking. "I don't know, soldier," he said honestly.

There was another moment of silence. "I don't know either, Detective."

The bomber dropped his arm, and a look of defeat settled into his face. After a moment, he stuffed the detonator into his vest pocket, carefully removed the jacket laden with explosive, and placed it on the ground between them.

Detective Barnes nodded his approval. "Good choice, soldier. Now take two steps backward."

The would-be bomber complied.

"Lie flat on the ground, and put your hands behind your head."

The man obeyed, and almost immediately four officers surrounded them. Two from the bomb squad began the careful work of disarming the bomb jacket. One pressed a knee into the suspect's back and quickly had him handcuffed and subdued for transport. The last was Captain Philips, and he went directly to Buck.

"I'm not a gambling man, Buck," the captain said proudly, "but I'd bet on you anytime, anywhere."

Suddenly a voice crackled on the radio of the police officer nearest to them. "Detective Barnes?" a voice called. Barnes recognized the voice as belonging to Hummel, one of the SWAT officers behind the house. He borrowed the nearest officer's radio and spoke into it.

"Barnes here. Go."

"Hey, Buck," Hummel said cheerily, "tell that lady we found her little brother. He's in our custody now."

"Good work, Hummel," Barnes said.

"And Hummingbird Collins is with him."

Detective Barnes heard an excited shout from the vicinity of his Chevy Malibu.

"And a third gentleman who says his name is Charles Robinson. All three are ambulatory, but Ms. Collins and Mr. Robinson are in need of medical treatment."

"Roger."

Another voice cut in, "On our way," and Buck saw two paramedics immediately begin jogging toward the greenbelt.

"One more thing, Buck. They're telling us that Johann Smidt has been disabled and that he's hidden inside that old church."

Now Buck started jogging himself. "Move in, people. Move in!"

— — —

Johann Smidt recognized the music that wafted toward his ears, but it was a cacophony of colors this time, an abstruse mixture of shaded reds and greens and oranges and blues and golds and more. He moaned. It felt good to moan in harmony with the music of the colors. He wondered at the blurry images in his mind, trying to make sense of where he was and why the colors were singing such an odd tune this time. He opened his eyes and found himself staring up, upside down, at the boat of the damned.

He licked his lips, trying to soothe the dryness that coated the inside of his mouth like cotton.

A greenish-hued, muscular man stood at the end of the boat, long donkey ears stretching away from his head like horns, pointy gray mustache quivering in ecstasy on his face, clawlike toes gripping the bow of the boat for balance.

"Charon," Smidt whispered to the air above him. "Beautiful Charon, boatman of the damned."

The green demon only sneered, whipping a pole with ferocity toward the naked and condemned humans rushing toward the stern of his boat. Johann Smidt smelled their fear, found the fragrance a perfume that mixed with the sulfur of a fire nearby.

He heard a roar, an inhuman appetite feeding itself in timbered tones that echoed around the room. He realized then where he was, lying at the foot of his very own masterpiece on the wall of the Baptist church. Overwhelming pride filled his insides, warming and leaving him empty at the same time. His body felt both feverish and chilled, and for more than a moment he heard a heart pounding in time to the melody of the colors.

He tried to stand, but the stench of burning flesh filled his nostrils suddenly, eating away the nasal passages and digging into his sinus cavities. The force of the smell was something he felt physically, and it toppled him again.

He watched as Charon's wicked pole swung lazily, as if in slow motion, off the wall, extending its reach beyond what Johann would have thought possible. Too late he realized that the boatman was swinging for him, and he felt the crashing blow implode at his temples, rolling him four or five lengths across the floor. The colors were laughing now, weaving hungry giggles into the dissonance that they called a song.

He felt a blast of warmth, like a furnace being stoked.

Johann crawled until he felt the front pew of the church with his hand. With effort he pulled himself up onto the pew, then collapsed into a seated position that allowed him to stare in wonder at his own masterpiece. He put his hands to his throbbing temples and was mildly surprised to find there was no blood. But the aftereffects of Charon's mighty blow still lingered, making him feel as though it were an earthquake that still had smaller tremors to push into his head.

The painting swam with life before him, and he was transfixed by its terrible beauty. Bodies writhed and struggled as they wrestled with the destiny of eternity. Now he heard—no, he saw—the screams; the colors were not singing, they were screaming, and their mouths sprayed him with hot spittle that felt like pellets of boiling lava. He tried to speak, to scream in unison with the music they were making, but his mouth would not respond correctly, and the sounds became stuck behind his teeth, dripping back into his throat in long succession until they lodged painfully there. He swung his arms and kicked his legs, but nothing would release the pressure of the screams that trapped themselves inside him.

He stared at Charon, laughing and waving his pole, saw the boatman share a look with someone, and turned to see who it was.

Minos stepped off the wall, clothed only in a serpent of unimaginable width. Minos stroked the serpent as if it were an aphrodisiac of pain. Johann felt the screaming finally gurgle its way to the surface, saw the pleasure it gave to the face of Minos. He heard—no, saw—his scream echoed in the feasting demons that swam across the painting, and so he screamed until he simply could scream no more.

He heard a great whooshing sound and felt a hot wind wash over his face, blistering his skin and stinging his eyes with pinpricks of fire. The vision of Minos blurred and dimmed, then returned and doubled. He blinked, trying to center the blurry double vision into a single Satan. He didn't see Charon's second blow until it was too late, until it hit him with such bone-crunching force that Johann felt certain it had cracked his skull. He found himself sprawled again on the floor. This time he clawed his way back onto the pew using only his right arm and leg. For some reason, he was alarmed to discover, he could no longer use the muscles on the left side of his body.

He gasped breathlessly, hearing the noise of the colors grow louder and louder until he thought it would pierce his eardrums. He closed his eyes and tried to shut out the sound. When he opened his eyes, Minos stood before him, drinking in the artist with malevolent eyes. The burning stench seemed to emanate from his pores, but the lord of the damned was unaware. The serpent undulated wordlessly up and down Minos's torso, awaiting command from its master.

Minos leaned over and stared appraisingly at Johann. After a moment he reached out and placed a finger under the artist's chin, gently adjusting the position of his profile. Johann started to speak, but Minos frowned and shook his head. Minos spat, careful to avoid coating saliva on Johann's shoes. Finally he spoke.

"He'll do."

Johann felt an unfamiliar sense of panic. He watched helplessly as the serpent began weaving its head toward the artist's face. He heard—no, saw—the serpent hissing a foreign language into the air. All at once the serpent's tongue flicked out and touched Johann's cheek. The poison from that tongue had immediate effect, causing a numbness to spread over the entire left side of Johann's face. He felt his insides rumble and involuntarily spewed them out onto his own lap. Minos and the serpent seemed unconcerned. He felt the numbness travel and become a poisoned stiffness settling into his neck, and he wondered, if the serpent's tongue had been so powerful, what the serpent's fangs could do . . . would do.

Suddenly Minos was leaning before him again. "Do you know who I am?" he said.

"Minos, lord of the damned," he gurgled in reply. The demon before him grinned but shook his head.

"No."

Johann's mind was filled with a parade of unpleasant images. "Jonathan Shelby?" he croaked.

"No."

"Satan?"

Minos looked flattered. "I thought you didn't believe in things like that. But no. Not even him."

"Who?"

"Johann," the demon said with hungry eyes. "I am, of course, your father."

Johann felt a lurching in his chest, found it hard to breathe the fetid, smoking air that surrounded him.

"You let me come to this place," the demon said. "Even now I am in unimaginable suffering. Even now I feel my insides rotting and my bowels aflame from the poison this serpent has pumped within my soul." Minos leaned in close, so close his breath burned like acid on the right side of Johann's face. "Even now," the demon hissed.

Johann let his gaze travel past the demon and back to the canvas, back to the wall that he had spent the better part of his life adorning. He saw the hole, the entrance to hell that he himself had painted in the ground at the bottom of the wall. A flash of fire surged through the hole, washing heat over his entire body once more.

"I blame the mistress." Johann choked. "I blame the mistress I was born to serve."

"Blame whoever you want. You're still the one who is here."

"But—"

"Quoting Michelangelo poetry won't keep you from that which you've prepared for yourself, my son. And now, Johann," the demon continued, "now we shall be here together. It is our last judgment."

The snake uncoiled from Minos's sturdy frame and wrapped itself around Johann's neck. He felt himself lifted off the pew, heard—no, saw—the demonic cacophony of colors singing and eating and clicking like pincers on a thousand crabs. He felt a searing pain in his right leg and saw that a green, snakelike demon had already begun feasting on his flesh there. He wanted to struggle, wanted to cry out, wanted to beg the Christ in the center of the picture for forgiveness and redemption. But in the end he did nothing but let himself be dragged without ceremony to the fiery hole. He could not even close his eyes when they heaved his soul into the blazing furnace below.

And then the unpretty horrors truly began.

SEVENTEEN

Hummingbird Collins grinned widely when the bell on the door of her family's bookstore rang and two people walked inside. One was a tall man, dark-skinned and handsome, with a touch of gray at the temples of his tightly curled hair. The other was a young man with light skin and a grimace she'd grown to love like the laughter of a child.

"Ready! Kinseth! I was worried you two weren't coming this week."

Kinseth came over to give Hummingbird her obligatory hug. Ready just smiled and shook his head.

"He had thirty-one questions this week," he said with a nod toward Kinseth. "We spent two hours on them, and we still only covered the first three."

"More for next week." Kinseth shrugged. Then he went past Hummingbird, walking toward the seating area in the back where he began unpacking his supplies.

"He's getting to be a regular theologian then?" Hummingbird said to Ready.

"He's got the curiosity for it."

"What's he asking about this week?"

"Psalms. Been reading them over and over, I guess. I never

should have told him to write down any questions he had while he was reading from the Bible."

Hummingbird laughed. "No, you just never should have told him that you'd answer all his questions."

Ready raised his eyebrows and nodded in agreement. "Kid stumps me every week. And then we have to spend hours going back and forth, looking at other Bible passages that might explain something or looking up stuff in Internet commentaries or even trying to decipher parts of the original Greek or Aramaic texts."

"You know you love it. And him."

Ready looked sheepish. "Okay, it's true. But still, sheesh! The kid's insatiable."

Hummingbird leaned over the cash-register counter and pulled out a fancy envelope. It had Ready's name on it but no address.

"T.W. left this for you. Said he wasn't exactly sure how to mail it to you and asked me to give it to you next time you came in."

"What is it?"

"Invitation to their wedding next month."

"Wow, is it that time already?"

"Yep. Peg says Easter is a time of new beginnings and that she can't think of a better time to start a marriage."

"Smart girl."

"Yep. Oh, and did Buck Barnes find you?"

Ready sighed. "No. What does Mr. Constant Investigation want now?"

"He just thought you'd want to know that the congregation that owned that old Baptist church has decided to demolish the building. They're going to donate the land to the city so that the government can plant a flower park there—you know, a big park that's a garden of all kinds of flowers, with walking paths through it and stuff."

"Took them long enough to make that decision. I would have figured, what with all the protests from victims' families, they would have decided to demolish it sooner."

Hummingbird nodded thoughtfully. After they'd escaped from the church back in October, they'd found SWAT officers on the greenbelt behind Kinseth's cul-de-sac. The SWAT people had called Detective Barnes, and his people had raided the church within twenty minutes of their escape. They'd found Johann Smidt sitting on the front pew, dead, with an unholy look of horror on his face. The coroner's office had said that Smidt had suffered a massive, drug-induced stroke and then a heart attack and had died on the scene. Hummingbird had never found out exactly what was in the syringe that the nameless woman at the church had injected into Smidt's neck, but it had definitely been lethal.

After news got out about Smidt's macabre work of art on the altar wall of the Baptist church, victims' families had come out of the woodwork. Anytime a person painted on the altar wall was identified as someone who was missing or had been murdered, the clamor to tear down the building had grown. Most people felt that keeping the painting intact was disrespectful to those who had suffered. Hummingbird had to admit she agreed. There were also a few new trials going on, as some people appeared to have been incorrectly convicted of crimes that Smidt had actually committed.

"What about the tunnel that ran underground from the church over to the house on Kirby Court?"

"Buck says that since it's city property, the Lehigh city council will make the decision on that one. But the current word is that they're going to collapse the tunnel sometime during the summer and fill it in with dirt and grass like the rest of the greenbelt."

"That all Buck wanted?" Ready said. "Am I supposed to call him or something?"

"Well, he also said to tell you that the counselor you recommended is working wonders for Jonathan Shelby."

"Good. That woman has helped a lot of people through drug addiction and all sorts of battles. I'll be checking in on the Shelbys myself again soon."

Hummingbird thought she detected something more behind his words but let it pass. She nodded toward his jaw. "Face is looking good."

"Thanks," Ready said. "The doctor Buck recommended also works wonders. And how's that hand of yours?" Hummingbird opened her palm and held it out toward Ready. "Barely even a scar left," he said.

"Yeah," she said. "It has healed up well. Better than I expected it to."

"Any trouble drawing or painting with it?"

"Nope. No residual damage at all." She sighed. "You know, Ready, I still find it hard to believe that you attended the memorial service for Johann Smidt's father."

Ready shrugged. "Nobody else came. Buck said probably because no one wanted to be associated with the crimes that took place in that house. It was just a basic, civil ceremony, and then the body was cremated at government expense."

"So why'd you go? The old man was just as guilty of terrible crimes as his son was."

Ready shrugged again. "Seemed a shame that anyone would go into eternity unobserved."

Hummingbird nodded contemplatively. "Heard you went to Johann Smidt's cremation too."

Ready just shrugged, then appeared intent on changing the subject. "Buck having any other successes in his investigation?"

"He says the computer at the house was wiped clean, though the IT experts at the FBI were able to recover the first page of a manuscript for an article in a scientific journal. It was layered deep underneath the erasures on the hard drive."

"Oh?" he asked casually. "What was it?"

"Buck said it had some absurd title having to do with psychobehavioral implications and artistic temperament. And there was something about an experiment in progress, but with only the cover page to the article, the information was rather sketchy."

"How about those two who held us at the church? Are the police having any luck finding them?"

Hummingbird shook her head. "According to Buck, they never existed. No traces of them whatsoever, except for our descriptions and the sketches I made of them. Which reminds me, it looks like I'm going to be a police sketch artist on a freelance basis from time to time now. So that's at least one good thing that came out of this whole ordeal."

Ready grinned. "Congratulations, Humm," he said. "Can't wait to see your artwork displayed in post offices all around the nation."

Hummingbird gave him a playful slap on the shoulder. "Yeah, you're just jealous because Kinseth is already a better artist than you are."

"That may be true." Ready laughed. "But at least I make a better cup of coffee."

Hummingbird wrinkled her nose. "Really? That's what you think. Have you *tried* your coffee?"

Now it was Ready's turn to pout, but after only a moment he sighed and admitted the truth. "Yeah, I guess that's true. But you know, there's always the next pot—and who knows what magic might happen then, right?"

Hummingbird smiled. She looked up and saw that Kinseth was now standing next to her again. "Ready for today's art lesson, honey?" she asked him warmly. Kinseth nodded and grimaced. "Watch the store for me, Ready?"

"Will do."

Hummingbird walked back to the table where Kinseth had set up his art supplies. She loved this part of her week. Ready was so reclusive she hardly ever saw him, except when Kinseth somehow managed to draw him out of hiding. Nowadays Ready and Kinseth usually spent Saturday mornings talking over whatever the young man was reading in the Bible at the time. Then they'd come to the shop for an hour or two, and Hummingbird would give him an art lesson.

Elaina Roberts, Kinseth's older sister, had shed a few tears of joy over the arrangement. She was so grateful that anyone would take more than a passing interest in her brother. "His looks scare most people off," she'd said tearily. "But he really is a wonderful young man, mental disabilities and all." Ready and Hummingbird had to agree. They found they enjoyed being Kinseth's friends as much as he liked having them for friends. It was a good thing for everyone involved.

Hummingbird sat next to Kinseth and flattened out a sheet of sketch paper. "Okay," she said, warming to the subject. "Today we're going to practice pencil drawing."

Hummingbird made herself take a mental snapshot of this moment, of Ready busying himself behind the counter, of spring beginning to show itself outside her windows, of Kinseth's captivated face, of the pencil and the blank sheet of paper that waited before her. Something about this particular capsule of time felt, well, it just felt . . .

Pretty.

EPILOGUE

It is December 23, 1888, that history most often remembers in association with the artistic genius of Vincent van Gogh.

He painted nothing that day, however—at least nothing on canvas. Instead, he sliced off the bottom portion of his own left ear, wrapped it in newspaper, went to the front door of a local brothel, handed over the ear, and asked for it to be given to a prostitute named Rachel. His instructions were that she should "keep this object carefully." Then Vincent spent Christmas recovering in a hospital.

Much has been said about the artist's altered state of mind at this time, about his struggles with sanity, and about the gruesome nature of his gift. But little has been written about the response this fragment of Vincent's flesh received from the willing and desirable Rachel.

Here's what I believe: I think she must have been flattered . . .

EXCERPT FROM THE VAN GOGH SPLINTER CORRESPONDENCE,
LETTER 1

— — —

SATURDAY, APRIL 4, MIDNIGHT

Number 39 stood on the front porch, blanketed in the darkness of the night and positioned directly in front of the camera that hid itself beneath the unlit porch light. Number 61 stood behind him and off to his right. He noted with satisfaction the absence of a doorknob, then held up his right palm toward the camera lens so the soldier on the inside would clearly see the number 39 he had inked there for his benefit.

A mild spring rain drizzled behind them, unseen in the darkness, rain that imbued 39's subconscious with the constant feeling of dampness in the soul. Number 61 stood patiently, motionless, absorbed in her own thoughts. They had waited the full six months before reappearing, even though it had been obvious after only two or three that those imbeciles at the Lehigh police department were never going to be able to connect them with the Johann Smidt affair. Still, 39 was nothing if not thorough. And six months could pass quickly when it was spent planning the next phase of experiments.

The front door opened after only three minutes or so. A young man nodded deferentially to them and welcomed them into the dryness of the house. The young man had a bland, average look about his face. European stock of some sort, though hints of a Native American background hidden somewhere in his family tree peeked out through his eyes and in the bone structure of his nose and chin. His hair was, as expected, cropped short. What was unexpected was its color—an Irish red that gleamed with healthy fervor.

"Welcome, sir," the young man said respectfully. "We had no idea when or where you would show up next. I'm honored that you chose to come here."

"Yes," 39 said casually. "I do love Seattle in the rainy season."

They had planned it well, the original three who had started this little experiment. Number 39 had come into things later than many, but he knew it was now up to him to see the experiments through to the end. And he would do that, no matter the cost. Even when it meant he had to eliminate those original three himself. And a few others. Even when it meant he had to use their money and recruiting methods to maintain safe houses and soldiers in a dozen places across the nation.

They said the Nazis were monsters, 39 mused, conducting all manner of cruel experiments on unwilling subjects. But when World War II was over, those same governments that condemned Nazi research also gobbled up Nazi test results. And when 39 and his comrades were done, they would do the same again. Of course, it might take a lifetime and maybe another one after that. But it would be done. And now that the Lehigh phase was over, it was time to begin a new phase that built on what they'd learned there. Seattle seemed like the right place for that to happen.

Number 39 took a moment to examine the living room of his new home. It had been decorated with normalcy in mind. Gray carpet, a large couch and a love seat, a big glass coffee table in the center of the room. A coat rack and a bench stood behind the entry, and a narrow wooden table pressed against the back wall just before the hallway to the first-floor bedrooms started. It was cluttered with the most current issues of several popular magazines. Anyone—any stranger, that is—who was invited into this room for coffee and conversation would never know that the house was anything other than a suburban home occupied by hardworking members of the community.

Art prints hung on the walls—not real art, though. Mundane, mass-produced paintings and framed lithographs that one could find in any discount retail store in the nation. They were all prints of the same artist, however, and 39 found that to be an interesting fact.

"What's your rank?" 39 asked without looking at the young man.

"Ninety-two, sir."

He gave a halfhearted nod toward 61. "She is Sixty-one," he said. "Follow her orders unless they conflict with mine."

"Yes, sir." Number 92 nodded deferentially toward 61, but she ignored him. She was now inspecting the paintings on the walls. Number 39 joined her, first examining a dark painting filled with browns and blacks and expressive shadows surrounding spare points of light. Within these colors five caricatured figures dressed in nineteenth-century styles circled a simply set dinner table. Number 39 glanced at 61.

"The Potato Eaters," she said in response to his unasked question.

The art print next to *The Potato Eaters* was a sharp contrast, with bright blues and swirling white colors punctuated by glowing yellows that filled a dazzling sky. The print fairly exploded with color and kinetic energy, as if the original had been painted in an absinthe-fueled burst of creative inspiration that barely contained itself within the artist who held the brush.

"Starry Night?" 39 asked. Number 61 nodded.

He turned his attention back to the young soldier who was waiting patiently at their side.

"How many in this house?"

"I'm the only one, sir. This site has been dormant for several years. But I have contact information for up to six others who are on call and assigned to this location."

"We'll only need three of them to start," 39 said. "Contact them in the morning."

"Yes, sir."

Number 39 looked at 92's hands, now clasped and hanging in front of the young man's belt buckle. He noticed with satisfaction that the nails were worn and dirty and that the tips of the fingers appeared to be stained by darkened colors that once may have been blue or gray or even red. An unhurried smile spread over 39's face, a look that was faintly echoed in the expression and posture of Number 61.

"So," Number 39 said with a slow drawl, "I understand that you are an artist . . ."

READER'S GUIDE FOR PERSONAL REFLECTION
OR GROUP DISCUSSION

A NOTE FROM THE AUTHOR

Not long ago I visited a bargain bookstore (yes, I'm cheap!) and saw a beautiful coffee-table book on the life and work of Michelangelo Buonarroti. I was instantly transfixed, so much so that I bought the book on a whim, brought it home, and immediately began churning through its pages. It was here that I first discovered Michelangelo's scary beautiful masterpiece, the *Last Judgment*. This violent, graphic painting adorns the altar wall of the world-famous Sistine Chapel in Italy.

If this painting were a movie, it would be rated NC-17 on the basis of nudity and violence alone. Yet it also breathtakingly depicts an artist's interpretation of literal events described in the pages of Scripture itself. It achieves an impression on the viewer that is both repugnant and holy. This apparent juxtaposition of values was fascinating for me—and it sparked within me an exploration of the concept of God's presence in art, in suffering, in beauty and ugliness, in life, and in eternity.

The result, as you can guess, was *Unpretty*, the book you now hold in your hands. (Hey, I'm a novelist! What else did you expect?) It is my hope that you found this book both entertaining and thought-provoking and that it helped you (like Kinseth) to consider where you belong in Michelangelo's terrifyingly beautiful painting of the end of the world.

Writing this book raised many questions for me, and I'd like to share a few of those questions with you. Even though neither of us may have all of the answers, I hope you find it worthwhile at least to think about the questions.

May God bless and keep you,

— — —

1. Which character in *Unpretty* is most like you? Why?

2. If you were casting a movie of this book, whom would you pick to play the main characters? Why?

3. In your opinion, what is the role of art in religion?

4. From what you know about Michelangelo's *Last Judgment*, do you think it is an appropriate decoration for a church wall? Defend your answer.

5. It has been reported that all societies of man—from the most primitive to the most technologically advanced—harbor a widespread fear of snakes. Michelangelo tapped into this fear repeatedly in his depictions of demons. To what do you attribute this near universal fear?

6. How would you define the term *unpretty?*

7. When have you felt unpretty? What did you do about that?

8. How do you define beauty? Be specific.

9. Why do you suppose humankind is drawn to beauty? How do we pursue beauty in modern life?

10. What is God's role in the creation of beauty? His responsibility?

11. Jonathan Shelby believed that even in the depths of torture and captivity, God was somehow watching over him. Do you agree with him? Why or why not?

12. In our world today many justify brutality and violence as a means to achieve a beautiful outcome. Do you agree or disagree with that perspective? Explain.

13. Ready Robinson's "Urban Monk" is largely a fictional construct. Still, if you were to create "Vows of the Urban Monk," what would you include?

14. Hummingbird Collins struggled to overcome a paralyzing fear of unknown threats to herself and to her family. If you could have spoken to her at that time, what advice would you have given her for combating her fear?

15. Would you say that fear is a positive, negative, or neutral emotion? Is it a sin?

16. How does faith influence fear?

17. What is God's responsibility when we are suffering?

18. What questions about God did this book raise for you?

19. Michelangelo stirred controversy by blending Greek mythology (Minos, Charon, the River Styx) with biblical descriptions of Christ's *Last Judgment*. Do you see Jesus's second coming as a mythological idea or a future-historical certainty? How does that view affect the way you live today?

20. Where do you belong in Michelangelo's painting of the *Last Judgment*?

FOR FURTHER REFLECTION

To dig more deeply into the spiritual themes explored in *Unpretty*, get a Bible and check out the following Scripture passages:

- Psalms 139

- Romans 8:15–28

- Romans 8:37–38

- Hebrews 4:15–16

- Nahum 1:7

- Psalms 23

- 2 Corinthians 4:7–10

ABOUT THE AUTHOR

Who is Sharon Carter Rogers?

On one level, she is, of course, the popular author of the thrillers *Unpretty* and *Sinner*. Some readers believe, however, that Sharon is not the author's real name and that she has hidden her true identity. True? Pure speculation? A publicity stunt—a "mysterious author who writes mysteries"? Ms. Rogers refuses to confirm or deny, but Internet rumors about her background have included the following:

- She is a former English teacher, now a homemaker.

- She is a group of Christian romance writers who got together to experiment with a more gritty style of novel.

- She is actually Dean Koontz, or some other well-known author, who wanted to write something with a spiritual emphasis but did not want to confuse the market about their "author brand."

- She is a former covert military agent and skilled combatant.

- She is married to a Steven Rogers.

- She has never married for fear that her work would put her loved ones in danger.

- She is married to James Barnes.

- She is an elderly woman living in Connecticut.

- She is an aspiring actress living in Southern California.

- She is blonde.

- She is brunette.

- She is a redhead.

- She is bald, and wears wigs that are blonde, brunette, and red.

- She is a former mob moll who now lives in the witness protection program.

- She is a high school drama teacher in Alabama.

- She doesn't exist at all.

Regardless of the rumors, there is one thing we can be sure of: Ms. Rogers is an astonishingly good writer of fast-paced, suspenseful mystery novels.

So who is Sharon Carter Rogers? Perhaps it doesn't matter, as long as she keeps delivering high-octane entertainment like *Sinner* and *Unpretty*.

To contact Sharon directly, you can send her an e-mail through the MySpace.com social network. Her profile page is at: www.MySpace.com/SharonCarterRogers.